# Child of the Lion

## By

## Steven E. Farley

ISBN: 1-4033-2891-9 (e-book)
ISBN: 1-4033-2892-7 (Paperback)
ISBN: 1-4033-2893-5 (Dustjacket)
ISBN: 1-4033-2894-3 (Rocket Book)

Library of Congress Number 2002105676


This book is printed on acid free paper.


Printed in the United States of America
Bloomington, IN

1stBooks – rev. 07/23/02

# Prologue

The great black maned lion raised his head, ears cocked windward. He was crouched over the carcass of an impala. Blood covered his massive muzzle and dripped from his lower lip. It was a fresh kill the four lionesses had brought down. They waited patiently in the tall grass of the Serengetti plain for him to vivisect the animal and eat the choice portions before they came in to feed.

But the lion had caught an alien scent in the soft breeze, a tension in the air. He searched the expanse of rippling grass in the hot afternoon sun. Though uneasy, he continued his careful removal of the pouch and entrails. With deftness a butcher would respect, he removed the viscera without breaking the sack, and carried it in his mouth a few paces. He clawed the grass and earth over it, covering it completely.

Returning to the kill, yellow eyes flaming, he menacingly darted toward some waiting hyenas who scurried off. He trotted back to the kill and devoured the heart, liver, and kidneys along with the fat clinging to them. As he ripped into the thin skin at the anus, he exposed the tender meat of the buttocks. His claws, sharp as honed steel, held the carcass as his pointed canines ripped large chunks from the animal, which he gulped down without chewing. Once more, he rose and padded a few paces, his head held high into the wind. The breeze rippled his luxuriously thick dark mane. His black tufted tail arched high over his back. The lionesses sensed his apprehension. They stood and joined him, sniffing the air.

The impala lay forgotten. The boldest of the hyenas crouched low and slunk several steps toward the carcass. The lion turned swiftly, and with a reverberating roar, charged the scavenger. The hyena ran, his disjointed gait almost tripping him as he fled. The lion stopped and roared once more at the retreating hyena, then circled the crisp grass and lay quietly, his head barely clearing the grass. The four lionesses moved to the kill, tearing at it. Only when they had eaten their fill did they move aside as a pair of woolly cubs wobbled up

The lion looked for a place to settle into his afternoon nap. He usually slept eighteen hours out of each day. His pride of four lionesses seldom needed his help in the hunt. They were young and in their prime. One had already produced a pair of cubs and another would give birth soon.

He had fought the old male, an all yellow lion with a modest and scraggly mane, from whom he had taken over the females. But he was an old one; his incisors broken, and he limped from an old spear wound. The young, black maned lion had watched him carefully for several months before challenging him and the fights were long and bloody. The old lion was crafty and wise but tired; finally, under the attacks of the younger male he had abandoned his pride. Later, when the old lion had fallen ill and a group of jackals had killed him, the lionesses had driven off the jackals, and eaten of him. Two of the lionesses were his daughters.

The resting lion glimpsed movement in the tall grass. As if on signal, he and the females crouched low, their heads just above their paws. The mother of the cubs brought her foreleg down on the backs of the young ones. They flattened out in the straw colored grass, their dappled coats blending into the mottled landscape. The lion raised his head slightly, eyes and ears pointing down wind.

A group of Africans single-filed into view. The lion caught the scent of man and lay quietly under the shade of the thorn tree. Only the most sensitive ears could have heard the soft tread of the men as they came closer. They stopped at the kill.

"Simba," the one carrying an unlighted torch muttered, pointing. The others silently looked around. They moved off quickly, trotting now, spears and shields held alert. The lion watched them go. He did not like the man scent and avoided it whenever possible. But if they had come too close, especially if they had made eye contact with him, he would have charged. Content now, he rolled over on his back and let the soft breeze cool his distended belly. He closed his eyes against the sun's glare and the buzzing flies.

# Chapter 1

The young army lieutenant paused a moment, then grasped the base of the unlighted torch firmly, and continued the long torturous climb up Mt. Kilimanjaro. Dusk would come soon and the last steep part of the climb was ahead of him. The thin cool air made him gasp for breath but he didn't dare stop. A dozen African soldiers straggled behind him on the twisting path up the mountain. The twin peaks flattened out as he approached. Soon he could see the depression the collapsed volcanoes had made. He veered to the right toward snow covered Mt. Kibo, the highest of the two peaks.

He lowered the heavy torch and sank on a pile of rocks, his lungs expanding under his throbbing heart. The last rays of the sun cast oblique shadows across the southern plain. Kilimanjaro rose like a sleeping giant in the middle of the flat country, its peaks covered by clouds most of the time. But this evening was bright and clear' with a view of the rain forests to the west, and toward the east the glint of the Indian Ocean. He could see the pink reflections of Soda Lake in the Ngorongoro Crater, the elephant forests of Lake Manyara, and the vast expanse of the Serengetti. He looked south towards the capital city of Tanzania five hundred miles away.

Das es Salaam. "Haven of Peace", the name translated into English. The Persians had come first, long before recorded history, then the Arabs with their slave ships, raping the country along the fifteen hundred-mile slave route into the Congo. The lieutenant turned his gaze westward. A double line of coconut palms marked the route where his people had been shackled, whip-driven, and starved all the way to Bagamoyo by the sea. They had been crammed into dhows there and sailed across the Zanzibar where they were sold. The palms grew from coconuts dropped by the Arab slavers as they marched inland. Livingston's body had come out by the same route.

"I am more gratified by having brought an end to the slave trade," Livingston had said near the end of his life, "than by having discovered the source of the Nile." The black men who had brought him out had first removed his heart and planted it beneath a tree in his beloved Africa. Then they had filled the body cavity with salt to preserve it for the long journey back to England. It was ironic that his

1

last journey on this alien continent should have been on that same route, worn by the callused feet and faltering steps of his adopted African brothers.

In 1502 Vasco de Gamma had planted the flag of Portugal on the East African shores, declaring the whole land for the king. The Chinese had traded in the distant past, eager for ivory to gild their palaces and rhino horn as an aphrodisiac. In modern times the Arabs were succeeded by the Germans who, in turn, forfeited it to the British after the first World War. Finally, this night, the British will relinquish their rule. Freedom. Uhuru!

Darkness settled quickly on the peaks of Kilimanjaro. The lieutenant walked over to warm himself at the sputtering fire the soldiers had built. A rude bowl filled with umgali was handed him. As he twirled a ball of the white maize with his fingers and settled it far back on his tongue, he wondered how long before his palate could adjust to the bland diet. His years at Sandhurst in England had spoiled his taste for the simple fare of his childhood. The soldiers' animated talk was interspersed with bursts of laughter.

"After midnight I'm going to move into that house on Oyster Bay—the one with the high wall around it."

"All right. I'll take the pink one next door."

"Midnight," the lieutenant thought. *Midnight, tonight. December 9, 1961; after forty-eight years of British rule, freedom!*

It would be a year, of course, before the last of the British officials left Tanzania, but tonight was the first giant step, the beginning.

"And I can walk into the yacht club and order a beer," grinned one soldier.

"And we'll never have to scurry off the road when the big British cars come speeding by," another replied.

"Ah, my brothers," the lieutenant smiled gently, "let us not confuse dignity with pomposity. It is dignity we seek and freedom from poverty, ignorance, and disease. That is more important than where we drink our beer."

A corporal stood facing the young officer. "A day comes when the people prefer death to insult! Why should we not drink our beer wherever we want in our own country?"

The lieutenant clasped the older man's arm. "We are fortunate to have, got rid of them without bloodshed, but, if it had come to that, I would surely have killed as many as I could."

*How easy it is to inflame an insulted people. Even an educated African will pretend to love European while his heart is bursting with hatred and envy, Perhaps it's not good for our people too become over interested in this independence. The problems become formidable if they see it to quickly. A British house one minute after midnight! And what will come next?*

The lieutenant looked at his watch. It was near the time. He built a cairn of stones on the highest point, waving off the others who wanted to help. He soaked the head of the torch in paraffin and set it upright in the center of the cairn. The soldiers stood in a circle around the torch, quiet now. The lieutenant glanced at his watch again and walked to the embers of the camp fire and drew out a glowing stick. He cupped the hot end in his hands and blew on it. The flame flared. He walked back and stood by the torch. He counted the seconds as they ticked by on his watch.

"Midnight," he shouted, as he held the flame to the torch. The paraffin caught and blazed. The soldiers whooped and started dancing and chanting around the flame.

"Uhuru," the lieutenant shouted, as he leaped down from the cairn and joined in the wild dancing. He leaped high, shaking off the last vestige of Colonialism.

*****************************************

Shortly before midnight the band played the closing notes of, "God Save the Queen". The sports arena at Dar es Salaam was filled with 75,000 Africans. At one side of the platform stood a small contingent of British soldiers standing at attention behind a half dozen British ministers, their white dress uniforms bright with ribbons. On the other side of the platform stood a group of Africans, some in western suits, some military, and a few in the collar-less "Mao" pajama suits. The speeches were over. Britain was surrendering yet another part of her shrinking empire.

The great crowd was silent watching the British flag fluttering in the gentle ocean breeze. The bright stadium lights dimmed. Two British soldiers turned to the flag pole, unbound the cord, and slowly lowered the British flag. As they caught the colors a murmur ran through the crowd. The lights were almost out and the crowd strained to see the flag pole.

Four uniformed Africans stepped forward and affixed the green, black, and gold flag of Tanzania to the cord. The colors slowly ascended as the lights came up. At the top, a sudden gust of wind caught the flag. It straightened and dipped. The lights came on full and the band began the rhythmical Tanzanian National Anthem.

"Uhuru!" shouted the crowd, as they leaped and danced, filling the large arena. The eyes of the British High Commissioner were wet as he glanced at the leader of the TANU party. The slightly built African's eyes were moist, also. They exchanged looks, moved instinctively toward each other, and clasped hands.

# Chapter 2

Blake dropped anchor a hundred yards off the Dar es Salaam pier. He wiped the sweat from his receding forehead with a clean white handkerchief and used the other end to polish his wire rimmed glasses, then set them back on his nose and sighed. Shifting his huge frame in a chair on the afterdeck, he accepted a steaming cup of tea from his cabin boy.

"Dinner, Bwana Captain?" the boy asked, in Swahili.

"Later," Blake grunted, "after my shower."

He looked around the harbor. It seemed strangely quiet even for that late hour. There were few ships; one was an Indian passenger boat, her paint peeling and rust streaking her sides. Blake's nose wrinkled. His years in the British Royal Navy compelled him to keep a trim ship, even though his was but a medium sized schooner. He could not tolerate slackness in any vessel. He admired the Danish freighter, pristine white, lying at anchor to his starboard. A few small craft dotted the neckless shaped natural harbor. Blake decided to wait until morning to check through customs.

It had been a long journey from the Island of Rhodes, through the Suez Canal, and down the long coast of East Africa. He had sailed short-crewed all the way, picking up a stray hand in one port, and losing him in the next. Only the cabin boy, long removed from his African tribe, and glad to earn passage to Tanzania, had remained the entire journey.

Blake sat in his sweat-streaked shorts. He rubbed the thick black hair on his chest and shoulders and swatted at a mosquito.

*How long has it been?* He had joined the Royal Navy at the very onset of the war, leaving school in Liverpool to do it. There was a full six years of service until after the war ended. He glanced across the harbor toward the east where his old home, Zanzibar, lay, and visualized the white rambling house with the elaborately carved wooden doors and the heavy spice scent of drying cloves overlaying the humid air. *The land, were I was born and haven't seen for over twenty years.*

The Moslem cry to evening prayer came faintly from the town. He sensed a restlessness in the air, but there was still no activity on the pier. Showering, he ate a light dinner, and went directly to his cabin and bed. Only faintly, some time in the middle of the night, he thought he heard voices and music coming over loud speakers, but he turned and buried his head deeper into the pillow.

Next morning he rose at dawn, puttered with the engines, tested them, and nodded in satisfaction as they purred smoothly. He washed his hands and sat on the afterdeck drinking his second cup of tea. The cabin boy brought his breakfast of fruit, scrambled eggs, and skillet biscuits. He picked a boll weevil out of the biscuit. *Time for fresh supplies.* When he had finished and was preparing to lower the dinghy over the side, he noticed the Coast Guard cutter leave the pier and head towards him.

When the cutter pulled along side, Blake leaned over and took the ropes from the boat man's hands and tied them fast to the schooner. Two Africans, one in military dress and the other in a white "Mao" suit, stepped from the cutter onto the afterdeck of the schooner.

"May I see your passport and papers, please?" the latter asked.

Blake disappeared below deck and returned with a plastic folder. He laid it on the table and zippered it open. The African opened the passport and his eyes widened.

"Mr. Blakely, may I introduce myself? My father worked for your father on Zanzibar many years ago, on his clove plantation. Do you remember? My name is Maasseemma. We were the only members of the Masai tribe on the plantation. You used to let me go fishing with you when I was just a lad."

Maasseemma smiled and extended his hand. Blake took it, studying him closely.

"And this is Colonel Ogendo, head of immigration for the port," he said, indicating the uniformed official.

Blake shook his hand and called for the cabin boy to bring two more folding chairs and tea. The three men settled around the small table.

Blake studied the Masai carefully as Maasseemma examined the papers and passed them one by one to the Colonel. Blake noted the Masai's features, so different from the coast African's mixed Arab and Negro blood. His color was lighter than that of the Colonel, his hair close cropped, nose less flattened, and in an almost straight line from tip to forehead. His small shell-curled ears lay flat against his head, teeth even and white behind chiseled lips. He handled himself

6

with the sinuous grace of his people, the lean frame rested easily against the chair.

Looking at Blake over the rim of the heavy tea cup, Maasseemma saw a powerfully built man with black receding hair, dark brown heavily lidded eyes behind glasses, a surprisingly well sculpted nose, and thin compressed lips.  It was a face, Maasseemma intuited, belonging to a man who could be both deliberately as well as casually cruel, but there was a twinkle in the eyes that softened the first impression.  His burnt arms and legs were massive and covered with thick black hair.  Only the bulge above Blake's belt line betrayed his approaching middle age.

"And they call us monkeys" Maasseemma thought, conscious of his own smooth body where even the underarm and pubic hair was tightly crinkled against his golden skin.

"We heard you had settled in Greece," Maasseemma said.  "I was sorry to hear your father had died during the war.  And your mother—?"

"She's well," Blake replied, glancing at the Colonel who was going through the papers a second time.  "She's settled in Liverpool with my younger brother, but I had a yen to return and settle in Africa.  Thought I'd do a bit of trading with the Camore Islands.  By the way, who do I see in the British Commissioner's office for a license?"

"Ah, my old friend," Maasseemma interjected, "do you not know what day this is?"  He noted the blank look on Blake's face, and continued.  "Just last night, at midnight, the British withdrew their rule.  So, today is the first day of Uhuru for Tanzania.  We are free of foreign rule. At last.  At last!"

"That was just last evening?"

Yes.  Didn't you hear the loud speakers in the sports arena, the band playing?"

"Only vaguely.  I was very tired.  I've been short of crew and haven't had much sleep since leaving Mombasa.  And now, the Africans think they can govern themselves, eh?" Blake's grin was derisive.  "I thought the United Nations had recommended a twenty year transition period a few years back."

"That is true," Maasseemma replied, "but we have stepped it up a bit.  We feel we are ready now, and we have a full year to take over completely. I, myself, am a graduate of Stanford in the United States, and there are more educated Africans now. We will manage."

The Colonel leaned forward and glared at Blake, "To suggest we are not ready to govern ourselves is like saying, 'You are not ready to live!' Now we have hope where before there was only despair; dignity, where before there was only humiliation!"

He had spoken in Swahili, aware from Blake's expression that he had understood. The language sounded musical to Blake's ears. It was spoken in a monotone with little inflection, but Blake disagreed with other Europeans who contended it was an impoverished language.

"As surely as the tick bird follows the rhino," Blake replied in Swahili, a smile playing around his mouth.

The Colonel was taken aback at the pure accent and the age-old saying. He was accustomed to Europeans who troubled learning only a bit of kitchen Swahili. He returned to a serious examination of Blake's papers.

"What of you, Maasseemma?" Blake returned to English. "Went to university in the States, you said?"

"Yes. As you may know, my father was one of the few Masai to leave the tribe and go to work for wages. He did this so my mother could have clean water, so his children could be healthy. He was a very wise man, ahead of his time. Even so, when I was ten, after your father left Zanzibar and returned to England, our family returned to the tribe. He wanted us to know tribal ways. I became a warrior, then a shaven-headed 'old man'."

The Masai rose and moved to the railing of the boat. He looked across the bay to the open water, and continued as if talking to himself, "One day, my father took me to the missionary school, where the priest took a special interest in me. I worked very hard. Later the priest found a scholarship for me at a Catholic college in the States. I stayed there for two years, then transferred to Stanford in California. They had better courses in political science. I wanted to be ready for my people when the time came." He turned back to Blake with a smile. "And now it is here."

"But the Masai have always seemed so happy," Blake countered. "How do you intend to help them."

"The Masai are living in the twelfth century," Maasseemma grew serious. "They have dirty water, when with a little work, they could have clean water. Today the standard of the U.S. of A. is a part of Tanzania. It would be wonderful if we could put this country on another planet and give it a hundred years to catch up, but we can't do that. The Masai know that it is possible to have clean water and good houses, but they don't accept the discipline required. Clean water and good houses require work. Work!"

Blake refilled the tea cups, adding generous amounts of tinned milk and sugar. "But it also requires technical skills. Where are your Masai engineers? The Americans and the Russians are going to the moon while the African dances and eats roots."

Blake stirred his tea with a bent spoon. "Germany, and Japan, too, were virtually destroyed in the war, but they have rebuilt themselves because they have the necessary skills."

Maasseemma sat heavily and bent his head over the steaming cup of tea. He was about to speak when the Colonel interrupted. "So, we may have to borrow skills for a while. We cannot train everybody all at once. Under the British my mother could neither read nor write but I have taught her. Now she can read signs and she can write her name. She does not have to use her thumb print for her name."

"It is easy," Blake returned the Colonel's hard gaze, "for a foreign power to leave by the front door and come in by the back door, and you will not like that either. What will you do when this country grinds to a halt? Who will keep your trucks running and your trains repaired? What will you do even if every family had a tractor? There would be no parts and no one to keep them in repair. Like it or not, you need foreign technology, and you will need it for a long time."

Maasseemma interrupted. "We do not need tractors, Blake. We hope to teach the people to use the plow instead of the hoe. That is a big step forward."

Colonel Ogendo jumped to his feet, letting the papers fall to the deck. "Should we have to choose between being dominated by a white or an Indian minority and driving that minority out of East Africa, no thinking African would hesitate to make a choice. We have independence now and we do not have to tolerate the Colonial arrogance any longer!"

Blake had scooped up the papers during the Colonel's tirade, turning his back to the man as he sorted the papers on the small table.

"The white man," the Colonel continued, his voice rising, "behaves like a man seeking to control a sleeping giant with his hands

9

at the giant's throat. This fear drives him to suicidal madness and he tightens his grip until the giant wakes up feeling pain."

The Colonel spun on his heel and started toward the cutter. Over his shoulder, he spat, "Permission denied for disembarking in Tanzania. Go on to Zanzibar, Englishman. They issued your passport. Let them deal with you."

Maasseemma looked apologetically at Blake as they watched the Colonel jump over the side and into the cutter. "Remain here. I'll get word to you."

Blake stood watching the departing boat cut across the harbor. His eyes narrowed. "Damned gibbering monkeys," he muttered. "Bugger me about, will they?"

That night the cabin boy slipped over the side of the schooner and swam toward shore.

# Chapter 3

Blake woke early the following morning after a fitful night's sleep and began preparing his tea. Although he had heard the cabin boy slip over the side in the night, he had not tried to stop him. Just as he finished his second cup of tea, the Coast Guard cutter pulled along side. Two uniformed soldiers greeted him and handed him a letter. He opened the sealed envelope and read, "Please accompany these men to my office. Maasseemma."

Blake showered and changed into long trousers and a clean white shirt. He gathered up the folder of papers, and climbed onto the cutter. As Blake entered the small office in the port authority building, Maasseemma came from behind a battered desk and extended his hand.

"I am sorry about yesterday," he smiled. "Please sit down."

Blake lowered himself gingerly into the rickety brown plastic chair. "Were you able to get an emergency visa for me?"

"One for only twenty-four hours. That was the best I could do. I'm sorry. I'm afraid you will have to go on to Zanzibar if you wish to return here. Perhaps later—."

He offered Blake a cigarette, which was declined, and while lighting his own, said, "Your father was good to my family. One time he brought medicine from Dar for my mother when she was sick. He was very kind to us when she died. I wish I could do more for you."

"Where does Zanzibar stand at the present time?" Blake asked.

"It's very unsettled. The Sultan claims they are independent. He also claims a twenty-mile strip of the Kenya coast as part of Zanzibar. We do not know if he will elect to join Tanzania or Kenya or remain independent. It is a problem."

Maasseemma stood up and studied a large map of Africa scotch taped to the wall behind his desk. "There are times when I wish we could put a grapple in Zanzibar and tow her far out into the Indian Ocean! It is an alien monarchy, with sons dabbling in politics, subject to an alien influence. And, as always, when the pipes are played on Zanzibar, all Africa east of the lakes must dance."

"Do you suppose it would do any good to talk to someone in the Commissioner's office?" Blake asked.

"I could call Bob Slade for you. He'd be the man to see, but I doubt if he could help you. It's too bad you antagonized Colonel Ogendo. He is sure to be a minister when the government is formed. You must get used to the fact, Blake, that the old Colonial days are over."

He picked up the phone and made an appointment with Slade for four that afternoon. "You must be out of the harbor early tomorrow, Blake, but keep in touch with me. I'll let you know if there's any change here, but for now—."

Blake nodded as they shook hands. "Appreciate what you've done."

Blake walked past the large Lutheran Church, a reminder of the days of German occupation. He turned away from the bay, and quickly covered the two blocks to the New Africa Hotel. Seating himself at a sidewalk table in the outdoor restaurant, he ordered coffee and a large breakfast. As he waited to be served, he discovered he was between two occupied tables. On his left were two Europeans and on his right, three Africans. The cafe was crowded and the tables were close together. Without straining he could catch the conversation from each table.

The Africans spoke in Swahili; "Do you think Julius Nyerere will take leadership now?"

"He must. We trust him. He is not out just to fill his own pockets. He cares about this people, this country."

"All the British wanted was to line the pockets of the British Empire."

"And the Asians to line their own."

"Yes. Nyerere says we do not control our continent and that is true. He says the best thing that can happen to us; would be for the United States, this power with a good ethic, to understand us.

"But they will side with the British, the white man. You'll see. That's why Africa must be for the Africans. There is no other way."

"Just a year ago I came to this hotel and ordered a beer. My brother African brought it to me. Then, the manager, a European, came running up. 'This is terrible,' he said. 'We don't serve Africans here.' I would like to see him now, if he should say this. I would see he was fired."

"You are right. No longer shall the white man insist on this vulgar doctrine of, 'The divine right of Europeans'!"

On Blake's left the voices of the two Europeans grew louder. "What they don't realize is that the wilderness of Tanzania begins at the end of the runway at Dar. The contrast between the primitive and the modern, one never quite gets used to it."

"Do you know of any independent country where there has not been a silent scramble for power and money? 'Make yourself rich as quickly as possible.' And if this is questioned, you are questioning people's freedom."

"I was in Leopoldville last week and heard a story going around. As you know, when the French left the Congo so quickly they had to hire foreign mercenaries to guard the public buildings. It seems a young Mukongo turned to one of the white soldiers who was on sentry duty near the university and asked, 'Is your country independent?'

'Yes.'

'Since when?'

'Five years ago.'

'Only five years and you're white already?'

Both men laughed and Blake smiled over his sausage and eggs.

"Did you see night before last—the big Uhuru thing—that all the African officials rode to the ceremony in big chauffeured cars? I wonder how their people feel about having to scramble out of the road for *them*?'

"They'll find out, I'm afraid, that their own African leaders can be more cruel than any white of the old school. They'll buy and be bought in return. Not Nyerere, maybe, he's a rare one, but can he control his ministers?"

The men rose to leave and one added, "Well, I'll be getting the 'golden handshake' the end of the year. Twenty-eight thousand pounds; for the unused part of my contract. Not bad, what?"

"Not bad at all. I think I'll stay on a while. They're going to need all the white man's know how before this is finished and I think they'll pay handsomely for it when all's said and done. After all, most of them don't even know how to flush a toilet!"

Blake glanced at the three Africans. They had overheard the conversation and sat sullenly over their coffee.

"Mbwa hawa," one muttered. "Those dogs."

Blake paid his chit and rose. He turned off onto a side street and entered a small shop. A young Asian girl spoke pleasantly to him and called the manager.  A Mr. Singh appeared and Blake introduced himself.  They spoke briefly, then Singh ushered him into a back room behind heavy curtains.  Blake withdrew a thick wad of bills from his plastic case.  The Asian counted them carefully and counted out a large pile of Tanzanian shillings.  Blake placed them carefully in his case after stuffing a few in his pocket.

"What will you be doing here, sir?" Singh asked.

"I hope to do some trading with the Camores from Zanzibar a bit later on.  I've a schooner in the harbor."

"Ah!" Singh's eyes lighted up.  "May I recommend you to my cousin in Zanzibar?  He has some very interesting merchandise he would like to get into French hands.  The color is blue and does not take up much room."

"Tanzanite?" Blake's eyebrows rose.

Singh put his finger to his lips, and rising, drew the curtains back slightly, glancing about the empty shop.

"Jeru does not understand English but one must be careful.  In any case, she has stepped out for a moment.  Singh seated himself next to Blake and continued in a low voice.  "The blue diamond.  Yes.  We have a direct connection at the mine—another cousin.  He brings them to me rough and I get them cut here.  But things are going to get very tight in Tanzania, I'm afraid.  My usual route will be no longer possible in a short time."

"Are they of good quality?" Blake asked.

"I will show you."  Singh crossed the room and stepped behind a heavy drape, Blake heard the sound of a wooden panel being moved and the metallic clink of a safe door.  Singh returned with a carved wooden box and removed a draw string bag from it.  He spread a black velour cloth on the corner of the desk, and shook the bag above it.  Three stones fell softly on the velour.  Blake picked up the largest of the three stones, a beautifully faceted circle the size of a silver dollar, and held it up to the single dangling light bulb.  Its blue fire reflected through the facets and bounced off the walls and ceiling as Blake's stubby fingers slowly turned it.

"This one could rest with the crown jewels," Singh said.  "The only precious stone discovered in modern times and the price will go up as people begin to demand it.  Can we do business?"

"It depends.  There is risk, you know.  I have spent enough time in jails to wish to avoid them.  But, if the price is right—?"

Singh nodded. "I think we can do business. My cousin will make the arrangements with you. I think there is enough in it for everyone. Can you take these to him?"

"Yes. I will not be searched when I leave Dar. I came in on the Coast Guard cutter and will leave the same way. I do not have to stop at customs. I sail for Zanzibar in the morning as far as I know now."

"Here is my card. I will write on it the address of my cousin. His name is Singh, also, of course."

"Of course," Blake laughed, as he picked up the three stones. "Has there ever been a sikh by any other name?"

Blake unbuttoned the top of his trousers, turned the waist band down, and zipped open a flap hidden underneath. He placed the stones in a straight row, tucking them into the flap. The zipper stalled on the largest stone, but soon went shut.

"How do you know I won't just take off with these?"

"I know," Singh rose and came from behind the desk, his small frame came no higher than Blake's shoulder. "I know of you, Captain Blakely. A cousin of mine served with you when you were a mercenary with the Sheik of Abbu Dabbi. The world is not large enough for you to run with the Tanzanite. I am sure you know that?"

Blake laughed. "Yes, I know that. You have a cousin—."

"You are right. You could not leave Africa alive. So, good sailing. I am sure Mr. Singh on Zanzibar can help you in other matters, also. He has many interests."

Blake hesitated at the heavy curtains. "The girl, there." He nodded toward the shop. "Her name is Jeru, you said?"

"Yes. She is not a relation, a stray without family. Perhaps when you have completed arrangements with my cousin on Zanzibar I will send her there with more Tanzanite. She is young, a virgin, but she is well trained. We shall see."

Ushered into Bob Slade's office promptly at four o'clock, Blake took his measure of the man and decided he liked what he saw. Slade's reddish brown hair framed a ruddy Irish face.

In spite of his bluff clipped speech, his eyes and relaxed full mouth bespoke a gentle nature.

"Glad I had some notice of your coming, Captain Blakely," he greeted Blake in a deep resonate voice. "It gave me time to glance through your dossier."

Blake winced when he saw the size of the file folder on the desk with "A. J. Blakely" penned in red on the front. After they were seated, Bob opened the folder and riffled the pages. "My, you've had a varied background," he teased, smiling. "Makes very interesting reading. Always managed to get out of your scrapes, though, didn't you?"

"There were a few close ones," admitted Blake, smiling in resignation. "I've been forcibly detained a few times, but only for brief periods."

"And what brings you back here? Don't think the new TANU government is in the market for mercenaries at the moment."

"I've a schooner now," Blake relaxed in the deep over stuffed chair. "I was running between Greece and Italy the past few years but trade sort of petered out in that area. So, I thought I could find something profitable between here and the Camore Islands. I know the French administrator for that territory, but they've rather forgotten the islands, if my information's correct."

"You've a Zanzibar passport, right? That limits you somewhat, especially with the change in government and the status of Zanzibar at the moment."

"I'm aware of that. I thought I might ask you for an emergency British passport, at least until things get cleared up around here."

"Don't think we'd get far with that. You elected to drop British citizenship after the war, you know. We might try for a United Nations passport if you like, but that will seriously jeopardize' your being able to stay in Africa. Is that important to you?"

"Yes, it is, rather. I'm set on staying. Even with the changes here I think there's a future for me in Tanzania. I'd like to give it a go, anyhow."

"Then I'd suggest you plan to operate out of Zanzibar at present, at least until things are a bit more settled."

Blake rose to leave, extending his hand.

"I say," Bob interjected, "why don't you put up for the night at our home? I doubt you could get a hotel room in Dar tonight with everyone in town for the ceremony last evening. We just sent our two children off to school in England this year and Ann, my wife, feels rather out of it these days. A little interesting company would be most welcome. Can I count on you?"

Blake nodded. "I'd enjoy that. I need to get my land legs after that long voyage. It'll be good to sleep in a bed that isn't moving about."

"Meet me here at 6:30. I'll call Ann and have an extra place set for dinner." "Thanks," Blake said, as he left.

Two hours later, Bob Slade drove his small Pugeot up the Oyster Bay road that hugged the gentle surf. He turned in toward a row of beach front apartments.

"We're living here temporarily," Bob explained. "The family has a coffee farm up near Arusha where I've lived most of my life. I took this job with the government just a while back. Guess I'll stay on for the year of transition, then go back to farming. I must admit, I've missed it, the highlands. Ann was jolly glad to hear you're coming," he added, as he slid the car into a ground floor parking place.

They walked up a flight of cement stairs. The apartment door swung open and Ann stood with outstretched arms to greet Bob. Blake almost ran into her. Ann dropped her arms in the confusion and shook hands with Blake.

"Goodness, I almost hugged the wrong man," Ann laughed. "Umm. From the looks of you, that wouldn't have been so bad."

"Enough, woman," Bob laughed as he moved toward the bar to mix drinks. "Let's sit on the balcony, Blake. I'll bring the drinks out here. Ann, I'd have introduced you if you'd only waited. This is Captain Blakely."

Blake turned and shook hands with Ann again in mock seriousness. "Blake, if you would. It's kind of you to have me on such short notice."

He watched Ann as she sat in the deep patio chair. Her long blond hair was pulled back and caught in an elephant hair clasp. She had merry blue eyes set in a classical face. She was tanned but retained the creamy complexion so commonly bestowed on English women. Her full long skirt fell becomingly about her slender figure. She looked fragile and very feminine, but Blake recognized that underneath she was as capable of shooting a marauding elephant as she was of sitting helplessly with a cigarette while a man rushed over to light it for her. That was what Blake was doing just now.

"You don't smoke," she stated.

"No. Never got started. I was a swimmer in public school in England and it was just understood smokers didn't make the team."

17

Bob appeared with frosty drinks. "To Uhuru," he toasted, as they took their first sip.

"Do you think they have a chance of making it?" Blake asked.

"I wish I could say," Bob replied. "They've far to go. Basic concepts like cash crops and land ownership will have to learn plus most of the technical skills, of course. They think the European is selfish because he looks out only for himself. They have a saying, 'He behaves like a European' when anyone refuses to share what he has."

"You know," Bob reached out for an appetizer the house boy had brought, "if an African has three of four hundred goats, he'll slaughter one at the week-end, and everybody will be welcome. To them, it's a terrible disgrace to have someone leave their house hungry. But, on a cash economy, what is not used for the family is sold and the money is used to buy only what the family needs."

They sat silently for a while, watching the billowing triangular sail of an Arab dhow as it crossed the path of the setting sun. Bob continued, "We've introduced a new concept of land as a marketable commodity. Such a system is completely foreign to the African, completely wrong. For centuries the African viewed the land as belonging to the community. His right to land was only the right to use it, and it never occurred to him to try to claim it."

"I wonder if he's not right," Blake responded, "I've seen so many developing countries go this route, thinking it's bringing them up into the twentieth century. They start growing cash crops and sell them to the western countries so they can get foreign exchange, and then they buy food from these same countries to supplement what they grow, and—."

Ann broke in. "That's right. They pay such high prices for what they buy they really don't show a profit. They might be better off if they went back to their old ways and did without transistor radios and coca cola!"

"You sound like an old African hand," Blake smiles.

"She was raised on a north Kenya cattle ranch," Bob laughed, "Until I managed to get her off a horse long enough to marry me and come to Tanzania. First time I saw her she was chasing an eland on her horse and nearly ran into a rhino. Some girl!"

"A tobacco farm's pretty tame by comparison, isn't it?" Blake queried.

"I miss the stock, but since the farm's outside Arusha near Ngorongoro Crater, we see our share of game. Our first night at the farm after we were married a leopard carried off my pet dog who was lying in the doorway. Poor little thing; I heard her whimper when the leopard seized her. The only evidence was a wet spot where she had urinated."

"The long rains were sparse last year and we cut the coffee trees back," Bob said, as he served fresh drinks. "Two years 'till we get a crop again. That's why I agreed to take government work for a while. The rest of the family can run the place for a couple of years."

After they were seated at dinner Blake turned to Bob. "Tell me about this Julius Nyerere. I know he was educated in Scotland and has translated some of Shakespeare into Swahili, for whatever that's worth, but what sort of person is he?"

"He's typical of the 'leap' we see occasionally in the locals these days. He comes from the small Zanaki tribe, so he's not as threatening as a Kikuku or a Chagga would be. His father had twenty-two wives and one of his brothers, even today, has eleven. His teeth are filed according to tribal custom. But Nyerere's a Christian and that may account for a lot of what's different about the man. I'd say that of all the newly sprouted African leaders, he shows the most promise. He seems to be totally without personal ambition, a rarity these days, even among Christians; a truly humble man, in the best sense of that word."

Bob leaned forward, his hazel green eyes intense, "His task is formidable, of course, trying to bring together one hundred and twenty-six tribes, all with different languages, and all claiming allegiance to the tribe over any central government. But he's been the leader of the Tanzanika African National Union for some years and managed independence without violence. He's a man trusted by the African and the European alike, and there aren't many like that."

"What about the Asian?" Blake smiled.

They all laughed. "You know the Asian," Ann replied. "He's so clannish, and cunning, and downright dishonest often times. They have bought a lot of houses in Dar and charge very high rents for them, but if you rent, that's who you have to rent from. And they're the shop keepers of Africa. The Africans hate them."

After dinner they went into the living room for coffee and brandy. As Blake lighted Ann's cigarette, he said, "I've seen articles in papers and magazines in the twenty years I've been away but stories coming out of Africa are usually about some tribe who dressed up in lion skins and went raiding, or about an M.P. who wanted to know if there really were mermaids. It's hard to get the real news."

"Quite," replied Bob. "The reporters write what they think makes a good story. I met an American reporter once in England and he said, 'Tanzania? Isn't that one of those countries that changed its name?' And that was all the information he had about the whole country."

"You'd think the Yanks would be closest to this country since they fought Britain for independence to become a nation," Blake replied. "But I think something went wrong with the U.S. someplace."

Ann broke in. "Yes. They'll go to any length to save some missionaries, but they don't seem to care how many Africans the mercenaries kill! God! Mercenaries; those haters of the human race!"

There was a strained silence. Ann read the stricken look on Bob's face. "Our guest—Captain Blakely—," he stuttered.

Ann reached for Blake's hand. "Oh, I'm so sorry. I didn't realize—."

Blake laughed at her embarrassment. "Quite all right. It's been some years since I was a mercenary, anyhow, and most of it was training troops, really. I worked for a Sheik of one of the Persian Gulf countries, the oil rich kind, and taught a bit of soldiering. Now and then, one of the Bedouins would start something and I'd take a helicopter out to the desert. I'd fire a shot over their heads and if that didn't do it, I'd pick off the man in front. If that didn't stop them, there was always the machine gun. But it seldom came to that, actually."

Noticing Ann's discomfort, Blake continued in a lighter vein. "The Sheik had a camera installed in the woman's dressing room at the yacht club, hidden, of course. They had lots of Yanks as well as British engineers working there. Well, when this Sheik sees the wife of one he likes—and he's become pretty well acquainted with their, ah, attributes in a short time—he invites her to tea. If she's a good girl and cooperates, he gives her the equivalent of a hundred pounds or so. If she's *too* good a girl and doesn't cooperate, she's on the next plane out of the country. Her husband can stay or go, as he likes. If the Sheik really likes her, he finds some excuse to send the husband out of the country for a month or so. The wife, of course, remains.

They all laughed. "By the by," Blake added, "if you like to dive or do some fishing, come over to Zanzibar later on. I've a fine schooner and we can have some fun. I'll let you know where to reach me."

"I'd love that," Ann exclaimed, her eyes shining. "With our two little ones off to school, it would be a good time to do some diving. I wouldn't dare do it with them around. They'd want to go, too. Wouldn't that be great, Bob?"

"Indeed it would be. Nice of you to ask, Blake. Maybe I can talk her out of another child. She's been hinting at that lately; the empty nest and all."

"Oh, no you don't Bob. I can dive pregnant or no. We've waited far to long as it is."

"See, Blake?" Bob frowned in mock seriousness. "I'm not just hen pecked, as the Yanks say. I'm pussy whipped!"

The next morning Blake's schooner weighed anchor and sailed clear of the harbor, the bow pointed due east. The cabin door opened a crack and a small brown face framed by loose black hair peered out. Blake looked down and smiled, extending his hand to the slight young girl, who emerged.

"Come here, Jeru," he said.

# Chapter 4
# TWO YEARS LATER

"Go to my beach house. I'll be along shortly," Blake said over the phone. "It's the third one after you pass the Bahari Beach Hotel on Ocean Drive. I'll call Mohammed and tell him to look after you."

Dick Dirkson smiled, thinking of Blake's proper upper middle class accent. Although Dick was an American he knew that in families like Blakes' care was taken that children grew up speaking with a good accent, along with strict rules about what "simply was not done". The accent and education of a gentleman notwithstanding, he knew Blake's reputation as a scoundrel, and he knew it to be well earned.

"He's asked us to wait for him at his beach house," he told Penny when he joined her. He settled back on the comfortable divan in the hotel lobby. The Kilimanjaro Hotel was the newest and fanciest in Dar. Facing the ocean with bougainvillea trailing the grounds, it was dotted with gardens rife with colorful and exotic plants. People of all skin hues and national dress passed through its doors.

Penny turned an anxious face to Dick. "I'm so glad you were able to locate him for me. I've been told he is the best bird trapper in Tanzania and Hubert and I can sell all the parakeets we can get back in Liverpool. They've gotten frightfully hard to find lately."

"That might be due to the change in government." Dick replied. "I've found it much more difficult to do business here than before, when Tanzania was a British Protectorate."

Penny twisted in a too tight white summer dress. The air conditioning in the hotel was a welcome relief from the hot humid climate, but even so, her abundant black hair straggled a bit, and traces of dampness formed on her forehead. Her ill-fitting dress, to long for current fashion, covered a plump figure that could easily run to obesity.

"Ah, the British," Dick thought. *They must have their boiled potatoes and puddings every day, but what it does to their figures! She is striking, though, with those arched dark eyebrows that set off her dresden blue eyes so effectively.*

He had guessed her age in the mid-forties, but revised it when she mentioned she had married young and had a son shortly afterward. Alfred, a gangly fifteen year old, was with her. Alfred appeared at that moment, fresh from the pool, and strolled toward them, rubbing his head with a towel. He resembled his mother in a quite masculine way; shy, but with an' engaging warmth.

"Run and change, Alfred." his mother said, looking fondly at him. "We're in such luck. Captain Blakely is in town and has invited us to his beach house. We'll be leaving shortly."

She looked questioningly at Dick. "Shan't we?"

"Well, this *is* East Africa, so we're on East African time, and no one really knows what that means. As I told you, I had an appointment with a government minister for yesterday only to be told he had left for up country and won't be back until next week. So, we learn patience here."

He chuckled, then continued. "Blake, of course, is better about these things than the locals, but he's lived most of his life here and isn't entirely immune."

Alfred bowed slightly and turned toward the elevators.

"I'm so glad the tables in the dining hall were full and you were kind enough to let us share yours last evening." Penny exclaimed. "We've had such trouble getting young healthy parakeets in our little shop. I jumped at the chance to come here when Hubert suggested we should try to buy directly from a trapper. I've always longed to see Africa. I used to stand in front of the parakeet cages and talk to them. I would ask them what it was like in that beautiful mysterious country they came from. They would flutter their little feathers and blink their eyes as if they really wanted to tell me."

"Oh," she drew back, looking slightly embarrassed, "And you must think me absolutely bonkers to be talking like this."

"Not at all," he laughed. "I've been to East Africa many times, and I always feel a thrill when I set foot on the tarmac at the airport. Even here, one is overwhelmed by the colors, the smells, the strangeness. There's nothing quite like it anywhere in the world. I'm glad to be of help to you, especially since I've time on my hands. Blake and I met years back when my father was stationed in Liverpool. We attended the same school. It's been over a year since I've seen him, though."

"I'm from Liverpool. I think I told you." Penny said.

Dick nodded. "Yes. You did mention it. I haven't been back there since the war. Has it changed much?"

"The war made some change inevitable, but all in all, it's pretty much the same." Penny paused a moment, glancing at the elevator which failed to produce Albert. "Would you mind telling me about Captain Blakely? I've heard a bit about him, but it all seems rather contradictory."

Dick hesitated. He had doubts about anyone doing business with Blake, but he was undoubtedly the best contact Penny could make for buying birds. Also, he knew Blake could be most magnanimous when it suited him. He glanced at Penny, noting her eager, expectant look.

"No one in the business knows Tanzania like Blake. He'll not only help you in getting the birds but will help you clear customs and get all the necessary papers to transport them."

"That's nice to know," Penny replied, with a sigh of relief. "I've never before been out of England and I wondered if I should quite be able to bring it off—coming here with only Alfred and not knowing anyone and all. It was such good fortune running into you."

"Oh, here's Alfred." She stood up quickly and brushed a hair from the boy's shoulder. She turned back to Dick. "Thanks so much for offering to run us out there."

"Glad to," he replied. "It'll be good to see Blake again. He always has interesting stories to tell."

The heat struck them as they entered the small car and left the parking lot. Tall fronted palms lined the highway as it followed the curve of the sandy beaches. Most of the local people wore western clothes, but now and then one passed wearing bush garb; a woman in a brilliantly colored wrap-around skirt with a strip binding her breasts, a layer of material across her shoulders used to carry a baby slung on her back. A small head, black against the bright colors, lay contentedly against a shoulder blade and tiny feet dangled out below. Cotton of yet a different color cushioned the woman's head, topped by an easily balanced basket laden with bananas. A man took the lead armed with bright edged panga, and dressed in loose fitting white top and baggy trousers.

"I asked Blake about that one time," Dick said, nodding toward the couple. "He explained that in the bush a man never knows when he will be attacked by a lion or leopard and he must be unencumbered in using his panga or spear to protect his family."

"I wonder where one would expect to encounter a lion in the city limits of Dar?" Penny asked.

Dick laughed. "I suppose old habits die hard."

Penny's intense blue eyes were sparkling. "I should never get enough of this. What beautiful people! Is it like this all over Tanzania?"

"Somehow I like it better back in the bush," he replied. "Not that I've seen all that much of it, but in the remoter areas the people have remained more or less the same for centuries. You'd be surprised how many Africans in this city have never even seen an elephant."

Penny looked from one side of the highway to the other, anxious not to miss anything. "I've always wanted to see the strange places in the world, but I never really thought I'd actually be in Africa! Hubert's never cared much for traveling. I've hardly been able to get him to take a holiday, even as far as Brighton, but I've always had such a longing—."

*Dear Hubert. So steady and solid, but not very exciting, I guess. And ever since Alfred was born, not even interested in me as a woman. Sometimes I meet an interesting man and I wonder what would happen if I flirted with him—just the least bit. Oh well, I've got past the age for that sort of thing, I suppose. Just the same, I can't help but think about how it would be.*

They passed the Bahari Beach Hotel complex with its spacious lawns and guest houses and soon turned ocean-ward onto a sandy road. A neat rambling beach house, almost hidden by palms, lay near the edge of an escarpment with the surf of the turquoise Indian Ocean rolling gently below. A small grinning black man came running out of the house. The flowing robes of his dhoti flapped about him. A small brightly embroidered skull-cap sat atop his close cropped head.

"Welcome, Bwana," his head bobbed up and down. "Welcome, Memsahib, and young Sahib," He bowed as he opened the car doors. "Jambo."

This seemed to be the extent of his English since he lapsed into a rapid torrent of Swahili. Dick remembered that Blake seldom employed blacks who spoke English, preferring servants who would understand little of his business.

25

"Asanti," Dick replied, glad to find bits of the language coming back to him.

"Captain come soon," The African grinned, as he led the way through the house to a wide verandah where four wicker chairs surrounded a matching table.

"How long has Captain Blakely lived here?" Dick asked, thinking the luxuriousness of the surroundings somewhat beyond the means of the Blake he remembered.

Hovering over them as they sat around the table, Mohammed answered. "Bwana Dinwitty on leave. Captain stay here a while. What you drink?"

Dick laughed in spite of himself; *Good old Blake hasn't changed a bit. 'My beach house', Blake had said over the phone, and would be quite content to have me believe it, and not at all embarrassed if we found out otherwise.*

"What would you like to drink?" he asked. "Luncheon isn't served until around two o'clock in these parts, and it's just past noon."

"A double gin and tonic, please," Penny replied, "and a coke for Alfred."

Dick was a bit taken aback. She didn't strike him as a person who would drink double gins at mid-day, but he relayed the order to Mohammed, adding a beer for himself.

"Shall we see any animals about?" Queried Alfred. He was downing his second cake and Penny was starting her third double gin.

"Ordinarily not," Dick replied, "though they sometimes appear quite unexpectedly. I met a friend in London who used to live here in a house on the river that empties into the bay. His wife was swimming in front of their beach house when a hippo appeared from nowhere and clamped his teeth on her right shoulder. It lifted her out of the water and shook her as if she were a rag doll. Fortunately, when it let her go she splashed down in shallow water and managed to crawl ashore before she passed out. It took fifty-four stitches to sew her up, and they had to return to London for plastic surgery. She may never get the full use of that arm again."

"How awful," Penny gasped.

"What did they do to the hippo?" Alfred asked, excitedly.

"The police came out and took some pot shots at him," Dick replied. "They think they hit him three or four times, but he was still there last I heard."

At that moment Mohammed came running in. "Bwana Captain here," he cried.

And in strode Blake.

# Chapter 5

"Jolly good to see you again, Dick," Blake said, as they shook hands.  Blake's sheer size again struck Dick, but he noticed some excess fat had been added around his middle, and his hair line had receded even more.  Even so, that did little to alter the impression of brute strength and animal vitality.  Blake removed his wire-rimmed glasses and pressed the bridge of his nose.

Penny's eyes were wide as Dick turned to introduce them.

"Mrs. Lambert-Smith, may I present Captain Blakely, and her son, Alfred?"

Blake glanced sharply at Penny, a look that would go unnoticed to one not familiar with his ways.  "My pleasure," he smiled and nodded, turning to give a hearty handshake to the boy.  He moved with a feline grace Dick had always admired in a man his size, remembering Blake's early years as a champion swimmer, and that he had once been in training for the Olympics.  Too bad some minor scandal involving the disappearance of a watch, or a bit of money, had caused him to leave school before graduation.  Shortly afterward the war started and Blake was one of the first to enlist.

Blake moved with long strides to the railing opposite Penny.  Even when he sat, his muscles were ready to spring, his eyes darting about the verandah.  He looked at Penny with a rare softening of expression, the corners of his eyes crinkling, and his usually firm mouth relaxed in an easy smile.

"You're new to Africa, aren't you?" he asked Penny in his deep resonate voice.

He laughed at her surprised look accompanied by an embarrassed giggle.  "I can usually tell," he continued, "It's all new and exciting to you."

"You know, Dick," he added, "us old timers have been here so long we just don't see it any more until we start showing it to visitors.  Then it hits us all over again."

He turned back to Penny.  "And what brings you here?"

"I—we—that is, Alfred and I—.  I mean Hubert, Mr. Lambert-Smith, my husband—.

"I'll tell him, Penny," Dick laughed, sitting next to her and looking up at Blake. "The Lampert-Smiths have a pet shop in Liverpool, Blake, and she's here-."

Dick choked back laughter in mid-sentence. Blake sat angled on the railing and one of his testicles was hanging below his shorts. Dick tried to continue but his laughter came in short spurts and he barely got out that Penny was there to buy birds for their pet shop.

No longer able to contain himself, Dick rose and walked into the living room, calling Blake to join him. When they were together Dick explained the cause of Penny's and his embarrassment.

I'm perfectly aware of that," clipped Blake. "I can sit that way when I want to."

"Now look here, damn it," Dick's voice rose in anger. "This woman's a nice, married, naive, little middle-class shop keeper, and I feel responsible for introducing her to you, so none of your shenanigans."

"Very well," Blake nodded soberly, but his eyes twinkled. "Shall we have lunch?"

Blake set a gourmet table and was a charming host. He told one of his longish war stories in which he, as always, was the hero, but told with such humor one didn't seem to mind. Alfred listened with mounting excitement, breaking in to ask questions that Blake patiently answered. Penny sat wordlessly, hardly eating, her eyes seldom leaving Blake's face.

He had seated Penny next to him at the table. As he talked, he passed her the salt and pepper. His fingers pressed hers when they touched and Penny returned the pressure. Over after-dinner coffee, she felt Blake's leg touch hers as he shifted and relaxed in his chair. Startled, she started to move away, then with color heightening her cheeks, she moved her leg to return the pressure. Blake's narrative continued smoothly. His hand moved under the table and rested on Penny's knee. She moved her leg slightly, allowing his hand to caress the inside of her thigh. Her hand trembled as she raised the coffee cup to her lips, then sat the cup down with a clatter. Blake turned to her with an innocent look. She lowered her hand and pressed his firmly against her thigh. Little of all this was lost on Dick.

"I've really done it this time," Dick thought. *I shall return her to the hotel soon and after that it will be none of my affair.*

Dick rose, thanked Blake, and said they must get back.

"But my dear chap," Blake interrupted, "it's past three o'clock now and the curfew started at two."

"What curfew?" Dick demanded. "When did all this start?"

The twinkle in Blake's eyes belied his innocent expression. "My apologies. It hadn't occurred to me you didn't know. For the past several weeks no driving is allowed from two o'clock on Sunday until six o'clock Monday morning. Pretty stiff fine if you try it. Something to do with shortage of foreign exchange and importing petrol. Most likely," he added with a grimace, "one of those bloody government ministers casting about for something to make himself feel important."

"But what shall we do?" asked Penny, her hands fluttered as she picked the wrinkled dress away from her damp skin.

"No problem." Blake rose and led the way down the hall. "I've two bedrooms with twin beds. Dick and I can share one and you and Alfred the other. In fact, I think I'll turn in for a nap right now, so if you'd care to rest, please do."

Penny and Alfred went into the other bedroom, but Dick, sensing he would be unable to sleep, went out onto the verandah. *That damned Blake! Even as kids he always managed to involve me in his nefarious schemes. I never seemed to see it coming.*

He stood watching the tide inexorably going out. The twelve-foot tide, when it was low, left acres of interesting tide pools filled with small neon fish, sea anemones, and colorful coral.

Alfred soon came out of the living room. "I'm just too excited to sleep. Gosh, what a super chap, that Captain Blakely is. If I had my dibs, I'd never leave here." He walked to the railing and peered over. "Do you think it would be all right if I walk over toward the river? I can see where it empties into the sea just over there. It would be super if I could catch a glimpse of that hippo."

"Surely," Dick replied, trying to shake off his annoyance at Blake. "I'll go with you."

They crossed the sandy, hard packed beach, stopping at several tide pools. Rounding a cypress grove, they came upon the sluggish brown river, twisting like a giant lethargic snake.

"Let's sit here," Dick said, pointing to two tree stumps. They both watched the water closely until mid-center of the wide river the water rippled and parted. A huge shiny black back rose, followed by a head whose mouth opened a good two feet from top to bottom. The pink mouth sported enormous stumps of teeth that jutted wickedly beyond the huge lips. As the massive head lowered into the water, the colossal rear end erupted. The animal threw itself from side to side. A stream of offal shot in a ten-foot arc.

"Why does he do it that way?" asked Alfred, his eyes turning dark blue like his mother's.

"The main thing to remember about that," Dick laughed, "is if you're in a boat on an African river, get ready to move quickly. More than once I've had to strip and wash my clothes along side the dugout with the African boat boys laughing themselves sick."

Dick looked up the hill behind them. "An acquaintance of mine lives just there. Would you care to come up with me?"

"Would you mind awfully if I didn't?" asked Alfred. "I'd like to wait here. That hippo may rise again and I'd hate to miss it."

Dick climbed the stairs to the house and found the Lawrence's having their fiveses on their verandah. After a few pleasantries and offering Dick a drink, Lawrence launched into a vehement tirade. "So the curfew caught you and you're having to put up with that dastardly Blake, are you? Well, I hope you come away with your wallet! Did you hear what he pulled on us?"

"No," Dick replied. "I arrived just yesterday evening, but nothing would surprise me. What's he done now?"

"You know how he is," Lawrence said, sitting heavily in the chair. "Ordinarily I would never have loaned him my car. I've known him too many years for that. I ran into him at the yacht club. By Jove, he ought to be black-balled. I'm going to look into that."

Lawrence lifted himself from the deep chair. His face grew red. "To get on with it, I needed my boat motor repaired, and you know how impossible it is here to get anything like that done. When the Africans repair anything they return it in worse shape than when they got it. This whole country has been grinding to a halt since the British left them to run it by themselves!"

Lawrence paced the verandah. "But back to Blake, that blackguard!" His drink sloshed unnoticed from the rim of his glass. "He heard me talking to someone about getting the motor repaired and he offered to do it for me. With his stint in the navy, and having owned his own schooner, I felt just desperate enough to let him have a hand at it. When he heard we were going back to England on leave

31

he said he'd need a car to run around for the parts and all that. Josephine let him have the car against my better judgment."

He glared at his wife and she ducked her head. "When we returned after a fortnight, Ahmed here," a nod of his head indicated his house boy standing by the bar, "took the keys from Blake when he returned the car. Blake had been sitting here waiting for him while Ahmed was at the market. Blake told him the car and boat motor were in the garage and Ahmed checked through the garage window and the car was there."

He sat down heavily. "Now, let me tell you what we found when we returned." Lawrence's wattles quivered. "The boat motor hadn't been touched, and of course, still wasn't running. Then when we went to start the car we discovered the whole car motor was missing! Imagine!"

Agitation lifted him from the chair again. He angrily thrust his glass at Ahmed to be filled. "When I stormed over to where he was staying—a little chicken coop of a place, shacked up with one of those Asian girls, of all things—and confronted him, he gave me that innocent look he gets when he knows you've been buggered and said, 'Look, I parked the car in the garage and gave the keys to your boy. What happen after that is no concern of mine. As for the boat motor, it was working perfectly after I repaired it.'"

Josephine broke in. "There was absolutely nothing we could do about it. Ahmed had accepted the keys without thinking to check things out. After all, why should he? The car was locked away in the garage, and even so, Ahmed hardly knows one end of a car from another. That's another reason we know Blake took it. Ahmed wouldn't know how to go about removing a motor."

"That bastard," Lawrence fumed, as Dick stood to take his leave. "I hope the people he's house sitting for have a house to return to."

Blake sat on the dimly lit verandah with a brandy and coffee after the others had retired that evening. As he gazed at the incoming tide under the strong moonlight, he turned sharply, hearing a muffled sound. Penny came hesitatingly out of the living room.

"Oh," she cried, seeing Blake. "I'm afraid I'm not dressed properly." She pulled at her thin slip. "I'd not expected to stay the night." She paused a few feet from Blake and stood nervously.

Blake rose, indicating a chair. "Sit down. You're perfectly all right. We're much more informal here, the heat and all."

Penny sank into the large wicker chair, tucking her legs beneath her.

"You've good legs," observed Blake. "Don't hide them. Here," he shifted the chair closer to the railing. "Stretch out a bit and put your feet up."

With a grateful smile, Penny relaxed and looked out into the soft inviting African night. "How utterly beautiful. I've never known a night like this. I watched the moon rise from my bedroom window. It looked twice the size I've ever seen it before and it was so red! Listen to the waves breaking."

She stood up enthralled and leaned over the railing. Blake studied the outline of her figure; her long dark hair contrasted with her pale skin and the white of her slip. "How would you like to take a swim?" he asked.

"Could we? I'd adore it." Her brow furrowed. "I just realized I haven't a bathing costume with me. Would it be frightfully improper to go in my undies?"

"Not at all improper," Blake laughed, rising. "Just a moment. I'll fetch a beach towel."

They went down the steep stairs along the escarpment, Blake guiding Penny with a slight pressure on her arm. He spread out the large towel and dropped his shirt on it.

"You can leave your slip here," he said, and went, without a backward glance, into the water. A slight phosphorescence followed his wake. Trembling, she pulled the slip off over her head, and giving a shake of her long hair, stepped into the warm sea water. After swimming a few strokes she felt turbulence in the water near her. Suddenly remembering the story of the hippo she panicked and floundered. Blake came up almost beneath her and caught her, half raising her out of the water. As she coughed and sputtered her arm fell about his neck and his hand slipped up to cover her breast. She drew back sharply, gasped, and choked.

"Relax," he commanded. "I'll get you to shore."

The pressure of his hand on her made her whole body feel warm and aware of the surging of her blood. Blake's feet touched bottom and he swung her up into his arms.

Her eyes looked up into his with a hungry yet scared gaze. She stared at his huge bronzed hand against the white of her bra. "Thank you," she murmured, "but you really—".

"Be still," whispered Blake. "I'm going to kiss you and I can't do that when you're talking."

He lowered both of them into the shallow water, shifting his body on top of hers. His weight pressed her into the soft wet sand. Her hair, ebony in the bright moonlight, framed her face and shoulders.

"Come up onto the towel," Blake said, as he pulled her to her feet. She lay on his arm and his lips came close to her ear, taking her ear lobe and nibbling it. "I want to take you," he whispered, "make love to you properly."

"Oh, I'm not sure," she twisted away from him. "I've never known any man but Hubert, but—I've never felt like this before. I just don't know."

Blake turned and lay on his back. Suddenly she felt cold, wishing for the close warmth of his body. They lay quietly for several minutes, then he said, "I'm going back into the bush the next day but one for more trapping. Would you like to come?"

"I'd love to, but I'd want to bring Alfred, if that's all right."

"Very well," he groaned. "I've two tents."

"Come," he said, springing to his feet and reaching a hand down to her. "We've teased each other enough for one evening. I'm not going to take you, anyway, on this dirty wet towel with both of us covered with sand."

"You can decide how you feel after we've made camp Tuesday night. I've never forced a woman in my life, and I don't intend to start now."

"May I call you Blake, Captain?" Penny asked.

He strangled a booming laugh. "Indeed you may, Mrs. Penelope Lambert-Smith. And now goodnight."

He playfully slapped her buttocks, letting his warm palm linger a moment on the downward curve of her rump.

She lay for a long time in her bed listening to Alfred's even breathing interspersed with the sound of the surf. She turned her head to watch the moon moving behind a palm frond, and drifted off to sleep remembering the feel of Blake's hand on her behind.

# Chapter 6

Blake's land cruiser slowly ground from pothole to pothole, jostling the three passengers in the front seat constantly. Penny wished she had asked Alfred to sit in the middle so she could be by the window. The dust from oncoming trucks and busses rolled past in blinding clouds, settling layer upon layer of red dust on sweaty faces and sweat streaked clothing. Blake's arm moving in a constant arc, trying to avoid the worst of the potholes brushed her right side, making her constantly aware of his sheer maleness. They had stopped by the roadside for a box lunch earlier. She saw Blake whip off his thin shirt and stand so Appendai, his gun bearer, could dump a bucket of water over him. His chest, back, and arms were covered with a mantle of thick black hair. She had felt a tingle in her groin as the water poured over his dark burnt skin, the rivulets parting the matted hair on his massive chest. She and Alfred had splashed water on their faces and hands, getting just clean enough to eat.

Alfred had been only a bit more wide-eyed than she, as they drove past trotting ostrich and craned their necks to see the heads of giraffes. Once they had halted over fifteen minutes while an endless line of migrating wildebeest crossed the road. Small villages, the few mud and wattle huts topped with palm fronds and an occasional corrugated roof lay deserted, baking in the hot afternoon sun. Shortly they began to climb, feeling some relief from the heat as a moment's breeze came down from the distant forest.

"We've made it," Blake grunted, as he turned the car sharply off the deeply rutted road near the edge of the forest. The truck following with the supplies and four Africans pulled to a halt some distance away. Appendai slid agilely off the top of the Land Cruiser. For the first time Penny noticed the gun he swung easily as he moved. He was narrow as an arrow, the corded muscles pulled taut across his rib-grooved ebony chest.

"Look at him," Blake gazed admiringly at Appendai's fluid movements. "He's the strongest African I've ever known. The other boys call him, 'The Gorilla'. He's been with me for years now and I only hope I don't outlive him."

"We'll all need a swim," Blake laughed as he looked at his bedraggled passengers. "Go behind the truck and change into your bathing costumes while we get the vehicles unloaded, and we'll be off."

When they reassembled and got into the car, Blake turned straight into the forest, climbing steeply. When the tree trunks became too thick to allow them through, they stopped.

"It's just a short walk from here," Blake said, helping Penny from the car. "I liked you better in your undies," he added in a low tone. His eyes flicked over her heavy black suit.

She felt the blood rising to her face. They had had dinner with him the night before and danced under the African sky at the outdoor bar atop the Twigga Hotel. He had acted the perfect gentleman, never holding her to close, nor had he referred to the previous evening. She began to wonder if she had imagined it, but remembering his demanding mouth on hers, and the pressure of his body holding her, she knew it had not been a dream.

After he had teased her a bit about being so protective of Alfred, he had introduced the boy to the young daughter of friends of his and urged him to invite the girl to dance. Penny protested her son's inexperience, but Blake insisted. When Alfred returned to the table from shuffling around the floor; he admitted he needed some dancing lessons. Blake laughed. "Get your mother to teach you. She's a natural."

The rumbling sound of a waterfall drowned out the muted bird calls and money chatter. In an opening in the thick green forest, tree trunks intertwined with hanging ropes of interlaced vines. They glimpsed white water cutting a deep gorge down the face of a steep mountain. At the bottom lay an emerald pool, the heavy dripping branches of the surrounding trees, wet with the spray of cascading water, cradled it like a jewel set in jade.

"How exquisite," breathed Penny. Alfred ran to the pool's edge and looked back at Blake inquiringly.

"Jump in," Blake motioned with his broad hand. "It's perfectly safe."

As Alfred's head disappeared into the water Blake turned to Penny. In a low voice, he said, "If you want to finish what we started the other night, I'll be waiting in my tent when Alfred's asleep."

"Oh, I don't know. I really shouldn't," Penny stammered. "I—you—Alfred—."

"Hush," Blake spoke softly, laying his finger on her lips. "If you want to come, fine. If you don't, I'll respect that."

He spun on his heel, peeled off his shirt, and appeared to fly as his huge body arced in the air, cutting the water in a dive that hardly rippled the surface. Penny anxiously searched for him to come up. After what seemed countless minutes she saw Alfred rise out of the water as Blake's head and shoulders appeared under him. Alfred fell forward, and when he came up they all laughed uproariously.

"Are you coming in?" Blake shouted, his left eyebrow lifted as he looked at Penny.

"Oh yes," she cried, "but I think I'll just slip in."

The water felt delicious. Blake gently splashed her dust-streaked face.

"I'd almost forgotten what you looked like under all that dust," he laughed. His eyes darted to the left. He had caught a movement. "Get out quickly," he said, loudly and urgently.

Penny and Alfred followed his eyes. A huge, shiny, black rock was slowly rising to the surface near the center of the pool. As they stared, mesmerized, the protruding eyes of a hippo slowly broke the water. Penny felt a hard shove from Blake. She floundered, screaming, "Alfred, Alfred, hurry!"

In a moment they sat breathing heavily on the mossy bank of the pool. They stared as the hippopotamus raised his heavy head, opened his mouth, and roared a primitive challenge. Penny shrank close to Blake. He put his arm around her and another about Alfred's shoulders.

"It's all right now," he spoke in a soothing deep voice. "He won't come out of the water, but we'd better get back anyway."

"I'm really sorry," he said, as they drove the short distance to camp. "I've been in that pool dozens of times, and have never seen a hippo anywhere near it. Anyhow, we're all safe," he added with a reassuring smile.

"Dinner was splendid," sighed Penny, as they relaxed around the outdoor table in front of the cook tent. "I'm amazed you could set a table like this here in the middle of nowhere." She drained her brandy glass and extended it to Abhurdamoni for a refill.

Blake smiled. "Abhurdamoni's the best bush cook around. Several people have tried to entice him away from me, but he won't leave."

Penny realized that, all day, she had been struck by the almost adoring attitude the Africans had toward Blake. They were polite to her and Alfred, but they treated Blake as if he were a god.

Blake had lost count of the double gins she had had before dinner and this was the third brandy. He watched for any signs of inebriation but could detect none. He had poured his brandy in his coffee mug and was sipping slowly. The Africans had finished cleaning up, and were hunkered around the large camp fire that glowed hotly near the entrance to the two sleeping tents. The murmur of their subdued voices was broken by occasional spurts of laughter and strange sounding chants.

"Oh, look," cried Penny, as she pointed to a place behind Alfred's head.

The moon, flattened like a ripe watermelon, slowly pulled itself up through the tree branches of the dark forest. The stars dimmed out as the broken plain took on the lights and shadows of penetrating moonlight.

"I could never have imagined so much beauty."

Alfred turned his head slightly. "What's making that crushing noise?"

They listened a moment, then Blake spoke. "That's old Jumbo, an old tusker who's almost tame. He often comes around."

"Do you mean an elephant?" gasped Penny. "What shall we do!"

She jumped up and looked around, suddenly realizing there was no place to go except maybe under the truck.

"It's all right. He won't harm us," Blake laughed, pulling her back into the camp chair. "Old bulls carrying a lot of ivory are driven out of the herd by the lead cow. Elephants are matriarchal, you know, and the lead cow is the boss."

Blake settled back in his chair. "Sometimes when I take a job with the game department to crop an elephant herd I have to hunt these old fellows. The young bulls who aren't yet big or strong enough to mate seem to know what I'm about and move so that they stand between my gun and the old one. Makes it hard to get a shot at him. Elephants are the smartest animals I know"

At that moment the huge gray beast appeared, moving silently as a shadow into the moonlight at the edge of the jungle. He stood as if carved of stone, the dew glistening on his great thrusting tusks; only his giant ears moved, jerking forward at right angles to his body, straining for the slightest sound.

"Don't move," whispered Blake, "and keep talking normally. My gun's a long way off."

Alfred giggled nervously. "How can you keep talking normally when three tons of elephant stands there eyeing you?"

As silently as he had come, the elephant melted into the shadows. No one had seen him move. One moment he was there and the next, he wasn't. They were wordless for a long space of time.

"But why," Alfred asked, at last, "was he driven out of the heard?"

Blake glanced at Penny, then turned to Alfred. "When their ivory gets to long and heavy they have difficulty mounting the cows whose rumps get gorged by the sharp tusks." He looked at Penny, his eyes twinkling. "I don't imagine any female would enjoy that, do you?"

Penny rose, turning to Alfred. "It's late, dear. We'd better start for bed."

She turned to Blake, looking at him sternly. "Thank you for a perfectly wonderful day." Her eyes softened. "Thank you for taking such good care of us."

Blake stood silently, looking deep into Penny's eyes. Her gaze faltered and she looked toward Alfred disappearing into the tent. He turned and spoke to Blake. "Yes. Thank you very much, Sir. I think," he stopped, embarrassed, "I think you're a super chap."

Blake caught Penny's hand as she started to the tent. Without looking at him, she mumbled, "Don't expect me tonight."

Penny lay for hours looking through the mosquito netting tucked in around her cot. The sloping tent top was blurred with the silhouettes of monstrous beasts. She listened to her son's even breathing, barely making out his form in the diffused moonlight. The far away boon of drums mingled with the raucous scream of a hunter animal who had missed his prey.

She rubbed moist palms on the thin sheet that covered her. Her hands moved up and held her breasts, gently massaging them until her nipples were rigid, making hard points that thrust through her bra against her nightgown. She slipped one hand beneath the elastic top of her panties, feeling the warm darkness below her round stomach.

"Oh God," she gasped, as she swung her legs off the cot. She sat immobile, listening for Alfred's disturbed breathing to resume.

"Oh, dear God, what am I doing," she thought. *I'll leave this tent and run smack into that big elephant or a lion or—. Good heavens! There're probably snakes about, too! And it'll be just what I'll deserve.*

Holding one arm tightly across her breasts, the other lifting the long cotton nightgown, she tiptoed out into the waning moonlight. She paused at the entrance to Blake's tent.

"Is that you, Penny?" she barely heard his soft voice.

She raised the tent flap and slowly entered. Blake struck a match, holding it on the wick of a citronella candle. The flame sputtered, casting giant jerking shadows on the tent walls. Penny stood at the foot of the cot like a frightened creature ready to flee at any moment. Blake threw back the sheet, hearing her gasp at his nakedness. He moved on cat's feet, silently and swiftly, and with a deft movement, lifted the nightgown over her head.

"You sleep in your underwear?" he asked, suppressing a grin.

"Oh yes, always," Penny whispered, her last word muffled as Blake's mouth covered hers. He drew back, searching her eyes, and began to undress her.

"I knew you'd come."

"I guess I knew, too."

"Come to the bed," he said, as he led her toward the cot, snapping the hooks on the inside of the tent as he passed.

"Come here," he sighed in mock exasperation, "I'll take those things off you."

She lost her balance, tripping on the panties about her ankles, and fell over Blake. He reached down, twisted them off her feet, and twirling them about his head, spun them across the tent.

"So much for that," he laughed, as she snuggled close to the warmth of his body, trying to suppress her laughter. His hand moved in ever increasing circles until it thrust hard against her.

"You're ready for me," he whispered. "I'm too randy to wait any longer!"

With a hard kiss, he said, "I'm going to take you now." Moving quickly on top of her, he thrust deeply.

Her gasp was almost a scream. He moved his hand to cover her mouth when he realized she was completely limp, unconscious. He threw back the net, and kneeling by the cot, massaged her wrists and temple. He lit the carbide lamp, wincing at the harsh light. She looked so pale. Blake dipped a washcloth into the basin of tepid water, wrung it lightly, and pressed it to her forehead again and again.

He was becoming frantic. It would be first light soon and there was no way he could get her back into her own tent without waking Alfred. It would be impossible even to dress that limp form. *Alfred may learn the facts of life sooner than his mother intended.*

Finally, she stirred. Her face was white, drained of color. Blake quickly extinguished the lamp.

"What happened?" she faltered, close to tears.

"You fainted," he replied, helping her to sit up. "Do you have a habit of fainting?"

"I've never fainted before in my life!" Her voice shook, fighting tears. "What happened?"

"Why, I just started to make love to you and—."

She cut in. "I remember now. You *did* something to me. What was it?"

"I told you. All I *did* was start making love to you—."

She interrupted. "That was it! Why did you do that? Hubert never did anything like that!"

"Penny, my dear, he must have. After all, you've had a child."

"Oh, no," Penny covered her face with her hands. "He just—you know—he just sort of stroked me with his—with it."

"But how could you ever have got pregnant?"

"I don't know. I just always thought that was how it was done." She shuddered. "He never, never put it inside of me."

"My dear, what you've missed!" Blake countered. "I suppose a woman could conceive that way, 'though I've never heard of it happening like that. But why miss all the fun? Now," he added, pulling her to her feet, "it will be dawn soon, and you need to get back to your tent before Alfred wakes. Here," he handed her the nightgown, "slip this on and go get some sleep. We'll stay in camp tomorrow, you and I. Appendai can take Alfred and do some scouting."

He gave her behind a playful slap as she slipped the gown over her head. "Off with you."

41

"Let's take a drive," Blake said next morning.

Penny was a bit disappointed. They had been alone for over two hours. Alfred and Appendai had gone out to explore the area and search for birds, and the other Africans were away on odd jobs. Only Abhurdamoni was left in camp, and he was busy puttering in the cook tent. Blake had not referred to the previous night. She looked longingly at his tent, at once excited about what had happened to her there and frightened, too. Maybe he was too disgusted with her to bother.

Reluctantly, she went to the car. They set off in a new direction. As they drove, a herd of impala crossed the rutted road in great leaps. One small fellow with dainty black horns was asleep on the road. As the car approached, he leaped straight up, windscreen height. Coming down on stiff slender legs, he leaped again, and yet a third time before he surged forward.

Turning toward the flat country, Blake said, "The game warden for this area asked me to check on some possible poaching on the lake. He gave me the keys to the launch so we'll have a little boat ride, if you're game."

"I'd love that," she replied. "Is it far?"

"No. Right here," Blake replied, as he turned sharply through a grove of trees and parked alongside a large lake that disappeared around a bend of the forest. The boat was chained to a tree that Blake unlocked and in which he deposited two petrol cans and a gun. As he turned from the car carrying a small boat motor, Penny asked, "Do you have to bring the gun? I'm so afraid of guns."

Blake's lips tightened. "In the bush you'd do well to be more afraid of not having one."

The wake of the boat cast a flat road bordered by turbulent water. Penny shrank back as she saw more than one crocodile slide silently into the water. Two hippos rose up, mouth to mouth, and remained as if glued together for several minutes. A large herd of elephants waded out into the lake, taking great trunks of water, and throwing it backward, gave themselves liberal showers. The tick birds resting on the elephants' backs hovered just above the spray, then fluttered down to peck insects along the deep crevices in the broad backs.

"How could anyone shoot those beautiful animals?" Penny mused.

Blake seemed not to hear over the drone of the motor. Overhead a flock of vultures glided in gradually smaller circles. "Some poor little thing is dead," thought Penny. *"I hope it isn't our dear wee impala."*

Blake turned the boat into the shore, getting out to pull it through the eel- grass. Great winged herons and a painted billed stork rose in wing flapping flight.

"Wait here," Blake said. "I'll return shortly."

Penny sat in the still boat while the panorama of wild life displayed around her. A pair of Goliath herons watched her warily through the tall grass. The root of a mangrove moved. Penny leaned toward it, peering. The root detached itself and slithered into the water before she realized it was a huge snake.

A gun shot cracked from the direction Blake had gone. Penny jumped, nearly upsetting the boat. She heard two more shots in rapid succession, then silence, except for the chattering of monkeys and shrill parrot calls.

"Whatever shall I do?" she thought, panic overwhelming her. *Blake may have been shot, lying somewhere, even dead. I'll never be able to start the motor much less run this boat, and all those hippos and crocodiles—.*

She whirled and cringed as a great crashing came from beyond the trees. Blake broke through the undergrowth and Penny went limp with relief.

"Quick," he said, as he tossed some animal skins and an elephant tusk in the boat. "Grab a petrol can and follow me."

Penny scrambled out of the boat, clutching a heavy can tightly as she hurried after Blake. They traveled a worn twisting path and entered a small clearing. Blake pulled back the flap of one of the two tents.

"Look at this," he said, pointing to two stacks of skins.

She saw leopard, zebra, water buck, and others she could not identify. Beneath them, on the tent floor, were dozens of elephant tusks and horns of all sizes. Dried fish hung from a line stretched near the tent top.

"I'll get this one. You start on the other tent, the one with the canned goods in it," Blake ordered.

"Get what?" Penny asked, bewildered. "I don't know what you're about."

"The petrol." Blake locked her eyes with his. "Splash the petrol on the supply tent."

Seeing her hesitate, his voice boomed. "Now! Move!"

The flap was off the supply tent. Stacks of canned goods lay along the edges of the blanket littered floor. Stepping back, she threw great splashes of petrol on the tent sides, some of it going inside the tent. Her can was nearly empty when Blake ran over and took it, throwing the last bit on the tent top.

"Go around to the leeward side—around in back," he snapped.

She had barely rounded the tent when she saw Blake running from one to the next with flaming rags tied onto a stick. The tents exploded. Penny ran back several steps to escape the heat, then stumbled over something, sprawling sideways. Trying to push herself up, she felt something hot and sticky on her hand. She looked down. Her hand was drenched with blood. Screaming, she leaped to her feet and stared down at an African covered only by a loin cloth with a large bloody hole in his back.

She ran blindly away from the blazing tents only to stop short as she saw two more figures lying face down on the path, flies already drawn to the pulpy mass of a face shot off, the other with an arm blown away. Her face contorted in horror.

"Blake. Blake!" she screamed.

He was by her side in a moment, holding her trembling body, and softly stroking her hair. One hand held the gun while his eyes searched the surrounding forest.

"It's all right, girl. It's all right," he spoke soothingly, leading her by a circuitous route away from the tents. "I don't think there are any more of them."

"Bad show, what?" he said, as he seated her gently on a moss covered mound near the boat.

"Blake! Why, why?" she was near hysteria. "What happened to those three men?"

"I shot them," Blake said, simply.

"Shot them! You mean you just pointed that gun and murdered three men? For the love of God, why?"

His eyes narrowed to slits' his lips clamped in a thin line. For a moment she was frightened of him and drew back.

"They were poachers," he said. "Come now," he pulled her to her feet. "You've blood on your shirt. It wouldn't do to go back to camp that way, would it?"

He pushed her trembling fingers aside and unbuttoned her blouse. "Sit here for a bit while I rinse it for you."

"You understand," he said, as he swished her shirt in the lake water, "it doesn't do any good to arrest them. I tracked one for two weeks through the Selous one time; brought him all the way into Dar in chains. The judge fined him fifty shillings and let him go. It cost a lot more than that just to bring him in."

"But, Blake," she protested, her voice still shaky, "I know it's wrong to poach but this is their land and their animals. Is it so wrong for them to want to feed their people?"

"You don't understand," he said, wringing out her blouse and spreading it on a bush. "They leave the meat to rot. They can't carry it out. They're only after the hides and the ivory, trophies to sell on the black market. Furthermore, look."

He walked a few paces up the path, bent over, and picked up a small metal ball. He rolled it around in the palm of his hand. "This is from an old muzzle loader. They'll wound ten animals with these and not bother to track one of them, for every one they kill. You'll know what I mean," he continued, tossing the ball up and catching it, then slipped it in his pocket, "when you're attacked by an enraged cape buffalo and have to shoot him, then discover he has a great gaping wound in his shoulder that's crawling with maggots."

He helped her struggle into her damp blouse. "We'd better get back. It's nearly time for lunch and," he kissed her quickly, "I want an hour in the bed with you before Alfred and Appendai return. You're going to find out what it's really like to be made love to."

Before he started the boat, he said casually, "If anyone asks, the Africans got away. The skins and ivory in the boat are evidence and we needn't mention the other."

"What if the bodies are found?" she asked. "Someone might discover them."

Blake shook his head. "No. Even an elephant disappears in forty-eight hours here, except for the largest bones. There'll be no evidence of those chaps by this time tomorrow."

"What do I feel about this man," she thought. *He can be so tender and so exciting. No one has ever made me feel this way before, so alive, so vital. But he just murdered three men! Is it Africa that has made him like this or do Europeans who are like him come here because they are different from other people? I'm so confused. I don't know what to think.*

On the return drive to camp Blake slowed down when they passed a large herd of zebra. Several of the females had nursing young and Penny asked Blake to stop so she could watch them.

"Those are Grevy's zebra." Blake said. "Different types of zebra are stripped differently."

"They look so much like horses it seems as if they could be tamed," Penny replied.

"Been tried," he answered, "but I don't know of anyone who's managed to get the wildness out of them. They have a vicious kick and they bite, too."

The herd became agitated. The big stallions stopped grazing and turned in one common direction, ears forward, bodies tense. Some tall grass fifty yards away moved, then exploded. A lioness burst through the low scrub at top speed. The herd moved as one, galloping in dust raising clouds. A new born colt dropped behind, unnoticed. The lioness leaped on him, and with a powerful bite in his neck, brought him to the ground.

Blake eased the car closer to the kill. A large black maned lion came up in a slow lope. He crouched at the kill and tore at the belly of the zebra. The lioness backed away, her yellow eyes gleaming. Three cubs came out of the tall grass and stood by her, waiting.

"Why does she let him eat first when she made the kill?" Penny asked.

"That's the way they do it," Blake replied. "That's his reward for fathering the family. Pretty neat, if I do say so. His other two or three mates will eat next, then the cubs. The males seldom hunt, but they always get first choice."

Penny watched the huge lion tearing away at the entrails of the small creature and shuddered. She visualized the three men lying in the forest being torn apart, even the bones being crunched by the powerful jaws of hyenas.

The lion raised his head and snarled at them. His face was crimson wet. Blood dripped from his lower jaw.

# **Chapter 7**

The black maned lion had reached his prime. He weighed over four hundred and fifty pounds. His long coarse mane extended well back over his golden withers and ran in a thin line beneath his belly. He and his pride did not migrate and game was getting scarce. During this height of the dry season, most of the grazing animals had gone to the high country to find grass. The lions had been content for some time to run down smaller game, but they were almost constantly hungry. The cubs were rail thin and fretful. The lion always ate first, then the six females, a ritual as set as a state dinner.

The cubs mewed as the pride walked to the water hole, a small pool surrounded by mud as the water receded, sucked up by the hot sun. They circled carefully to avoid stepping in holes left by elephants and cape buffalo. The lion stood alert and watchful while the pride drank then flattened himself to lap the dirty water.

The lions sought the shade of a thorn tree and lay in the skimpy grass. Shortly, the male rose and padded over to one of the females. She crouched low on the earth, presenting her hind quarters to him. He mounted, holding her just in front of her hind legs with his fore paws curled under her. Her tawny body flattened under his weight and her eyes closed.

He mounted three more lionesses in turn, a brief five minutes apart. The remaining two females were not receptive, and slid from beneath him, turning on him with low growls. He walked over to a sleeping lioness and nudged her from a choice place in the shade, biting her neck lightly to urge her going. Now, he stretched out to sleep, but the cubs, their empty bellies keeping them awake, tumbled over him, biting at his heavy mane with needle teeth.

The lion rose and shook himself. Night would come soon and he felt a primal urge rising. He trotted off toward the north, leaving the lionesses where they were, traveling about five miles, and climbing steadily. He found three lionesses tearing at a koodoo. They drew back as he approached and he crouched over the carcass. He flipped the heavy animal over with a swipe of his fore paw, holding the animal's head with his back claws, and ripped into the flank, exposing the dark meat beneath the sleek hide. He ate part of the hip in a few gulps, then turned away.

Now, he prepared himself for the attack of the male of the pride, but could not locate him. The largest female walked close to him, rubbing his side with hers as she passed. The other females pressed against him, rubbing his mane and flanks. Then the big one presented her hindquarters to him. He mounted her, giving a few brief thrusts, then mounted the others in turn. Without pausing to rest he turned southward and joined the first pride well before dawn. He slept the better part of two days.

He now had two prides and he made the long trek between them every few days. In the following years the Kikuku, living in a small village on his route between the two prides, called him a Kikuku name that meant, "Father of Lions". They pointed him out as he doggedly trotted across the plains, head low, his tufted tail barely clearing the short grass.

# Chapter 8

Penny picked at her lunch, glancing, in spite of herself, at Blake's tent. He followed her eyes, then chuckled quietly. "You're as randy as I am, aren't you?"

Her denial ended at her lips. She ducked her head and grinned, giving a quick nod. Something of the excitement of the morning, even the dead men, had strangely impassioned her.

Blake reached for her hand. "Come," he said. Saying a few words to Abhurdamoni in Swahili, he led her into the tent.

Her eyes took a few moments to recover from the glare of the afternoon sun. In a moment she saw Blake, the mosquito netting drawn up, lying on the cot in his shorts, his shirt crumpled on the floor.

"Take your clothes off, sweetie," he spoke in a deep soft voice.

Her clothes dropped one by one on the floor. She stood at the edge of the cot, conscious of his eyes covering each part of her body.

"I'm afraid I've gotten a bit fat in recent years," she giggled.

"A skinny woman is no use to God or man," replied Blake. "Now lie down," he added, moving over to make room for her. "I want you to take off my shorts."

*********************************

"I'll let you rest a while," he said later, as he stood and looked fondly down at her. Her lips, red and slightly swollen, were parted, her breath exploding in short jerks.

Blake walked to the small table and picked up a slender candle. With his pen knife, he began carving the blunt end.

"When I was a boy on Zanzibar," he mused, "when my father, owned a clove plantation there, the Sultan had a large and closely guarded harem. I found a niche in the wall that enclosed a shallow pool fed by a fountain. I gouged a small hole through the wall with my pocket knife." He held up the candle, gauging it carefully, then continued carving it.

"I saw everything through that hole, but the best were the evenings that the Sultan had all his wives brought out. Some were so

49

young they had bare nubbins for breasts, and no body hair on them at all. The Sultan gave each of the women—they were all starkers, of course,—a candle that they put in their bottoms. A palace eunuch lit each one. While the Sultan sat on a low cushion, the women splashed around in the shallow pool trying to put out another's candle. It was quite a spectacle; all those naked cavorting women!"

He seemed content with the candle now, and holding it, sat on the edge of the cot. "The last one with her candle lit was led out of the pool and dried off with big towels by the other women, then covered with sweet smelling oil. I can still smell that fragrance."

Penny lay very still, her eyes fastened on the waxy shell color of the candle that glowed with the refracted light coming in through the small-screened window of the tent. Her nostrils widened at the pungent smell of the wax intermingled with the subtle scent of Abdurdamoni's cook fire. The afternoon quiet was broken, only by the faint buzzing of insects. At a light touch from Blake she rolled over on her stomach and closed her eyes.

\*\*\*\*\*\*\*\*\*\*\*\*\*\*\*\*\*\*\*\*\*\*\*\*\*\*\*\*\*\*\*\*\*\*\*

Alfred returned with hairy tales of being chased around a tree by a rhino, a leopard leaping out of the bush—which turned out to be a hyena at second look—lions aplenty, and hero worship for Appendai.

"Oh, Mums," his face shone with excitement, "he's just the greatest. He can track anything, and knows all about the animals and where they go and what they do. He could make me understand even without speaking English. He must be the greatest tracker in all Africa!" He turned to Blake. "Isn't that right, Sir?"

"That's absolutely right, Alfred," Blake laughed. "Once I took Appendai in the Land Cruiser and deliberately drove around in circles. Finally, after I, myself, was totally confused, I stopped the car and asked him, 'Which way is camp?' Without a moment's hesitation, he pointed to the left. I drove straight in that direction for five miles or more, and there it was. He's one of the best."

Blake sat with his shotgun lying in pieces on the camp table, carefully oiling the blue-black metal and the scarred wooden stock. He plunged an oil soaked rag on a rod through the barrel, and held it to the light to check the inside. "By the by, did you see any birds?"

"Yes. Lots," Alfred pointed toward the thick forest. "About noon we came upon them. There was a small pond and the trees around it were thick with them. I couldn't say how far away it is, but Appendai would know, I'm sure."

"I'm sure he will," Blake smiled. "Well, we've all had a busy day." He clicked the gun back together and winked at Penny. "I suggest we turn in so we can get an early start in the morning for bird trapping."

Next morning, they took a short ride, stopping at the edge of the forest and continuing on foot. Although the sun had been up only two hours, the walk made them all hot and sticky. Penny wondered how the five Africans could keep up such a pace, heavily loaded as they were. Even Appendai had two woven cages strapped on his head. They came to a watering hole and Blake signaled the men to drop their loads. Without pausing, they turned into the surrounding jungle and began cutting long poles, chopping the branches away with their sharp pangas. When they returned Blake explained the operation to Penny and Alfred.

"They're digging holes to set the posts in, then we'll spread nets over the poles by deck strings, letting the net hang down in bags between the strings."

He carefully unfolded the net from the box and spread it on the ground.

"You see, this net is a dark green to match the trees. It was made in Japan, and hard to come by. Most nets here are coarser and about one-half inch openings. This mesh is one-fourth inch, and of much finer material."

The Africans set the poles upright and began stringing the net's deck strings to the pole tops along the end of the watering hole. The net hung in deep folds between the poles.

"When the birds come in to water this evening," Blake explained, "they'll give this net a wide berth. They are always in a big flock, and generally follow a leader. But by watering time tomorrow morning, they'll have got used to it. After drinking they'll likely as not fly into the mesh and become entangled. At least some of them will."

He gave the trap a final check and left instructions to the Africans in Swahili. They started picking up the cages and placed them well away from the water hole in a small clearing.

"Do we wait here to drop the net on them, Sir," Alfred asked.

"No," Blake replied. "We'll come tomorrow and pluck them out of the net. No reason we can't sleep comfortably in our tents tonight."

He glanced sideways at Penny and she surpressed a smile while giving an almost imperceptible nod. Alfred looked disappointed.

After dinner, just at dusk, they heard a car coming. It stopped and a man alighted and came towards them. "Blake, is that you?" he called.

Blake hurried to meet him and shook hands with a tall blond Norwegian. "Lars! My God! It's been an age."

He turned to introduce Penny. "Mrs. Lambert-Smith and her son, Alfred. This is my old friend and partner in crime, Lars Andressen."

They shook hands all around and settled into folding camp chairs, drinks in hand.

"Blake," Lars said, leaning forward in his chair. "I want to get into old times with you later, but right now I have a problem, one that may appear at any moment."

Lars eyes' were so light a blue they mirrored the glaciers of his homeland. The fair complexion of the Scandinavian had reddened and burnt, but not tanned. His eyelashes and eyebrows were so bleached from the sun as to be invisible. A crop of abundant wheat colored hair sprang up as if on wires. His jaw was square below a slightly hooked but aquiline nose.

"Right-o," Blake replied. "What's the trouble? Incidentally, where are you camped? All I see is your car and your gun boy."

"I'm about six miles east of you," Lars said hurriedly, running his fingers through his springy hair. "I'm between contracts—still a mercenary, you know—so I thought I'd do a bit of hunting while there's anything left to shoot. I've got licenses for the big three, and had only the leopard left. To make a long story short, we had the blind all set up one night, and the bait hanging just right. But when the leopard showed up and I took a shot at him, he moved, and I only wounded him. We tracked him next day and he'd gone into thick bush. I don't know yet where he came from, but he went straight for my white hunter, Clive Malder, and nearly took his scalp off when he went right over his head. Then he was gone. We got Clive to the bush air strip and on his way to Nairobi. They're sending me another hunter in a few days. I still hope to find that leopard. Don't like the idea of his being out there mad as all hell."

"Poor Clive," Blake shook his head. "I know him. Good man. You can see why, as the saying goes, those chaps 'cost the earth and live like kings'. Was he still drinking your liquor before this happened?"

Blake rose to make fresh drinks. Lars looked at him, puzzled. "Well, yes, quite a lot of it, as a matter of fact. But what that's got to do with it?"

"Not a thing," Blake laughed. "It's just at first I thought that might be the trouble you were speaking of. When you ask a hunter how he's getting along with his client, he'll say, 'I'm still drinking his liquor'. That means things are all right."

Blake handed the drinks around and sat, holding his up to the glowing campfire, squinting at the amber liquid. "But if he says, 'I'm drinking my own liquor', that means he's having a rough time with some chap."

Lars laughed and shook his head. "No. That's not my problem."

"Then what is it?" Blake asked.

Lars glanced uneasily at Penny. "You might say—," he shifted his chair closer to Blake and lowered his voice. "You see, it's this girl."

Blake's laugh exploded in the muted African night. "I've never known a girl to throw you, Lars!" He turned to Penny. "In the old days we used to call him the Scandinavian stud."

Blake turned back to an uncomfortable Lars. "What is it? Some wench you've buggered about and now she's after you with a pistol?"

"It's not exactly a girl, Blake."

"What do you mean, 'not exactly a girl'? Either she is or she isn't." Blake continued to chuckle.

"Damn it, Blake," Lars smiled and relaxed a bit. "No. I mean it's a Masai girl."

"Oh, a Masai, is it? Why in hell are you messing around with a Masai? Don't you know you can get in big trouble that way out here in the bush?"

"Damn it to hell, Blake," Lars exploded. "I'm not 'messing around' as you put it. She's just *there* all the time."

"Lars," Blake replied with mock seriousness, "maybe you had better start at the beginning and let's get the straight of it."

"All right," Lars sighed and ran his fingers through hair that defied order. "When I say she's 'there' that's just what I mean. She

53

loped into camp shortly after Clive left, came to a dead halt when she saw me, and has dogged my footsteps ever since. None of the safari boys speak Masai, so I can't find out what she wants. She squats in front of my tent when I go to bed at night, and, no matter how often I wake and look out, she's right there. When I get up in the morning it doesn't look as if she's moved."

Lars extended his glass for a refill, and paused until he'd had a long swallow. "I've tried losing her when we take the car out in the bush, but by God, she can lope along at fifteen miles an hour for miles, and doesn't seem winded at all. Even when I'm able to go faster, it's just a matter of time before she shows up."

"And you know how they are, Blake," Lar's nose crinkled slightly. "I mean, she's a gorgeous hunk of female, damn near six feet tall and graceful as a gazelle, but, my God—. And I can feel her eyes on me all the time. She just stares. I mean, it's getting to me."

Lars glanced apologetically at Penny and Alfred.

Blake rose and stretched. "I know. Don't tell me. Her head's shaved and her whole body's covered with animal fat mixed with red ochre, and there's flies all over."

Lars nodded with relief, and rose, standing next to Blake. "Also, I don't know when an irate husband or father—or maybe the whole tribe—might descent on me. I thought you might speak the language and—."

"I think I'll have the chance to do that just now," Blake commented, his lips tight. He pointed to a spot just outside the circle of light. It took the others a moment to adjust to the deep shadows, and then they could make out only a vague outline.

"She did a good job tracking you after dark," Blake said. He turned toward the dim figure and spoke a few words in a strange guttural monotone.

Slowly the figure emerged from the shadows and seemed to glide into the circle of the spitting campfire. Penny drew in her breath sharply as she looked at the girl. She stood erect, head held proud as only a member of a free and never conquered people can. Her copper-oiled body danced as the flames reflected off it, sending color to the edge of darkness. Long beaded earrings hung suspended from the tops of her ears as well as her ear lobes, which stretched almost to the massive necklace that circled her long slender throat. The heavily beaded neck piece covered her from shoulder to shoulder, stopping just above her nipples.

Her breasts were extraordinarily firm to be so prominent. They jutted out from her torso, the dark nipples pointed as spears. A short beaded apron, slung low on her hips, covered only the front of her. Her buttocks were high and rounded, taut as ripe melons.

Her eyes were on Lars until Blake spoke, then she looked at Blake's face, direct and unblinking. After a number of exchanges in that alien dialect, Blake turned to the others.

"Above all don't laugh, don't even smile. A maiden scorned is not taken lightly with these people, any more than with our own."

He turned back to look at the Masai. The others' eyes followed his. The girl's face showed no expression. The bridge of her nose completed a straight line from forehead to tip with no indentation. Her cheek bones were high and her mouth chiseled. She looked as Egyptian as a Pharaoh's daughter; indeed, probably was descended from them. She stood utterly motionless, only her eyes moving from face to face.

"Did you find out what she wants?" Lars sat on the edge of his chair.

"Yes," Blake replied, "but as I warned you, not even a smile! All right?"

Lars nodded, holding his breath.

"She says," Blake took a deep breath, "that you are the most beautiful man she has ever seen. She wants to marry you. She asks— now, watch it," Blake commanded with his voice, looking hard at the three of them, "She wants to know how many cattle will you give her father for her."

Blake turned his head to the girl, his face twitching as he fought for control. After a moment, except for the muscles moving slightly at the corner of his mouth, he said, in all seriousness, "What shall I tell her, Lars?"

"My God," Lars shouted in exasperation. "How do I know what you're to tell her? Say something to get rid of her, I haven't had a good sleep for three nights. Can't you tell her to go away?"

Blake turned back to the girl. She stood easily, motionless, but looked at Blake inquiringly. They had an exchange. Once her brow furrowed and she glanced questionably at Lars. She spoke rapidly and lifted a long graceful arm, pointing to the north. With one long last look at Lars, her nostrils flaring, she turned and strode with great steps, and disappeared into the darkness.

Lars let out all his pent up breath. Blake settled back with a satisfied grin, reached for his drink, saying nothing. Then, he started to laugh, a low rumbling sound that grew higher and fairly convulsed him.

Lars could stand it no longer. Rising and standing over Blake, he said desperately, "For God's sake, Blake, tell me what you two were saying!"

Blake wiped his eyes with his handkerchief, trying to stop laughing. Penny and Alfred were giggling, and even Lars began to chuckle. Blake tried to speak, only to start laughing again. The Africans in camp crept near, their grins making white hash marks across their dark faces.

"I told her," Blake finally managed to say, "that you are of a different tribe; that in your tribe, it was the custom for the girl's father to pay with cattle."

He stopped to get his breath and wipe his eyes again. "She had some difficulty understanding that, but finally accepted it. She said she would go and ask her father how many cattle he would pay for you."

"Oh, no," groaned Lars. "What shall I do? I don't want the whole tribe on my hands."

"I'd advise," Blake responded, "that you move your camp as early as possible in the morning, toward the south. She said her people were camped four hours walk to the north. Fifty miles will get you well out of the way, and you'd be in the Selous where the hunting's good. They're not likely to follow since no natives are allowed there. I'll get word to your white hunter when we return to Dar, 'though I'll hate not finding out how many cattle they think you're worth!"

Blake started laughing again and they all joined in.

"Isn't it rather unusual, though," Lars commented, "for a young girl to be out on her own like that?"

"It would be," Blake countered, "for any other tribe; the Kikuku, the Moran, and so on. But a young Masai girl has a lot of latitude. Girls are a valuable property to the Masai, but quite independent until marriage. She's allowed to do pretty much as she pleases now, but she'll knuckle under later when she's married. They're a strange but magnificent people."

Blake continued, as he rose to make fresh drinks. "Their God tells them all the cattle in the world belong to them, so when they raid the neighboring tribes of cattle, they're simply collecting what is their own. The Kenya and Tanzania governments cannot get them to assimilate, nor come into the twentieth century. They're nomads, cattle herders, and live on the blood from the veins of their cows laced with milk and a spot of urine to keep the milk from curdling."

Penny gagged. "What's going to happen to them?" she asked.

"What really worries the government is not whether they survive; they're already shot through with venereal disease, but the health officers aren't running any penicillin out to them. For one thing, they can pierce the heart of a tree at thirty yards with a spear, and tend to use for target practice anyone who tries to come at them with a hypodermic needle—or a tourist with a camera, for that matter. Government officials are mostly concerned that they run their cattle on thousands of acres that could be productive farm land, so they may just let the Masai disappear. I've heard the men are already marrying out of the tribe because so many of their own women are sterile."

"To bad," Lars said, glancing at his watch. He shook hands all around. "Want to be sure we're all packed up and on our way first thing tomorrow. Sorry we didn't get to chat about old times, Blake. Maybe another time."

Blake walked with Lars toward his car. "That's a splendid watch you have there. Take it off a general during the war?"

"No," laughed Lars. "Matter of fact, the last Sheik I worked for gave it to me when I finished my four year contract. Solid gold, it is. Must have cost the earth, but then," he added, opening the car door, "with an oil income of over a thousand pounds an hour, I guess he could afford it."

The two men stood leaning against the car when Lars asked, "What happened on Zanzibar, Blake? Word got to me that you'd left there in rather a hurry. Thought you and the old Sultan were on jolly good terms, you heading up his army and all."

"Things were going well," Blake replied, keeping his voice low as he watched Penny and Alfred walk toward their tent, "until I made friends with one of his young brides. You know," he looked over to be sure Penny was out of ear shot, "he used to contract for them when they were just children, and kept them in the harem until they reached puberty, to make sure they'd be virgins when they reached his bed."

Steven E. Farley

Lars nodded. "But, Blake, you didn't—?"

"No. Not at all," Blake replied. "One of them found a niche in the wall she could scramble through, and she used to come to my house. She loved sweets and would sit on the edge of the table and let me pull her panties down and play with her. She was a cute little devil. You know, Lars, I've never touched an African but those Arab girls are quite different.

Lars nodded. "I feel the same way, except I've been some places for so long a time, they seemed to get lighter every day."

Blake laughed. "Something about the hair on the blacks always put me off," Blake continued. "But those cute little Arab girls with their big black eyes and tiny bones—well, I do like the young ones. But I swear, Lars, I never broke a hymen. I saw she was kept intact. Cute-little-thing. Probably ten or eleven but looked about eight or so."

"Anyhow," Blake glanced back at the tent again, "one afternoon a palace eunuch saw her squeeze through the wall and told the Sultan. The next thing I knew soldiers burst through the door, and I barely made it out the back, not moving to fast what with trying to get my pants buttoned. I got to the beach and found an old dhow setting sail. I swam out and they pulled me on board. I landed in Dar with twenty pounds in my pocket, and everything gone; my house, bank account, schooner, and passport."

Blake shook his head and sighed. "Since they were having trouble deciding who Zanzibar belonged to; the Sultan claiming independence and Nyerere claiming it was part of Tanzania, they weren't able to force me to go back, thank God. I'm not having to look over my shoulder now since the Sultan's been deposed and there's a new government on Zanzibar."

The two men settled in the front seat of the car and Blake continued. "All this has left me a stateless person and on my uppers financially, but I've still have my head on my shoulders. I say, old chap, could you see fit to give me a bit of a loan, for old time's sake?"

Lars surprised look took in the new Land Cruiser and the sturdy truck. Blake followed his gaze.

"Oh," Blake laughed, "those aren't mine. I borrowed them from a chap who's on leave. I'm trapping a few birds until I can find something better to do. There's not much money in it except I sometimes hide a tanzanite stone in the bird feeder and smuggle it out. Pretty good money in that, but I can't work up much volume."

"How much would you really have to have, Blake?" asked Lars. "I'm between contracts and three months to go before the next one."

"I really could use a thousand pounds if you could spare that, old chap," Blake replied, leaning over to clap Lars on the shoulder. "I'll return it to you as soon as I can and deposit it to your Swiss account. Shouldn't be long."

"That's a good bit," Lars protested. "I really can't spare that much right now, with this hunting trip and all. Couldn't you get by with five hundred?"

"Could you make it seven-fifty? I'll get it back to you quite soon."

"All right," Lars said, grudgingly. "For old time's sake, as you said, but I will need it back within the month."

Lars turned on the headlights and the two men stepped in front of the car. Lars held the wallet in the light, turning his back to Blake. "Here," he said, handing Blake a stack of bills.

"Many thanks," Blake said, sliding the money into his pocket. He grasped Lars' hand, moving his other hand along Lars' wrist. "Have a good trip."

Lars started the car, his gun boy leaping onto the roof as they moved off. Blake stood, watching them go, then held his left hand high, looking at the gold watch case gleam in the dying sparks of the campfire.

"And many thanks for this, too, old chap, he murmured to himself.

# Chapter 9

"Tea, Memsahib," Abhurdamoni, in his embroidered cap and flowing dhoti, carried the tea tray into Penny's tent.

She woke with a start, afraid at first she was still in Blake's tent. Seeing Alfred's form stir in the opposite cot, she was flooded with relief. She could not remember returning to her own tent the night before. *Perhaps I had a bit too much to drink.* The events of the past evening were still shambles in her mind.

"Bwana Captain says come now for birds," Abhurdamoni said haltingly. She saw it was still dark outside as he lifted the tent flap to depart. Penny and Alfred hurriedly downed their tea and started dressing.

The first light shimmered faintly in the east. Penny stood looking at the waning moon, a mere sliver in the dawn's light. The forest awakened with strange raucous sounds that seemed at once near and far away.

"Hurry," Blake said, as he came out of the cook tent.

He startled her. It was as if she had been jerked back in time.

"May I ride on top with Appendai?" Alfred asked, looking from Blake to his mother.

"It's a bit chilly, yet, dear," Penny replied. "Perhaps you can on the way back."

Blake grunted his disapproval. "You coddle the boy too much."

They drove in the dawn's silence to the edge of the forest, then continued on foot to the watering hole. The sun was up full now. The net was moving, jerking in the still air. Bright-frightened parakeets struggled frantically, beating their wings furiously. The four Africans rushed to the net while Appendai ran to collect the cages. They all busily plucked the birds from the net, working patiently to extract wings and tiny feet from the green mesh. Appendai held one bird up and inspected it closely, then let it drop at his feet. Penny rushed over and picked it up. Turning to Blake with wounded eyes, she said, "It's dead."

"Yes," he said casually. "Some of the older ones fight the net and kill themselves, but we've got a fine lot here."

Penny saw a dozen more birds thrown to the ground. She ran to each one, and picked it up tenderly, searching in vain for a heartbeat. Her eyes filled with tears.

"I had no idea trapping them was so cruel," she said brokenly. "If I had known how they were caught, I should never have brought them for our shop."

She looked accusingly at Blake. He shrugged. "This many or more die every day in the wild. There's no better way to trap them I know of." He turned away from her stricken face.

After supervising the loading of the cages, Blake said, "I had Abhurdamoni pack a picnic lunch. Let's eat it by the waterfalls. It's not far from here, and I'm sure the hippo's gone so we can have a swim afterwards."

"I didn't bring my—." Penny faltered.

Blake cut in with a hearty laugh. "I also had him put your bathing costumes in, so we're all set."

They had turned away from the water hole when they heard a great crashing coming from the thick undergrowth. They whirled to see a huge tusker coming at them, his trunk thrust forward, the curved finger-tipped end waving from side to side, his great ears extending at right angles from his head. The large gray shapes of the rest of the herd appeared behind him. His resounding trumpet made Penny's ears ring, as she stood paralyzed, watching the huge shape come toward her. She felt Blake's fingers bite into her arm as he twisted her around and snatched her away from the oncoming elephant, pushing her behind the trunk of a giant Baobab tree. Relief flooded her at the sight of Alfred there.

"Flatten against this tree," Blake warned. "There's room for all of us. He can't see us from here and he's upwind of us."

They heard the elephants splashing in the water. Alfred edged to the side of the tree trunk to get a look. "Stay back," Blake cautioned. "They may not be able to get our scent, but they can see us." Alfred drew back quickly.

"Your mother's no woman," Blake said, grinning at Penny. "She's no woman, acting like that. Why were you just standing there between that bull and his water? Did you think he was coming up to be petted?"

"I wasn't being brave," her voice quavered. "I wasn't *able* to move. He was so big, he looked like a moving mountain. But, oh, he is beautiful, isn't he?"

"He is that," laughed Blake. "But when they lift their trunks and put their ears out, they're ready to charge, and they can move damn fast, for all their size. That's a good time to get out of their way. I was afraid I would have to shoot him since you weren't moving, and I was wondering how I would explain that to the game warden!"

"What a funny old tree," Alfred broke in, running his hands along the smooth barked convoluted trunk. "What kind is it?"

"You were right when you said 'old'," Blake replied. "This is a Baobab, and it's said to be one of the oldest living things on earth. The Africans call it the upside down tree, since the branches look more like roots with leaves on them. The roots are shallow so water is stored in the trunk of the tree to last it through the dry seasons. You see how enormous the trunk is, though it isn't much higher than a thorn tree."

It was true the tree concealed all of them adequately and they'd even room to move around.

"The Africans treat this tree with great respect," Blake continued, peeking at the still watering elephants. "Many tribes believe their ancestors' spirits live in the Baobab. They chant and dance around a tree like this to communicate with the departed spirits. There are many tales in Africa about the Baobab. The Africans never cut them down."

Blake checked the elephant's position again. "They're getting ready to leave now, but we'll wait a bit longer. I see they've a new born baby with them, a good reason why papa was so agitated."

Leaning back against the trunk, he continued. "I was on safari a number of years ago when I heard a dynamite blast and turned off the road to discover what was going on. I found a group of Danes. They were here on contract to build the road connecting Dar and Dodoma, where the new capital will be someday. They could speak a little French, but no Swahili. They were trying to dynamite a Baobab after having failed to fell it with trucks and chains. The chief engineer said they had planted enough dynamite to topple a building, but there sat that tree, as if nothing had happened to it. It was dead center of the road they were building."

"A group of Africans came up from across the river. I asked the old chief what was happening. He told me they had moved their village to the other side of the river at the request of the Danes, but they were not given time to ask their ancestors' permission to take their spirits with them to the new village."

Blake laughed. "There are strange things in Africa and the longer I live here, the more credence I give them."

He glanced around the tree trunk again. It had been quiet for some minutes. "We can get to the car now, but move cautiously. They may not have gone far."

Huge holes were sunk in the soft mud along the water's edge, slowly seeping full of muddy water.

"That was one big fellow," Blake said, inspecting the tracks. "Wish I'd had an elephant license with me. His tusks would have run close to eighty pounds apiece. That's worth five hundred pounds each on the market today."

"Thank God you hadn't," breathed Penny.

"What happened to the Baobab tree?" asked Alfred, as they started toward the car.

As they settled in the car and started the drive back, Blake continued. "I asked the old chief how long it would take them to appease the ancestors and he asked for, 'same time tomorrow', as he put it."

I explained it to the chief engineer. I'm sure he thought me slightly bonkers, but since all else had failed, he agreed to wait. I made camp next to the Danes and we spent a fascinating day and half the night watching those buggers cover themselves with white ashes and paint designs over themselves with brilliant colors made from berry and root juices. To Africans, white is the sign of evil and death. Black is Life and all good things.

The witch doctor came out at dusk with all the fetishes stored in tin cans and the cans wrapped in hides. The drums were rolled out, and the women came along carrying rattles. All night they circled round and round that tree, dancing and chanting. By morning they had all passed out from pombe and b'hang. That's beer and marihuana in Swahili. We turned in for a nap, and about mid-afternoon, they sent a delegation around.

"'The ancestor spirits have gone across the river now,' they said. 'Tree will move.'"

"Just as the crew started to hook up the chains again, the old chief motioned them to stop. Eight Africans circled the tree trunk, tugged a bit, lifted it out, and set it down several yards away. Damnedest thing I ever saw."

"Blake," smiled Penny, "I never know when you're joking. Are you serious?"

"I wasn't joking," Blake said indignantly. "For instance, did you know an elephant has five sex organs?"

"Oh, Blake," Penny laughed, glancing at Alfred.

"Well, not five, really. Actually, he has one sex organ and four legs, but if he steps on you, you've been screwed!"

Early next morning the boys started breaking camp. Blake walked over to the folding table and joined Penny and Alfred.

"I've some friends north of here," he said, "the Slades. They've a coffee farm near Arusha. Would you like to stop there overnight? I think you'll like them."

"I'd like to, Blake, but what about the birds?"

"Appendai will take charge of them. He'll see they're fed and watered. We can get them on their way when we return to Dar. We'll be crossing the Serengetti plain to get there. You've not seen that yet."

"We'd love to, wouldn't we Alfred?"

"Super," Alfred replied. "We read about the Serengetti in social studies last year. It's a game preserve, isn't it? Will we see lots of animals?"

"This will give you an idea," Blake observed as they drove to a barrier on the south end of the preserve. A sign read, "Elephants Have Right of Way." Blake paid the entrance fee, and the car followed the straight narrow road. The plain seemed endless; only toward the north could be seen the faint outline of the Mountains of the Moon. A few thorn trees dotted the low scrub and grass lands. Herds of game grazed peacefully on either side of the road. The car slowed and stopped. Two rhinos stood fifty yards away, their needle sharp horns silhouetted against the sky.

"Watch this," Blake said. "They're mating." He handed Penny the binoculars. The male rose on his hind legs, his ponderous forequarters suspended over the back of the female, who buckled under his weight. His enormous penis was bent about center, the top thrusting upward with four nubs along the flat edge. The organ swung wildly from side to side, not connecting at all with the female. She moved out from under him and shook herself. She took two quick steps toward him, and swinging her head sharply upward, caught him in the shoulder with her longest horn. It broke the skin and blood trickled from the wound.

The male backed off and circled her, rising again over her hindquarters. Again, he failed to find his target, and again she moved from under him, and hooked him viciously with her horn. Penny and Blake were laughing so hard they couldn't use the binocs. Alfred took them, stared intently, then shouted; "He made it!"

Penny quickly took the glasses from him. Blake started the car, still laughing. "I guess when it's a yard long, and has a hook in it, and you can't see what you're doing, it's a bit difficult!"

"Blake!" Penny exclaimed, nodding her head toward Alfred.

"You're too protective," he muttered. "What better way could the boy learn? He probably knows more than you think he does, anyway. Isn't that right, son?"

Alfred nodded, his eyes bright. "Just wait until I tell the fellows in school about that!"

Blake stopped the car again as a band of olive green baboons crossed the road. The male in the lead stopped in the road, and facing the car, opened his mouth wide, showing his sharp long incisors, defying them. The troop passed over the road quickly. The last was a female with a baby clinging to her back.

"Even a lion hesitates to have a run in with those fellows," Blake explained. "With those teeth, they can rip a man apart."

Before he could start the car, a male ostrich appeared with a dozen, or more young birds. They followed in his wake into the tall grass.

"Both parents help raise the family." Blake explained. "The father takes care of the chicks when his wives go off to feed. Ever see an ostrich egg?"

Penny and Alfred shook their heads. Blake drove slowly, searching the grass lands. "There should be a nest near here. All the eggs don't usually hatch."

He pointed to a slight depression, the sides built up with dead grass. "There's the nest. Stay here."

Blake reached behind the car seat and picked up his gun. "Not supposed to get out of the car here."

He walked several yards and bent over, picking up a large ivory egg, only slightly smaller than a football. Penny watched him anxiously. She caught her breath as she saw a huge black maned lion rise from beneath a thorn tree, not ten yards from Blake. Two lionesses rose and stood beside him. Penny screamed and pointed. As Blake turned, three young males came over a small hill at a dead run. They went straight for the large male. Blake dropped the egg and swung the rifle to his shoulder. The three lions leaped on the lone male. The lionesses drew back. Roars and snarling of the fighting flurry of yellow hides, and flashing teeth and claws filled the air. Blake ran toward the car, glancing over his shoulder. Penny swung the door open and Blake bounded into the car, breathless.

"That was close," he gasped. "Those lions were in no mood to be interrupted."

"Why are they fighting?" Penny asked, white and shaking. Alfred was leaning out the window, binoculars to his eyes.

"One or both of the females must have been in heat," Blake replied. "Look, the black fellow's driving them off."

The big lion seemed to be turning in three directions at once. He swiped a powerful paw at one of the intruders, his teeth raking another. He turned and swung his talons at the third, holding all three at bay. As suddenly as they had come, the three lions turned and ran back over the rise, disappearing on the far side.

"Wow! That was super!" Alfred said.

"What a savage country," Penny shuddered. "You could have been killed."

"Lions seldom attack a human," Blake replied, "unless they've become man eaters, and that isn't often. But when they're fighting like that, they'll take on anything in their way."

He started the car and drove back to the road. "There's a stream further on. We'll stop there for lunch."

"Can we eat in the car?" Penny asked as they drove off the road and stopped near a shallow rocky stream. Two zebra were standing with their necks crossed, momentarily reflected in a pool of water.

Blake opened the car door. "We'll be all right. I've my gun." He opened the back to get the picnic lunch. They sat on a grassy bank under a tree beside the pebbly stream and spread out sandwiches, boiled eggs, and cheese. Penny opened a thermos of wine. They ate quietly. The zebras had jumped apart on their arrival, but remained, grazing nearby. They watched as a tall graceful giraffe approached the stream some distance away. His front legs straddled and went into a split as he bent his long neck to reach the water.

"Golly, how tall is he?" Alfred asked.

"Well over twenty feet, I'd judge," Blake replied.

Alfred sat with his elbow on his knee, his hand holding a ham sandwich, watching the giraffe. A sudden swoop of vulture wings flashed black and gray as the huge bird sailed down from the tree and snatched the sandwich from Alfred's hand. They all jumped up, the wine spilling. Alfred stood, stupefied, as he watched a trickle of blood left by the bird's claw running down his hand. Blake inspected the scratch.

"Wash it off in the stream while I get the first aid kit. Those fellows eat carrion, and we don't want that to get infected."

He returned with antiseptic and a plaster. Penny was fighting tears as she held Alfred's hand in hers. *"Now* can we finish lunch in the car? It could have been his eyes!"

"Hardly. Their aim is pretty good," Blake replied, putting away the first aid kit. "Cheeky fellow. Must be used to tourists."

"Aw, Mum, it doesn't hurt. I do hope it leaves just a bit of a scar. I'd like to show the fellows."

Penny was sullen as they drove through the last part of the Serengetti.

"That's Ngorongoro crater," Blake observed, as they passed a turn off. "You can't see the crater from here, but it's a natural valley for game, and it's full of it. There's a soda lake with over a million flamingoes in it. We'll see it another time."

They drove past a band of wild dogs running in hot pursuit after a small dikdik.

"Don't like to see them kill," Blake observed. "They're not big enough to put a quick end to an animal, and they often eat part of the animal before it's dead. That's why they hunt in large packs, and they're tireless. They can wear out almost any game. Only animal I really dislike is wild dogs; used to shoot them whenever I could."

A few miles further on, Blake said, "Want to have some fun?"

Alfred quickly agreed but Penny looked questioningly at Blake.

"Don't worry," he patted her arm, "I guarantee you'll be all right. See that herd of Cape Buffalo?"

He swung the car off the road, and raced between the herd and a thicket of trees behind them. The buffs tried to run into the trees, but Blake cut them off. Dust clouded and billowed down on them as they ran in a milling circle, galloping very fast, carrying massive horns easily. A young calf, not able to keep up, was cut off from the herd. Blake braked sharply, barely missing the small animal, and stopped. The buff was breathing hard. He trotted a few steps and leaned against the front tire.

"Oh no," groaned Blake, "He's substituting that black tire for his mother. Just a minute, I'll move him."

The female buffalo stood, glowering beneath a tree fifty yards off, with horns lowered.

"Go to your mama, little fellow," Blake grunted, as he picked up the muddy calf, and carried him away from the car. He sat the animal down and tried to move away. The calf followed, and pressed against Blake's bare legs, leaving them mud streaked.

Blake turned toward the car, laughing. "Penny, drive the car slowly ahead. I'll catch up."

With a final pat on the calf's head, Blake turned and ran toward the moving car. Penny slid over as Blake leaped into the moving vehicle. The calf almost caught up with the car when Blake gunned away toward the mother buff. She was pawing the ground, and bellowing at her calf.

"There, I think they'll find each other now," laughed Blake.

Penny looked fondly at him. "You really are kind, aren't you? Seriously, though, I've had enough adventure for one day. Promise no more?"

"We'll be at the Slades soon and you can relax."

A short time later, they turned off the road onto a lane lined with frangipani trees, ending at a lovely park. Rose bushes and bougainvillea filled the large space surrounded by lush lawn. On the far side nestled a low rambling house. A large verandah spread the length of the front and one side. Beyond the main house was a cluster of small structures. Except for the rose garden dotted with brilliant peacocks, the house was surrounded by row on row of low coffee trees. Blake stopped the car beneath an umbrella like flame tree next to some children's swings on the thick lawn. Ann and Bob rose from the verandah, and walked to the car and Blake introduced them.

"We're a sight," Penny exclaimed. "We came across the Serengetti, and I think there isn't a square inch of me that's not covered with dust."

"You'll want to shower and freshen up," Ann laughed.

"We'll probably clog your drains," Penny sighed, "but it's a capital idea."

"I'll have Kumba bring your bags. That house first in line has two bedrooms and it's kept ready. Join us when it's convenient."

Showered and in clean clothes, they joined the Slades. Bob was putting on his hat, a broad brimmed felt with one side tacked to the crown, Australian style.

"I have to run over to the north acreage, Blake. Would you care to join Alfred, and me? There's a mare due to foal, and I want to check her."

Mayn't I, Mum?" Alfred asked. Penny nodded, glad to be able to sit a while in this peaceful and beautiful place.

"We've only the immediate family here now," Ann explained, as they sipped tea. "My father had a heart attack a few months ago, and the doctors advised him to move to a lower altitude. We're pretty high here, you know."

"Have you brothers or sisters?" Penny asked.

"Oh yes. My older brother, David, is a pilot, and he's flying now, crop dusting. The coffee's not ready to harvest so things are a bit slow at present. My sister and her family live in Nairobi. Her husband traps animals for research and zoos. Since he traps monkeys, too, I call him my brother-in-law who's in the monkey business!"

They both laughed, then Ann asked, "How long have you been in Africa?"

"Only a bit over a week, but it seems like years. So much has happened. I don't know whether I'm more excited than scared or the other way around. Blake—."

Seeing Penny hesitate, Ann said, "Oh my, he's one of a kind, isn't he? I imagine he's really showing you Africa."

"Indeed. Alfred and I came over here so I could buy parakeets for our pet shop back in Liverpool, but I never expected to see all this! It's so exciting."

"I've lived in Africa all my life. I don't think I could live anywhere else, though the way things are going here, I don't know what's going to happen."

"What kinds of things?"

"The government's trying to start land reform. They're 'buying out' many of the farmers, and settling Africans on the land. It's called the Ujamaa Village plan. But the Africans don't know how to run a farm, or a dairy herd, and they just go downhill. And what good is payment to us when we can't take the Tanzanian shilling out of the country with us or convert it before we leave?"

A small boy with bowed unsteady legs appeared on the verandah followed by an African girl.

"Adam," Ann held out her arms. "Did you have a good nap?"

With his tightly curled honey blond hair and china blue eyes, Adam looked angelic.

"What a darling child," Penny exclaimed. "Do you think he'd let me hold him?"

"I'm sure he will. He goes to anyone. We call him our vagabond."

Penny held out her arms, and Adam leaned over to be picked up. "You're adorable," Penny cooed, as Adam's busy fingers clutched a hand full of hair. "I've always wanted more children, but Hubert, my husband, didn't seem to—."

"I'm glad Bob likes children," Ann replied. "Our two older ones are in school in England, and I just had to have another. Bob acted grieved about it, but he's really crazy about Adam. He very nearly delivered him! He was due on a Tuesday, and Bob needed to go up country to a sale. There was a mare there we wanted for our breeding stock, and he was going to buy her for me to replace my old gelding we'd had to put down. I asked my doctor if I could go with Bob, and all he asked me was what kind of car we would travel in. I told him a Jeep.

"'Does it have a back seat?'" he asked. "I told him it did.

"'Well then,'" he said, 'you could have it there, if worse came to worse. Bob's had a lot of experience with animals. I shouldn't worry if I were you.'"

"So I went to the sale. I just had to see the mare. I'm so fond of riding, and it turned out she was a beauty."

"And the baby?"

"Quite. On the way home, on Monday, I went into labor, but we made it to the Lutheran hospital in Moshi in time. What a ride!"

"I'm afraid I'd not be that brave, but what a wonderful life you've had. You know," Penny looked away, saying wistfully, "I just go to that store every day, and look at the animals and the birds, and wonder about where they came from. Not the dogs and cats, of course, but the birds and the monkeys; things like that. One time we even had a bush baby. I hated it when he was sold. I'm thirty-six now, and too old to have more children. Hubert's a dear, but he doesn't think about much but the shop. Sometimes I—."

She stopped and looked at Ann. Her warm expression encouraged Penny to continue. "Sometimes I wonder if life isn't passing me by. I seem to long for things Hubert never thinks about. I've dreams of living in a place like Africa, and—yes—even meeting a man like Blake."

Penny looked down and bit her lip. Ann reached over to pat her hand. "I understand what you're trying to say. I think I should feel the same way."

"Dear Ann, I'm so glad we met. You're so easy to talk to. I think I'm falling in love with Blake, and I feel he's interested in me, too. I've never met anyone like him. He's fascinating."

"Penny, I'm so glad for you. Yes, Blake is fascinating, but I can see your dilemma."

Penny batted tears from her eyes. "I truly don't think I can go back to life in Liverpool and —Hubert—now. Though I don't think I'd ever be brave enough to risk having a baby in the back seat of a car, I think I could learn to live here, even though it's so strange and different."

Ann agreed, and reached out for Adam. "Let's take a walk. I'll show you around. I'm sure you could manage in Africa, if that's what you want. Of course, we all love and miss England. I remember when I was a little girl, what my mother went through establishing this rose garden. She always said it was like having a bit of home with her here. I think Blake would be a very lucky man to have you."

Penny smiled her thanks and reached for Adam. He clasped his arms around her neck and gurgled.

At the edge of the lawn Ann paused, looking at Mt. Kilimanjaro. The cloud-shrouded peak suddenly came into view.

"Oh, it's beautiful!" Penny gasped. A long shudder shook her. She felt a deep sense of foreboding. It was almost a physical pressure. She glanced at Ann, but she was gazing at the sunlit snowfield on the mountain.

"What's wrong with me?" Penny wondered. *"Probably to much excitement in one day. Already I miss Blake. Whatever shall I do when I have to leave?"*

\*\*\*\*\*\*\*\*\*\*\*\*\*\*\*\*\*\*\*\*\*\*\*\*\*\*\*\*\*\*\*\*\*\*\*\*

Inexorably, inevitably, it came; Blake and Penny's last night together. Alfred was staying with a young friend, a family Blake had introduced them to with a son about Alfred's age. They had danced after dinner at the Twigga, but Penny suggested they leave early. She could think only of departing on the plane the next day. Back in Penny's hotel room they made love, long and deeply satisfying. They lay in bed, Penny's head on Blake's shoulder.

"I can't bear to think of leaving tomorrow," she said, her eyes welling with tears.

"Then don't."

"What do you mean, 'don't'? What else can I do?"

"Stay here. Stay with me."

Penny propped herself on one elbow and stared at Blake. "But my dear! I'm married and there's Alfred and—"

He sat up, took Penny's hands, and looked deep into her eyes. "Penny, I want you. I want to live with you. I want to marry you if, and when you divorce Hubert. Do you understand what I'm saying?"

He got up and mixed drinks for both of them. "I knew," he continued, "as soon as I walked into that house and saw you, you were the woman for me. You've let yourself drift into middle age prematurely. You haven't been made love to properly or cherished, and you're more a business partner to your husband than a woman, a wife."

She nodded. "But Alfred?"

"He's in boarding school, isn't he? Ready to return in a few days?"

"That's true, but I see him on school holidays and all."

"Then have him here on the holidays. I've a bit of extra money. Lars remembered a debt he owed me, one I'd long ago forgotten. He repaid it in British pounds and I can nearly triple that on the black market here in Dar. Since the Asians have to leave the country, they're willing to pay very high prices for foreign currency. The Africans hate them and the government's going to force them out. Also," he added, "I'm sure to find something soon that's more permanent than trapping. It just takes a little time."

Blake set his drink down and put his arm around Penny, his face buried in her throat, "Please. Please, Penny. Stay here with me. I want to make you young again. I want to take care of you and see you come alive as a woman should. Stay with me."

"Oh, Blake! I do so want to! You can't know how much. Let me think a minute."

She rose and slipped on a robe. Going to the table and mixing a very strong drink, she stood at the window, looking out at the harbor lights. As they listened to the deep ships' horns, she turned to Blake, her face aglow. "My love, this is like a dream. You and Africa—. I'm afraid to pinch myself for fear I'm dreaming. I want to stay here more than anything in the world, but I can hardly believe it's true!" Her brows knitted. "Blake, you've not told me the most important thing of all."

He smiled. "I can't think what that would be. I've asked you to come live with me, to be my wife. What more can I say?"

She walked over to the bed. "You can say—," she started.

Blake stood up and stopped her words with his mouth on hers. Holding her close, he moved his lips to her ear. "I love you, Penny. I love you very much."

"My dearest," she whispered. "I love you more than I ever thought it possible. For the first time in my life I really feel like a woman. I'm so filled with it. I'm ten feet tall with wings on my heels! How could all this happen in only two weeks?"

They clung together, laughing, and fell into bed. Much later they lay in each other's arms, unwilling to end the magic with sleep.

"Were you ever married, Blake?" she asked.

"Yes. It was a young marriage that happened just before the war started. She got pregnant the first month, but I had to leave long before she delivered. I saw the child, a girl, only once during the six years I was away. When I finally returned to Liverpool, I found her living with a Polish fellow, had been for a year, quite openly. Even my mother knew about it. I offered her a divorce and she accepted. I haven't seen her since, or the child, 'though I heard a few years ago

I've a grandchild now. I've never blamed her; we were simply parted to long."

"All this was in Liverpool?"

"Yes. My mother's lived there since my father's death. They returned there when the war started, but my father couldn't get Africa out of his blood. He was never happy back in England. He died before the war ended"

"I'd like to meet your mother," Penny snuggled closer to Blake, running her fingers over the thick mat of his chest. "I've been thinking. I really owe it to Hubert to tell him about all this in person, and I'll need to get Alfred back and try to make him understand. Then I should collect my things, things I don't want to part with."

"I understand, sweetie, but you will return? You will come back to me?"

"Yes, Blake. Yes! Ever' so soon. I promise."

# Chapter 10

Blake received a cablegram from Liverpool the following week. "GOD LOVES ME. HE WANTS ME TO BE HAPPY. HE TOLD ME SO. WILL ARRIVE DAR TUESDAY TWO PM. PENNY."

"Bloody cablegram must have cost the earth," Blake muttered to himself as he folded it carefully and put it in his wallet. *Ten days from the time she left. That's pretty good.*

Penny's feet hardly touched the steps as she descended from the plane. Her eyes searched the crowd for Blake before she realized she would have to clear customs first. Her three large trunks and several pieces of luggage took an interminable time to be inspected. Once released to immigration, her passport was inspected' by a young African in so leisurely a manner she wanted to yell at him.

"Your return air ticket?" he asked, extending his hand.

"I haven't one. I'm not returning. I'm staying here."

The official smiled at her radiant face, then caught himself. Frowning, he asked, "Who do you know here, Madam?"

"Captain Blakely," she said, proudly.

The official's eyes narrowed. He shook his head.

"Captain Blakely. Blake Blakely. J. D. Blakely?"

The man stared at her, expressionless.

She tried again. "Captain J. D. Blakely. He traps birds. He—I—."

The official left his chair, taking her passport with him. He had a hurried conference with a man at a desk in the back of the room.

"What can be the matter?" she wondered. *Oh, I wish they'd hurry. I do so want to see Blake.*

At last the official returned. "How much money have you? Have you enough to return to England?"

"Return to England? I don't want to return, I want to stay here."

"I understand that, Madam. We want to be sure you have enough to buy a return ticket. It's the law."

"Oh my, yes. I've it right here." She pulled a bank envelope from her purse and hastily opened it, tearing the paper in her haste. She held out a cashier's check for three thousand pounds. "I've this and a bit more in travelers' checks." she hurriedly added.

The man took the check from her, scrutinizing it. He took it back to the man at the desk. Another official was called over. The men talked in low voices, glancing at Penny.

She grew frantic. *I can't leave to find Blake and I don't know any way to get word to him. What on earth could be wrong?*

Finally the man returned and handed her the cashiers' check. "Do you know anyone else here?" he asked.

"I've met ever so many people," she replied, frowning. "There's—oh, what is their name? We stayed the night with them a short time back."

Her mind was a blank. "Isn't Captain Blakely enough?"

"We would like another name, Madam, if you would." The man replied sternly.

"I know. I remember now! Slade, that's it. Robert and Ann Slade." She sighed with relief.

The official smiled. "The gentleman lives in Arusha?"

"Yes, in Arusha. They've a coffee farm." Penny tucked the envelope in her purse. "May I go now?"

He hesitated, then held out her passport. "Be careful, Madam."

Penny turned and hurried away, hardly hearing him. She searched the lobby frantically, not seeing Blake anywhere. She was in tears when she glimpsed Abhurdamoni picking his way through the crowd.

"Karibu, Memsahib," he smiled, his flowing dhoti as white as his teeth. "Karibu. Welcome." He took her overnight case. "Come, Memsahib," he said, starting toward the doors.

"Where is Blake?" she asked, feeling the tears start again as she followed Abhurdamoni blindly. She hardly realized he had stopped next to a tall Englishman.

"Mrs. Lambert-Smith? I'm Major Redwood," she heard a voice say.

She looked up to see a very tall man with thinning white hair. A black elastic band encircled his head and connected to a black eye patch. He was extremely thin, dressed in impeccable white shorts and shirt. White ribbed socks stopped below his bony knees. A military ribbon was pinned above his shirt pocket, confirming his rigid bearing. He bent forward at the waist in a semi-formal bow, and added in a high pitched voice, "Blake was delayed. Be in later this evening."

He extended a knobby hand. "Happy to know you. You'll be my guest for the present."

Penny tried to thank him, but burst into tears instead. The Major stepped back in dismay, then moved toward Penny, putting a long thin arm about her shoulders. "Oh, my dear."

She buried her face against his chest, her shoulders shaking. He led her haltingly through the front doors, pausing a moment to give Abhurdamoni swift instructions. They continued to the car. After settling Penny in the passenger side, he asked for her baggage checks. Through tears running down her cheeks, she fished them out of her purse.

"I'll see Abhurdamoni gets these," he patted her awkwardly on the shoulder. "I'll return shortly."

Penny nodded wordlessly, unable to speak. She turned her face to the back of the seat and wept uncontrollably. She was still sobbing when the Major returned. He noticed her soggy handkerchief. Withdrawing a large clean kerchief from his hip pocket, he handed it to her.

"There, there now," he said, starting the car. "Feel better once you're settled at my place. Shower and rest a bit, that sort of thing."

Penny blew her nose and took deep shuddering breaths. "I'm so ashamed behaving like a silly goose," she spoke haltingly.

"No apologies," interrupted the Major. "Long trip. Jet lag and all that."

Penny shuddered. "We had engine trouble over Greece, and I thought we'd be most awfully delayed, and then that man gave me such a bad time at immigration. They seemed upset when I gave them Blake's name, for some reason. I truly thought they were going to force me to return."

"Oh dear," she stifled a sob, "it's been a most difficult time these past several days, and then when Blake wasn't there to meet me—."

The Major turned the car onto the road into Dar. "All past now. Blake'll turn up shortly. My fault, his being away. We've a bit of business together. Let him tell you about it."

"I can't guess why there was so much difficulty when I mentioned his name," she said, puzzling over the past hour; the official's expression' when she mentioned Blake's name, the conferences. "He's not in any trouble, is he?" she asked, suddenly frightened.

"No, no. Nothing serious. Business he's on has nothing to do with that. Just—," he hesitated, "government's tried some time now to deport him."

"Deport him!" cried Penny. "But why?"

"One of those pesky political things, my dear," he spoke, soothingly. "Happens all the time in these countries. Nothing to worry about. Blake's smart, knows what he's about. Born on Zanzibar, you know."

Penny nodded, her tears gone.

The Major continued. "Some disagreement whether Zanzibar's part of Tanzania or Kenya or independent. Sultan favored Kenya, but couldn't get Tanzania to release the territory. Sultan was deposed, and a quasi-elected government formed. Holding out for independence. Lot of silly bother."

"What has that to do with Blake?"

He shifted uncomfortably behind the wheel. "When Blake was forced to leave Zanzibar—," he noticed her startled look. "All non-Africans were, you know."

She shook her head, not comprehending.

He hurried on, wishing he hadn't brought the subject up. "Confiscated his passport along with everything else he owned. Thought you knew, But old Blake's too smart for them. Got a good lawyer, and contended in court that the country who issued his passport was responsible for him. Had to return his passport or let him stay. Couldn't deport him with no papers, lawyer asserted. Judge agreed. Nothing Tanzania could do but let him stay since he wasn't permitted back on Zanzibar. Rather a stalemate."

"Then there's no way he could leave Tanzania, is there?" Penny puzzled. "He's no passport."

"Imagine he could get a U.N. passport, if necessary," replied the Major. "But if he did, Tanzania could deport him. Doesn't want that. Wouldn't be able to stay in Africa then. Couldn't ever return. Africa's too much in his blood for that."

"Then he's a stateless person," mused Penny.

"I should say, rather, but old Blake'll make out. To smart for them."

They slowed in the city traffic. Penny noticed a bank on the corner. "Would you mind stopping? I want to run into the bank for a moment. Thank you." she said, as he slid the car into a parking place.

She hurried into the bank and was some time in returning. When she did, she climbed into the car, out of breath, hot and sticky in the afternoon heat.

"I'm sorry to have been so long. Everything's so much more complicated here. I had rather a large sum of money, and wanted to get it deposited before it went astray. I had to go to three officials back there in order to open a simple checking account."

The Major grunted. "Rather. Rather."

"My, the sea breeze feels good," Penny sighed, leaning her head against the car seat. The city was behind them and the cooler air blew in through the window, drying her damp hair and sweaty face.

"Old Blake and I are outcasts here abouts. People seem to think Blake hasn't much ambition, especially being a public school boy, and all. Had a remarkable record in the Royal Navy. Decorated, you know. Been sort of a soldier of fortune ever since, living by his wits. Rather admire him for it. Jolly good company, too. Enjoy his stories."

"You mentioned you were both outcasts. What—." Penny stopped, and covered her mouth with her hand. "I'm sorry. I didn't mean to pry."

"Quite all right," he gave a short dry laugh. "You'll see soon enough, at any rate."

They had left the pavement and wound up a well-graveled side road. Penny looked at the lush tropical vegetation, the palms rose starkly beside the road, their umbrella fronds shading it for the fierce African sun.

"Ditched three Mosquitoes in the war," the Major continued, fingering his eye patch. "Shot all to hell by those Krauts."

His voice broke into her reverie. She had been about to say, "My Africa."

"East Africa seemed a likely place for a middle aged flier to start off. Lots of potential here then. Doing well under Her Majesty's protection. Started an air charter service, bush flying and all that. Hard work, but jolly good life. Wife wasn't too crazy about it. No children to keep her mind occupied. Used to tell her that. Took to staying longer and longer in London each year. Had to beg her to come back every time. Then, the Emergency. Mau-Mau, you know."

Penny nodded. She had read about it in the British newspapers, but at the time it was as if it was on another planet.

Major Redwood continued. "When Uhuru came—means freedom—she claimed she'd got afraid of the Africans. Nonsense, of course. Mau-Mau was way north of here. Kenya. Never touched here. Only five-six whites killed, anyhow. Mostly slaughtered each other—the blacks. Nevertheless, she'd got afraid of the Africans. Happens to white women now and then. No help for it. Fled off to England one day. Left a note. Never came back. For me, couldn't live anywhere else. Like Blake."

He glanced at Penny, cleared his throat, and continued. "Got to liking an African girl rather well. Looked down on by the local Brits, that sort of thing. Way they look at it, color's color. Sort of grew on me, she did. Full blood Kikuu, but educated. She got in the family way a few months back. About to ask my wife for a divorce when she wrote she'd sued for one herself. Soon as I could, I married the girl. Baby's due any time. Be great to have a son, especially at my age.

The car came to a halt under a spreading flame tree next to a palatial white stucco house. The Major handed Penny out of the car, and ushered her into a cool spacious living room. A tall raw boned black woman rose from a deep chair. Her hair was pulled tightly back from a high forehead and brushed out from both sides of her head. Her features were coarse, a flattened nose spread out above thick lips. She was one of the blackest Africans Penny had ever seen, and she wore an insolent expression. She wore a western cut cotton dress of a type that looks most awkward on an African, stretching tightly across her swollen abdomen, causing the hem of the skirt to hike up in front.

"Mrs. Lambert-Smith, my wife," the Major said, after he had taken the woman in his arms and given her a long kiss.

"Welcome to our house," the woman said, as she extended her hand to Penny. There was only a trace of an accent.

"What a strange pair they are," Penny thought, as she shook the woman's rough skinned hand.

"Thank you," she said. "It's most good of you to have me."

"We'll have a stiff drink and rest a bit before Blake comes," the Major said, moving toward the bar. "He should be well along before dinner."

Penny awakened from her afternoon nap to the cool of the late afternoon breeze. She rose and stripped for a second shower, leaning close to the mirror to check if the tears of the afternoon had puffed her eyes. She looked deep into her dark blue eyes, raised her heavy arched brows as she smiled at herself, and blew a kiss to the mirror's image.

"Oh, Blake," she whispered, feeling a stirring in her loins. She turned away from the mirror and shook her head. *I must stop this or I'll positively rape him first thing when he gets here.*

She showered and dressed, and went into the living room. The high ceilinged beautifully furnished room was quiet. Assuming her hosts were still resting, she walked across the verandah with its high backed wicker chairs, and non-down the steps that led to a steep path toward the river's edge. The water flowed brown-green, eddying around inlets along the shore. White herons flew into nests atop the flowering flame trees.

She had almost lost sight of the house when she turned to retrace her steps. She looked up and saw a figure standing at the bottom of the path. Blake!

He watched her as she ran along the path, moving from light to shadow. Her throat contracted. She wanted desperately to call his name, but couldn't speak. He hurried to meet her, stopped, and held out his arms. She flew into them and they whirled around and around, unable to stop laughing.

"I'm here," she managed to say, after a long kiss. "Oh, Blake, I'm really here."

"Yes. You're really here," Blake replied. He held her at arm's length, his face soft and yearning, eyes crinkling at the corners. "Here to stay?"

"Forever and ever," breathed Penny. They sat on the bottom step, watching the splendor of the sunset.

"Tell me about it," Blake said. "Was it rough for you?"

"I simply told Hubert what had happened."

"All of it?"

"All of it," Penny said quietly. "He surprised me. He really did. He said he had often wondered how I'd got on after Alfred was born. He'd never touched me, you see, after that, and we hadn't ever talked about it. I thought he didn't want any more children. I wasn't sure what to think. It's funny it took this for us to be able to discuss it. He said he'd never enjoyed it, and it was a relief not to have to bother with it anymore, now we'd had a child. Isn't that strange?"

Blake' surpressed a laugh. "That's so strange, I would never understand it." "He was unhappy about my leaving, of course. He couldn't think how he'd run the store, but I'm sure he'll find someone. He'd interviewed one applicant before I left."

She leaned her head back against Blake's shoulder, her eyes half closed. "He was quite decent about it, really. We went to the solicitor together and determined my share of the house and business. Hubert got a loan, and gave me my half in one lump sum. I had a bit tucked away in savings, enough to buy some last minute things, and my ticket here."

"What did you do with the settlement money?" Blake asked.

"I wasn't just sure what to do since you weren't here to meet me, so on the way to the house from the airport, I had Major Redwood stop and I opened a checking account."

"How much was it?" Blake asked, his eyes narrowing.

"Three thousand pounds." She looked at him inquiringly.

"You opened a checking account here? Here' in Dar? In Tanzania!" he exploded.

"Why, yes. I didn't want to carry it around with me, and—." She stopped and looked at him. He groaned and clapped his hand to his forehead. "My God, we'll go first thing in the morning and see if we can retrieve it. I'll put your name on my account at the same time. Your money will go back to England in your name. I'm quite able to support you," he added sternly. "Besides, that money's worth three times as much on the black market. Didn't you realize that?"

"Blake! I'm sorry! I didn't think. I hope it isn't to late. Of course, I'll do as you say, but as far as I'm concerned, it's ours to do with, as we want. I didn't mean to do anything stupid." Her eyes filled with tears.

"All right, dear. It's all right. But we'll still send the money back." He squeezed her shoulders. "Now, how about Alfred."

"He was a bit puzzled about the whole thing, but seemed to take it in stride. When I told him he could spend his long holidays here, he went off to school with a cheery, 'See you in Africa, Mum'. He likes you very much although he's quite fond of his father."

She sighed and reached for Blake's hand. "Hubert and I signed the preliminary divorce papers. The final ones will be ready whenever I return to Liverpool—after six months, anyway." She looked up at him shyly. "We can be married any time after that."

Blake nodded.

"Oh, and Blake, I met your mother. She's such a dear. I didn't know how to tell her, so I just blurted it all out. Before I left, she gave me this beautiful old locket. She said it had belonged to your grandmother."

Blake traced the chain down to the cleft between her breasts. "I remember it. She must have liked you very much to part with this." He rubbed a stubby finger across the heavily embossed gold, studded with small sapphires and rubies.

"And your brother," exclaimed Penny. "You didn't tell me you had a brother. I liked him so much, though you're not at all alike."

"Old bachelor," Blake said, darkly. "Stays home and lets Mother wait on him. Dreary little shop keeper, last I saw of him. We never got on well."

He stood, smiling again. "Come," he took her hand, pulling her to her feet. "We must find our host. I've exciting news for both of you."

Major Redwood rose from his chair, pre-dinner drink in hand, to greet them. His wife sat, spine curved, resting low in an easy chair surrounded by pillows, her feet on a large hassock. The position thrust her swollen belly far forward, held proudly like a banner. Abhurdamoni had their drinks ready, and they sat around the wicker table. The black woman made a feeble attempt to reach her glass, then sank back with a helpless shrug. The Major hurried to pick it up and hand it to her. He fluffed the pillows behind her back. "Comfy?" he asked, anxiously.

She smiled faintly and nodded.

"Well," the Major said, turning to Blake. "How did you find the place?"

"I liked what I saw," Blake replied. Turning to Penny, he continued. "Major Redwood is considering buying—or should I say leasing—from the government, a fishing camp on one of the large islands south and east of here. He's asked me to consider running it for him. You see," he leaned forward, his eyes searching her face, "he could extend his charter service to include a week or two of fishing and diving for his tour groups, cutting it at both ends. Might as well make all the profit you can, eh, Major?"

"Right. Just needs the right person to run it. Government's let it run down a lot since Uhuru. Indian manager they hired doesn't work well with the locals, or the guests either. Never do, you know. Needs a British chap. Boats need repair, too, I dare say."

Blake leaned back in the chair, and replied, "One or two may even need new motors. You know how blacks are with machinery. It ends up looking like they took a sledge-hammer to it. Probably did." He stopped suddenly, only then aware of the Major's wife, but she was smiling and nodding. Blake sighed with relief. "I think we have a deal, Major. It only remains for Penny to approve."

He turned to her. "It's isolated. We can go back and forth anytime on the charter planes, but except for a copra plantation on the far end of the island; there's little else but the camp and a few scattered villages. There'll be guests for company."

"It sounds heavenly, dear. I can hardly wait to see it. When can we go there?"

"Plane's taking the Minister of Fisheries over on Friday to give the Asian manager his walking papers. Could you run over then?" the Major asked. "Stay a few days to make up your minds."

They both agreed, then rose to go in to dinner, responding to the tinkle of a dinner bell.

"Bit of a 'do' tomorrow night," the Major announced, after he had solicitously seated his wife at the table. "Cock fight followed by a little something special." He cast a knowing grin at Blake. "Think your Missus'd enjoy it?" Leave mine here—her condition."

"What is it? What are you talking about?" Penny asked, looking from one to the other.

"You'll see tomorrow night," laughed Blake. "It'll be quite a show. Hope you're not easily shocked."

"I'll have a go at it," Penny laughed. "After all, I'm a part of all this, now."

# Chapter 11

Penny and Blake went into town early next day. They stopped at the sidewalk restaurant of the New Africa Hotel for coffee, waiting until the bank opened. Several people stopped to chat with Blake, who proudly introduced Penny as Mrs. Blakely. The people accepted her and asked no questions. She commented on this to Blake as they walked toward the bank.

"There's a different breed of Englishman here, Penny. They're the ones who found the British Isles to cramped for them and they like the vastness and the challenge of Africa. Before this country, there was India and Burma; anywhere the government colonized. They're used to making their own way and asking no questions. A man is accepted for what he is now, not what he was."

Their business at the bank was taken care of, Penny's money returned, and transferred to England, her name put on Blake's checking account. She stared at her new signature, "Mrs. J. D. Blakely", and smiled.

Suddenly, a strong sense of foreboding struck her. She tried to shake it off, telling herself it must be the let down after all the excitement. *Still, what am I doing here in this strange country and with a man I hardly know?* She looked down the street, seeing nothing but black faces. *Can a white ever feel at home here, or is the land to strange, to alien?*

It was long after dinner that night when the Major parked the car in a grove of coconut palms. It had been a long ride over bumpy roads from Dar. He held the door for Penny and Blake and led them to a circular palm thatch covered arena. Crude benches in three tiers surrounded three sides of a large pit. Clusters of black men squatted in-groups on hard polished clay with a few women gathered in the darkness at the edge of the light. Only a few of the better-dressed men were using the benches and they sat with their legs tucked under them Buddha fashion. Most of the others wore a piece of single multi-colored material draped over one shoulder that hung in folds down to their knees. One group sat in a circle opposite the open end of the arena playing finger drums and chanting. The thin raspy single notes of a steel stringed violin played a monotonous three-note tune repeatedly. Several of the men rolled cigarettes, passing them one to the other.

"B'hang'" grunted Blake, nodding toward the men, as they climbed to the top tier. "Like to try some?" he asked.

"It seems to be my night for new experiences," laughed Penny. "Promise you'll take care of me?" She looked questioningly at Blake. "I've never smoked marijuana."

"I'll always take care of you, sweetie," he said, descending the steps and approaching one of the men below. He conferred with him a few minutes, handed him some coins, and was given a fat rolled banana leaf.

"Seems you can't buy a small lot," he laughed, as he joined the others. He took a cigarette paper from his wallet and deftly rolled it around the dried leaves from the spread banana leaf. He lit the end and placed it at one side of his mouth, sucking in air along with a long drag, then handed it to Penny.

"Do it like I did and hold the smoke as long as you can in your lungs. Take only a small amount of air when you need to breath."

She took a puff and handed it to the Major. It was passed back and forth until Blake snuffed out the small stub

"What is it supposed to do?" Penny asked. "I don't feel any differently."

"Give it time. You should get a good jag before too long. You were really knocking them back after dinner. How do you manager all that brandy?"

Penny shrugged, not knowing what to say. She looked around expectantly, noticing for the first time the arena was lighted with oil flares placed around the pit. The shadows they cast were elongated and jerky. Penny looked again at the groups of men. The bright cottons looked alive with intense pigment. "I never realized before how beautiful the colors are."

The two men chuckled. "She's feeling it already," the Major said. Penny giggled, then the men started to laugh. She didn't know what was funny, but it felt good to laugh.

She pointed to one of the flares. "What gorgeous colors in that fire!" It seemed as if everything around her had slowed down. Even her speech seemed delayed in coming, and she heard the echo of her voice after each word was uttered. The flames spun out from the flares, reminding her of a film she had seen once of eruptions of gas on the moon. The fire was orange, vivid pink, purple; each color distinct, yet blending with the whole. Penny leaned against Blake, inundated with the flood on sensations, her eyes half closed.

"Look there," Major Redwood leaned across her to Blake, pointing to the opposite bleachers. "Bunch of damned tourists, Yanks, all sloshed to the gills. Wish I knew what bastard brought them here. I'd wring his neck!

The chanting stopped suddenly and an excited murmur rose from the crowd. Two brightly feathered cocks were brought out, held high over the heads of the men carrying them, and place in the pit. Penny was so enthralled with the flashing hues of their feathers it took her some moments to realize they were fighting. There was a flash of metal as the cocks drove their spurs at each other's heads. The spurs had been capped with needle point brass casings, and it was only moments before they drew blood. The eye ball of one cock was hanging below his eye socket. A man grabbed him, and put the cock's head in his mouth, sucking off the blood as well as the eye, which he spat on the ground. Penny felt herself wretch and hid her face in Blake's shoulder, eyes shut.

"It's over now," Blake said, after a few minutes.

She opened her eyes to see one cock, bloody and torn, held high over a man's head. The other lay, shuddering his death convulsions in the blood spattered pit.

"Please, Blake," Penny rose on unsteady feet. "Please get me out of here." She turned to the Major. "I'm so ashamed. This is the second time you've seen me behave badly. It really isn't like me."

"Quite all right, Ma'am," he replied. "The first time seeing cocks fight can be a bit dicey, I suspect."

They were bringing two more cocks in the ring as Penny and Blake slipped away.

"Blake," Penny said, as they stood under the soft starlight, "Forgive me. Go back in if you want. I thought I was going to be sick."

"No, my dear," he replied, putting his arm around her. "I've seen more than my share of cock fights. I didn't think how it would affect you. But, Penny, this is a raw new land for the white man. The African has survived here for untold centuries. Terror and tribal rule are in the marrow of his bones. If he's cut off from his tribe he's adrift, a nonentity. In a sense we are cut off from our familiar culture here, but we're of a different stripe. Nonetheless, it takes guts to be a white man in this country and hold on to what you've got. If you're to stay, you must remember that."

The word "if" chilled Penny. She had burned too many bridges, she suddenly realized. Besides, all she wanted was Blake; Blake wherever and however.

"Give me a little time," she said, faintly. "It's that it's all so new and strange."

"That's my girl. I'm sure you'll adjust sweetie, Africa requires a peculiar breed of women. English women, for scores of years, have followed their men, fathers, husbands, even sons, into the colonies. They've brought civilization with them while their men fought the wars and broke the ground.

She smiled bravely, looking at him. "I want to make you proud of me."

"I am proud of you, sweetie. Not many women could do what you've done these past weeks. Now," he added, "I think the cock fighting is finished. There's more entertainment—of a different kind—but I'm not sure you'll like it."

"What kind of entertainment?" she asked, trying to keep the shudder out of her voice.

"Let's have a little more b'hang," he said, rolling another cigarette on the hood of the car. They puffed away in silence. "There'll be women with animals, usually a dog, a goat, and a shetland pony."

He saw her eyes widen in the brief flare of the match as he lighted the dead cigarette. "What do you mean, with—? Do you mean—?"

"Yes. I thought you'd get a kick out of it, but now I'm not sure. I'll leave it up to you."

She hesitated. "Could we stand in the tent opening for a moment? I don't want to climb onto the bleacher."

They walked toward the tent, listening to the furious beating of a deep drum. Penny leaned against a tent pole looking into the enclosure. The Africans, reeling from the effects of b'hang and pombe, milled about in excited agitation. Two young black men ran naked through the crowd carrying torches, their bodies heavily oiled, muscles rolling beneath glistening skin. Penny gasped when one turned toward her.

"Are all Africans built like that," she whispered to Blake.

"Only ones from certain tribes," laughed Blake, "but they're known for it."

Two more Africans entered the arena dragging a struggling girl. All were naked, the oil making their bodies shine like polished soap stone. The men twirled and chanted to the drum beats, leaping high in the air, blocking the girl as she tried to slip past.

There was a commotion at the edge of the arena. A huge slavering Alsatian dog appeared, leaping and twisting, trying to free himself from the men who held him. Low growls came past his tightly muzzled jaws. The girl shrank back when she saw the dog, but the men caught and held her, turning her so her back was toward the animal, forcing her to kneel, and lay her head and shoulders on the ground. They held her there and the dog broke away and ran to her.

Penny turned away. "You were right. I don't want to see it. You may stay if you like. I'll go sit in the car."

Blake turned and caught her arm. "No. I've seen it before. We'll go to the car together."

"Are you terribly disappointed in me?" she asked, as they settled in the back seat.

"Not at all, don't be silly. Some people enjoy it, some don't. Besides, it's cozy here in the car with you. We can have our own private party."

It was an hour before Major Redwood joined them. He slid quickly behind the wheel and started the car. It roared off with tires squealing.

"Glad you were in the car. Whole thing could explode any moment."

Penny glanced at him. For the first time she saw him disheveled. His thin hair hung down over his eye patch that was askew. His shirt tail was half out, and his usually immaculate shorts were wrinkled and dirty. He tried to finger comb his hair away from his eyes.

"That little gal with the dog wasn't as timid as she seemed to be in there," he chuckled.

Penny felt Blake stiffen next to her, but she was distracted trying to wipe her hand on her dress. Blake looked down to see what she was doing, and reached in his pocket, handing her a handkerchief.

"We're all a bit untidy," she laughed, as she saw Blake trying to button his shorts in the cramped car. They drove in silence, unwinding from the prolonged excitement.

"There's bound to be a prostitute on the island," Blake mused, as if talking to himself. "If we decide to make a deal there, Major, it might be a good idea to show the guests a bit of something unusual. We can always get a few young bucks."

"Jolly good," he replied. "Most of your guests will be men, anyhow, and they pay well for that sort of thing. Any women probably be Americans or Germans, and they go for it as much as the men."

The first rays of dawn were lighting the east as the car turned in the drive to the house.

# Chapter 12

They flew in the small twin engine plane across the Indian Ocean's waters. The sea was quiet with only a few breakers foaming white as they broke over coral reefs. The pilot said something to Blake that Penny couldn't hear over the rhythm of the motors. She saw Blake nod, and the plane banked sharply to the right and lost altitude quickly. Penny gripped the arm rest. The plane dove like a pelican. The Minister of Fisheries was in the middle seat with Penny. He started to protest, but got no further than opening his mouth.

The plane leveled off at the last possible moment, and skimmed the surface no more than four feet above the water. Blake turned to Penny and pointed toward the window and down. She looked out. The pinnacles of reefs showed purple and orange. Even at this speed a few of the larger fish could be seen. The plane stayed low for miles. A manta ray was sighted, looking as big as a soccer field, then a shark's fin broke the surface, his slate gray body making a huge shadow on the shallow sandy bottom. A group of porpoise swam, arcing out of the water.

A palm fringed island appeared over the horizon. Flat, little higher than the sea around it, it was narrow but extended for several miles. The plane glided onto a small dirt landing strip, and taxied to a bumpy stop. A slender small Asian ran out from a low corrugated roofed building and opened the door of the plane.

"Welcome," he beamed.

Blake ignored his outstretched hand and walked past him. The Asian shook hands with Penny and the Major, pumping up and down endlessly, taking the chance to ignore the Minister who walked past.

"I'm Bemby," he beamed, as he bobbed up and down, repeating, "Welcome", over and over. Running ahead, he ordered the lounging Africans to bring the luggage. A small bus awaited them on the adjacent sandy road. Bemby slid behind the wheel, and after grinding away at the starter and killing the starter several times, got the bus turned around and headed down the road.

Penny looked at Blake, His lips were pressed thin, and his eyes behind his glasses, narrowed. "Doesn't anyone but a white man know how to treat a piece of machinery?" he muttered.

The car passed the entrance to a copra plantation, a few small native villages dotted with papaya trees and broad banana plants, the dark purple heart hanging beneath the small sugar bananas. A rosy breasted roller skimmed across the road, his plumage iridescent in the bright sun.

The road ended at a cluster of white washed buildings surrounded by frangipani trees and tall slender palms. Bemby rushed around the bus to hand Penny out. Blake glowered, but said nothing. Penny rushed to the edge of the bluff that stood between the buildings and the sea. Three other islands and a ring of barely submerged coral enclosed the bay water with loving arms, keeping the breakers and heavy currents outside. Palms lined the bluff's edge, their patulous fronds holding white helmeted, ivory beaked fish eagles sitting in a row. The birds watched the water endlessly, diving now and then into the placid water where fry roiled the smooth surface. Two large trees with pregnant purple fruit stood near the buildings, a bush baby curled asleep in the tall branches.

Penny turned, her eyes shining, and ran to the largest of the connecting buildings, where a thatched roof was suspended over low walls, leaving an open space atop the walls to the roof with a view spreading in all directions. Away from the bay rolling meadows dotted with fruit trees ended in a large grove of cashews interspersed with kapoc trees. The roofs of a small village were barely visible.

Penny sat in the circular room furnished casually with low tables surrounded by benches and raw hide leather chairs. Bemby relayed her double gin order to the waiting bartender. She stood, carrying her drink, and walked though the narrow opening into the adjoining room furnished with a long narrow table and chairs. Beyond, the kitchen stretched away from the bay view. Adjacent to the dining area was a long row of rooms, each with a small verandah partially covered by slanting thatched overhangs. She stopped at the first one and peered through the window. Bemby appeared at her side and bowed low.

"Care to see inside, Memshaib?" he asked, dancing from foot to foot.

"May I?"

Bemby whipped out a key and rattled it in the large opening in the door. He swept the door open, and with another bow, motioned her inside and quickly shut and bolted the door. The room was spacious, a large bed covering one end with a bright African print spread. Two chairs flanked a low table beneath the windows. At the far end a door led to a dressing room and bath. Soft light filtered through the screened windows. Bemby held a chair for Penny, then quickly brought the other chair next to hers.

Leaning forward, he said, "Have you ever tried any Indian peanuts?"

She had to listen very carefully to understand him with his thick accent and rapid speech.

"Yes, yes I have," she answered, thinking of the native market in Dar that she and Alfred had explored one afternoon.

"Did you like them?" he leaned forward eagerly.

"No, not really," she smiled.

"Why not?" he asked, surprised.

"Well," frowned Penny, "I—I guess—, well, they seemed to be burnt on one side and raw on the other," She smiled again, not wanting to hurt his feelings.

Bemby caught her hand, holding it in a strong grip with his small boned delicate hands. "Would you like to try my peanuts?"

She drew back, laughing uneasily. "Do you have some here?"

He brought his face closer to hers. "I thought we could meet in your room tonight."

Penny's eyes widened as she tore her hand away and sprang to her feet. "I'm sorry! I thought you said 'PEANUTS'!"

She moved quickly toward the door. "I'm sorry—no. Really, I'm not interested—really. Captain Blakely will be wondering where I am. You must excuse me."

She slipped around Bemby, unlatched the door, and ran down the hill to the water's edge. Dropping to the trunk of a fallen palm, and holding her hand over her mouth, she laughed with shoulders shaking and eyes wet with tears.

"Oh, dear," she thought, "what must he have thought when I said, 'burnt on one side and raw on the other!' I'd better not tell Blake until that little Asian is well out of the country. Blake would tear him apart!"

Blake and the Minister came up from inspecting the boats just as the sun began to sink. They all sat in the club room, drinking silently as the red balloon of the sun hung suspended at the far edge of the island, turning the softly rippling water into shimmering gold and silver. The clouds in the magnificent African sky blushed a vivid pink, then orange, then burnt sienna. The shrill gull-like cry of a fish eagle sounded loud as a clarion bugle in the twilight stillness. The sun sat on the line of the horizon, its bottom flattened in gross distortion. Like a pin-pricked balloon, it dropped in an instant, swallowed up by the darkening waters. The bush baby came awake, his bulging nocturnal eyes blinking in the last of the light. He swung from his long furry tail and began eating the lush purple fruit, his eerie cry shattering the night's stillness.

Blake turned to Penny with a tentative smile. "Well, what do you think of it?"

"There's a saying I read once," she replied, her deep blue eyes glowing. "I think it was carved in the marble of a Maharaja's palace in India. She rose and stood in front of Blake, holding his eyes with hers.

"It said, 'If there is a paradise on earth, this is it. This is it, this is it!'" She laughed, self-conscious at her own intensity. "I don't know what arrangements you might make with the minister," she nodded at the small black man, the only one present in a suit and tie, "or with Major Redwood, but, oh, I love it here. I should never, never want anything more!"

She bent and brushed Blake's lips with hers, and whispered, "As long as we're together, that is."

Blake laughed and pulled her onto his lap. "Well, you heard her," he turned to the minister. "That decided it for me. I need to be on the ocean again, even if it's just sport fishing and diving. I've missed it."

Penny lay long awake after she and Blake had made love that night. "An island," she thought. *And I'm going to live here. Me, Penny Lambert-Smith—I mean, Blakely.* She giggled. *Late' of Liverpool, England.*

They were back in Dar before the end of the following week. Blake and the Major agreed on the business end of the arrangement and Blake started rounding up equipment and supplies. Penny was entranced with the new baby boy the Major's wife had had while they were gone.

One afternoon Blake drove the car in through a narrow strip between two buildings in the center of town and parked in front of one of them. He mounted the steps that led above a ground floor bank, inserted a key in a door, and entered a small apartment. A passageway led out onto a wide verandah that had a kitchen on one end and a large cage of parakeets on the other. In between was a closed door with a window air conditioner rattling away in the afternoon heat. A small black man came out from the kitchen, barefoot, and his clothes in rags.

"Thomas," Blake greeted him as the little man bowed twice and shifted from foot to foot. "Are you still getting drunk and beating your wife?"

"Only when she needs it," Thomas laughed, and bent over slapping his thighs.

"Better be careful," Blake said, in mock seriousness. "Someday she'll discover she's twice your size, and turn on you!"

Thomas doubled over with laughter again. Blake's eyes sought the bedroom door. "The Memsahib?"

Thomas nodded and Blake quietly opened the door to the cool bedroom. He stood, looking at the delicate Indian girl who lay sleeping on the double bed. Her long black hair lay in braids on the pillow, her skin a creamy copper, her hands and wrists hardly larger than a child's. He sat on the edge of the bed and she stirred and looked at him. The sooty black around her eyes made the deep brown irises look even darker. Her eyes always looked liquid to Blake. Her tinted lips smiled as she looked at him, and her arms came up around his neck as he bent to kiss her.

"You've been away so long," she sighed. "I have been lonesome." She lay back on the pillows, looking at him fondly.

"Jeru, I've come to tell you something." He looked away. "I've got to leave Dar. I'm going to live on an island."

Her smile faded and she looked at him pleadingly. "For a long time?"

"Yes. I expect for a long time. And I can't take you with me. You wouldn't like it there."

She turned her head to the pillow, tears welling up in her eyes.

"I want you to know," he continued, stroking her bare shoulder, "that you have been the dearest, the sweetest little thing these past years. I've really become quite fond of you, and I'll miss you. But that's how it has to be. I'm sorry."

She rose from the bed and poured some water from a carafe, then offered the glass to Blake. He shook his head and she sipped the water.

"I want you to take this," he said, counting out a number of large bills from his wallet. He tried to hand them to her, but she turned away, so he laid them on the table next to the bed. "The rent's paid for the next three months after this one," he said, as he opened dresser drawers and piled clothes on top of the dresser.

"There's enough money here to keep you and pay Thomas for that time. There's more, too, for you to enroll in a secretarial school."

He picked up the money and spread it with his fingers. The girl stood by the bed, looking down. He caught her arm and turned her to face him.

"I mean it, Jeru. I want you to go to school. Your English is fine now, and you'll want to get employment. I don't want you passed around from one man to another the rest of your life, and that's what will happen to you. What are you now? Not sixteen yet, right?"

She nodded.

"And with no family, you need training to get a job. You're a beautiful girl, and you can make a good marriage if you hold out for it. Promise?"

She nodded, and opening a closet door, withdrew a suitcase, laid it on the bed, and began putting his clothes, carefully folded, into it. Blake checked the room, picked up a few things, handing them to her. He snapped the suitcase shut.

"I believe that's everything," he said. "Now, promise me, first thing tomorrow you'll go and enroll in typing school. I checked, and they're starting a new class next week. I want you to be in it."

She nodded again and stared at the floor. He cupped her chin with his hand, and lightly brushing her lips, picked up the suitcase and strode to the door. She stood watching him, fighting tears.

"Good-bye, Jeru, and good luck." Blake walked thorough the door, closing it firmly behind him. With a few words to Thomas, he was gone.

"After all, color's color," he murmured, as he descended the stairs to his car.

\*\*\*\*\*\*\*\*\*\*\*\*\*\*\*\*\*\*\*\*\*\*\*\*\*\*\*\*\*\*\*\*\*\*\*

They were back on the island within a week. Blake groaned at the amount of luggage Penny had brought from England. The two new motors and piles of fishing equipment, along with masks, snorkels, and fins had taken up the storage space in the plane. Penny took only a few things with her, and the rest was put on a shaky looking dhow along with Appendai and Abhurdamoni and their families. Penny watched the dhow set sail, low in the water, with children hanging over the sides. She fully expected never to see any of them again, including her three trunks.

She had called Liverpool to tell Alfred where she would be, but he was on holiday with school chums, and wouldn't return in time to reach her before she left for the island. She gave Hubert the call numbers of the short wave on the island and the Major's phone number in case of emergency. Hubert had sounded concerned about her. She thought again of their farewell at the airport. They both had tears in their eyes as they said good-bye. Hubert's last words ran through her mind. *If it doesn't work out, Penny, don't hesitate to come back. I'll always be here for you if you need me.*

She felt that was so much more than she deserved, having treated him so shabbily. She had pressed his hand and thanked him, trembling with the anticipation of returning to Africa and to Blake.

They settled in the fishing camp just as the rainy season started, during which Blake had assured her there would be no guests. "We'll have plenty of time to get the place in shape," he said, "the boats and motors running and—," he gave her a playful slap on her behind, "lots of time left over for making love."

Appendai and Abhurdamoni had built their rude houses in a few days, and had their families installed. Abhurdamoni quickly put the kitchen to rights, cajoling and shouting the kitchen boys into doing things his way. Penny had brought a Swahili dictionary from Dar, and practiced on the patient Abhurdamoni, who spent what time he could helping her with pronunciation. One word she especially liked was, "Karibu." It was the word for welcome. Literally translated, it meant, "Come closer". She liked using the lilting strange word when Blake slipped into the bed beside her.

"Every night you come to bed with your bra and panties on," he groaned, one evening. "And every night I have to take them off you." But she sensed he rather enjoyed it, and continued to wear them.

One morning the sun broke through the heavy clouds. Penny looked up from her studies to see Blake coming up from the boat house. "Put on your costume," he said. She was surprised since they usually had their daily swim in the afternoon when the rains stopped for a while. "It's time you saw the reefs," he continued. "It's a sight you'll not likely forget."

He ordered chicken sandwiches and a bag of mangoes from Abhurdamoni. They waded out to the boat where Appendai waited. It lay quite a distance off shore since the tide was out. The other boats lay in shallow water tilted on their sides. In the distance Penny saw a graceful dhow sailing toward a far island. Its single tri-cornered sail billowed out like a taut kite, making the cumbersome dhow slice through the water like a carving knife. The sound of the boatmen chanting carried the distance across the water.

"How utterly perfect," Penny thought, for the hundredth time. Her daily letters to Alfred used the phrase at least once in every letter.

As they reached the boat Appendai leaned over the side and picked her up out of the water and set her down in the boat. She again marveled at his easy strength. As the boat headed toward the far side of the bay, Blake fitted a mask for her, showing her how to hold it against her face to test the fit. He showed her how to take the snorkel in her mouth and tuck the shank upright through the headband of the mask. The rubber mouth piece was distasteful to her at first, but she quickly learned to breath through it and be comfortable with it. She adjusted the straps on her flippers and checked the fit. Appendai slowed, then stopped the boat, throwing out the anchor.

Blake held his mask tight against his face, then fell back off the gunwale. He reappeared, blowing sea water out of the snorkel, and motioned Penny to follow. She slid over the side, and started moving her flippers slowly, face down, she followed Blake toward the reef. She had been reading Blake's books avidly about the reefs and fishes in the area and she rehearsed in her mind her next letter to Alfred.

"There, a few feet below me lies a whole new world. It is like a riotous flower garden with everything in full bloom. The underwater mounds of coral are only a few feet from the surface since it is low tide. Undulating, opening and closing while feeding, plant-animals called anemones are imbedded on great shelves of miniature underwater mountains. These anemones catch small fish and devour them, but there is a small fish, the clownfish, (called that because of its markings) that is immune to them, and swims in and out at will. Huge brain coral teeters precariously at the end of a shelf, light and shadows playing about over its serrated surface. Elk horn swaying gently in the currant, and organ pipe antler, elephants' ear, green sponges growing from fat stems and a myriad of others I cannot as yet identify. There is red coral the Tibetans covet so much for their jewelry, bluish-purple-tipped and indigo coral, layer upon layer of coral rock, thousands, perhaps millions of years of patient building upon itself to achieve ten to twenty feet in height. And, oh my dear, the fish! Silent phantoms, propelled only by a fluttering fin and an occasional flick of the tail. First I notice the surgeon fish, lips protruding as if to say, 'kiss me'. Then a blood red intanga, about a foot long, dives up from beneath a coral shelf. As he approached, the pale purple spots laid in a geometric design becomes apparent, and the deep red fins are feathered with a bright orange-yellow. Two-tone butterfly fish swim by, dotted near the tail to simulate eyes; a protective device of nature so that when a larger fish comes at them, in what it thinks is head-on, the prey can streak off in the opposite direction and dive under a ledge! The Moorish idol, plate shaped with curved stripes in front and oppositely curved stripes in back that meet in a design midway that sprouts long trailing fins, twice the length of his body."

"There is a spotted coral. No, wait! It has an eye tilted toward me; such splendid camouflage. I have to peer several seconds to discern the outline of the fish, then only as it betrays its presence by the roll of an eye, could I be sure."

"The purples of the sea are fantastic, followed by the red, oranges, blues, and yellows. Floating along the top of the water one really learns to look. At first, what is directly underneath is so absorbing; yellow and black striped angel fish with fins like lacy organdy, coal black velvety mollies, rock cod as individually marked as a fingerprint, a cloud of inch long nearly transparent light and dark striped silvers—sargeant fish?—rock fish with tiny multipeed sized legs climbing on to the coral surface, the hermit crabs in shells with tiny feelers protruding outwards, and shells of all sizes and hues; spotted, pure white, plaid, striped, zipper opened, speckled, and horn rimmed."

"The water is marvelously clear, but held in wonder by the world immediately below my mask, it is some time before I realize the drama taking place on the periphery. The larger fish are swimming just on the edge of my vision, curious, but staying away. I float, barely daring to move in their direction. They move out a bit, but curiosity gets the better of them. They want to know about this strange alien creature. Slowly they come into focus, mostly rock cod, with a sprinkling of yellow fin tuna. In a deep crevice I see a large boulder. No, it moves slightly. Blake tells me later it is over two hundred pounds of sea bass. Its mouth is the same circumference as its body!"

"My eyes are stinging before I realize the salt water has seeped inside my mask, almost filling it. I tread water and empty the mask. Blake swims over, and motioning me to follow, dives down, and shows me how to press the mask and blow through my nose so I can clear it under water. Then he motions me to surface and jack-knife down. I try it, but bob along like a cork, flailing my arms and legs. He shows me again, and this time I am diving down, the flippers driving me down a coral wall. Something is different—yes—the sun has slipped out from under a cloud. All is sparkling! Shafts of light beams are waving through the water, dappling the coral. The parrot fish are the brightest of the lot. Sharp beaks munch on the outer edges of the rock hard coral. Except for shape, each one is different, adorned with unique colors and designs, and each so brightly marked it catches the breath. A medium sized blue-gray fish comes leading a group, and each has a spear shaped upper lip; a unicorn! I see pygoplities, (Blake tells me later) wearing meticulously striped Joseph coats; rare in aquariums, but in profusion here."

"I decide to pull myself down the wall of coral. I had not touched the coral before. It has a splendidly tactile feel, some to smooth to hold on to, others pebbly rough. I jerk my hand back because it strings! Black feathery fingers are growing out of a crevice, and I have touched them. Fire coral! Down further I go, needing fresh oxygen, but hating to reverse the dive. I nearly put my fingers into the open shell of a clam. Blake swims and pulls me away just in time. He takes a knife and cuts the clam out of the shell. I have to go to the surface twice to breath while he is down there with the clam. He pries the beautiful iridescent shell loose and hands it to me. Such a treasure! It is a foot across with fluted edges. On the way up I see a deadly lion fish, its beautiful, but a dozen poisonous fins waft with the current. We stare at each other for a moment, then with protesting lungs, I shoot to the surface."

"Blake meets me at the boat. 'Don't ever come up like that without exhaling,' he cautions. 'You can get an aneurysm that way.' I have so much to learn and I want to learn it all at once!"

After their dive they swam to the far side of a small coral outcropping, and came out of the water onto a narrow strip of sand. Tall wide winged water birds rose from the tufted crest of the butte, and flew, skimming the water on giant wings.

Penny sat down heavily, as if in shock. "That was the most fantastic experience of my life! I wouldn't have believed all that was right there, a few feet under the water."

"Thought you'd enjoy it, sweetie. I never get tired exploring it, and every reef's different. We'll have a chance to see them all."

He unsnapped the blunt ended knife from his calf, and waded out and around the exposed coral, starting to chip away at some embedded mollusks. "Come here, Penny, I've a surprise for you."

When she joined him, he held out a half oyster shell, the muscle resting in its own juice.

"Take it all down in one swallow," he said.

She held the pearly shell in the sunlight, looking at the subdued rainbow colors, then tilted it to her lips. The oyster was warm from the sun and tasted of the sea. She tilted it further and it slid down her throat. "Delicious," she exclaimed. "May I have another?"

"There's lots", Blake said, as he downed his oyster and pared more off the rocks. Satiated, they waded back to the narrow beach. Penny lay back and Blake sat looking at her.

"Do you know how much weight you've lost?" he asked.

She looked down and saw how loose fitting her bathing costume was. "Yes, I guess I have," she laughed. "Do you like it?"

"I like it," he replied, stroking her shoulder. He slipped the strap down below her breast, caressing it. "As long as you don't lose it here," he smiled. You look years younger."

Penny smiled, her teeth white against her golden tan, and laid her head on Blake's lap. "I'm so blissfully happy, and so in love. I feel like a whole new person."

"You're all the woman I'll ever want," he replied, and kissed her. "You'll never leave me, will you?"

She caught the hungry loneliness in his voice. "Never," she whispered, touching his lips with her fingers. "Surely there were other women after your divorce?"

"Oh, yes," Blake said, casually. "There was a French girl I met after the war." He looked at Penny, his eyes running down her body. "Sure you want me to tell you about her?"

"If you want to. I'm not at all jealous, and I've told you all about Hubert and me—what there was to tell," she laughed.

Blake stroked her body with a gentle touch. "I'd managed to scrape together the price of a schooner when the war was over, and I sailed to one of the islands off the coast of Greece. Got a profitable trade going smuggling cigarettes and contraceptives to Italy. Bought a house on the beach, met the French girl, and she lived with me for a time."

"How did you get on with her? Was she good in bed?"

"Good in bed, she was," mused Blake, cocking an eyebrow at Penny. "In fact, she taught me a few things. I was still pretty young and hadn't had a chance to get much experience while the war was being fought. She'd been around a good bit. Besides, the Greek girls were impossible to touch after they were married, and the unmarried ones wanted to keep their virginity intact."

"Anyhow," he continued, "one day I came into the harbor after a successful trip, and just as I was going to pull into the dock, I noticed a patrol boat anchored next to my dock space. I reversed engines and started out to sea again. The patrol boat started up and chased me. I figured they'd caught on to my operation, and me, and I'll tell you, Greek jails are not good places to be. They lock you up and lose the key, and they forget to feed you."

Blake laughed, caught up in his remembering. "We had a running gun battle, but my boat had an extra motor, and she wasn't loaded with cargo. They shot some cannon at us, but I zigzagged, and I didn't get a hit. I had fought a war in those waters and knew lots of small coves where I could hide during the days, and I sailed at night. I dodged in and out for several days, then headed for the Suez Canal. I managed to cross with some hefty bribes since I hadn't the proper papers to pass through. Then I sailed on down to Zanzibar, picking up a little freight on the way."

Blake squinted in the hot sun, and pulling Penny to her feet, resettled in the shade of a ledge. They lay with her head on his arm, and she wound and twisted her fingers through the thick hair on his chest and shoulders. "It's so long, I could almost plait it," she thought.

Blake closed his eyes, was silent for a bit, then continued. "I wrote for the girl to join me, but she replied she didn't think she'd like

Zanzibar. I signed over the house to her, and what I had in the bank, since there was no way I could get it out of Greece, anyway."

"Oh well," he sighed, "she was a hot tempered little thing, and I was getting tired of the scenes she drummed up every time she got bored. It always ended with my having to turn her over my knee and give her a good spanking, and that got tiresome. But it was good while it lasted, I'll have to say that."

"Who was your first girl?" Asked Penny. "Were you in love with her?"

"No," laughed Blake. "That was a strange one."

"I'm thirsty," Penny said, getting up to retrieve the thermos. She poured the last of the wine in the cup and offered it to Blake. He took a sip, handed it back to her, and lay with his head on her lap. She leaned back contentedly, sipping the wine.

"Now, tell me about your first girl."

"She wasn't a girl, really," Blake replied. "I was in public school in Liverpool, and one of the chaps in my class had an uncle who owned a sporting house. It was one of the fancier places with a white and gold piano, you know—. No," he laughed, "I guess you wouldn't. To get on, the uncle kept urging me to take my choice of the girls he had there. His nephew managed to try them all out at one time or another. We spent most of our weekends there during the school year."

Blake shook his head and turned over on his stomach. "I couldn't seem to get interested. They were whores, after all, and I'd see them taking all those men to their rooms. I've never yet made love to a whore, and never intend to. They would tease me. I was about sixteen or seventeen, as I remember, but I looked older. I started growing all this hair when I was fourteen."

"One evening I was sitting in the main room when a very classy woman came in and asked to talk to my uncle. They sat at the bar and chatted a few minutes, then he called me over and introduced me. We had a drink while we got acquainted. She spoke quite well, was around thirty years old, attractive. She asked if I'd had dinner and when I said no, she suggested we go to her house."

"We got in her big car and on the way she said she'd have to stop and make a phone call. I waited while she went to a pay phone. When she returned I asked her name again since I hadn't heard it very well when we met. I realized the name was Jewish, and when I asked her, she said she was. We drove to the outskirts of the city, and turned at a rather fine house. We went in and she fetched some jellied chicken and a bottle of wine from the kitchen. She said the servants weren't there on weekends."

"After we'd eaten, she suggested we go to her bedroom. We made love several times that night, and the next day, then she drove me back to the brothel. She said if I was interested, she would pick me up the following Saturday. This went on for three or four months. Then one Saturday, the uncle told me she had sent a message that she didn't want to see me again."

"I asked if he knew why, if I had done anything wrong. He said he knew why, but he couldn't tell me, except that it was nothing I had done, but that I was not to go near her house or make any attempt to get in touch with her again. He made me promise. I really didn't think too much about it. I was busy trying to qualify for the Olympic swim team and do my studies. Then I left for the summer to go back to Zanzibar with my parents."

"It was nearly a year later I was back in Liverpool in my last year of school when I was on a ferry and saw her again. She recognized me, and tried to avoid me, but I was curious and followed her."

'Why are you following me?' she asked, when I caught up with her beside the rail. 'Have you been following me all along? Do you expect me to give you money?'

"No," I replied. "This is the first time I've seen you in nearly a year. But I am curious, now that I've seen you again. No, why should you give me money? I'd just like to know why you broke it off?"

"She asked if I had tried to find her, and I assured her I hadn't, that in fact, I'd met a girl I wanted to marry. I told her I hadn't thought of her in months."

"'Well, then, I'll tell you.' she said."

"It seemed she and her husband had been married some years and had no children. They were both checked by doctors, and it turned out he was sterile; not impotent, but sterile."

Blake looked at Penny questioningly and she nodded. He continued. "They had decided she should get pregnant by a man neither of them knew or would be likely to run into, and she had gone looking and found me. She selected me because I resembled her husband, The phone call she had made that first night was to tell him to vacate the house."

Blake rose and shook himself. He went into the shallow water and picked up two sea urchins, giving one to Penny, and fishing the other one out and swallowed it. She started to pick hers out and drew back. "Ouch! They're prickly."

Blake speared the meat with his knife and held it out to her.

"Umm, good," she said, swallowing it. "Go on. Was that all?"

"No, there's more. After I thought that over, I said, 'I should think you'd have wanted a Jewish chap.'"

"'I thought you were at first,' she laughed. 'You could be, you know, with your dark looks, but I realized you weren't, of course, when I saw you weren't circumcised. By that time it was to late, and I hadn't the courage to go looking for another man!'"

"We both had a good laugh about it and she asked if I would like to see the child, making me promise I would never ask to see him again. I agreed, and we went to her house. I met her husband. He was a nice chap. The baby was two months old, a little boy, and looked exactly like me."

He shook his head and chuckled. "Come," he said, pulling Penny to her feet. "It's going to rain soon, and I want lunch."

# Chapter 13

The long spring rains ended and guests started arriving in the Major's small planes. They were European business men, for the most part, set for sport fishing and diving. Evenings were filled with drinks and conversation, the inevitable talk of 'the big one that got away'. Penny found Blake was fluent in French and Italian. He was busy most days taking out one boat, and Appendai the other. They returned every day around three or four o'clock, and hung their catches proudly on the scales. Blake brought Penny a camera and she dutifully photographed the men with their fish. Often they asked her to pose with the catch while they took a shot or two. Blake teased her about it, telling her she was getting better looking every day.

He had gotten the jeep in running order, and Penny made the trip to the far end of the island with Abhurdamoni to shop at the local produce market. Most other supplies came in by plane. Her Swahili was passable, although Blake and the Africans laughed uproariously at some of her attempts.

Alfred came for most of the summer, and Blake taught him to spear fish. He was proud as punch of a rock cod he speared weighing over a hundred pounds. He and Penny spent long hours together, and grew even closer. As time for his departure grew closer, however, Penny was flooded with a strange sense of foreboding. *Maybe the gods are jealous; maybe no one deserves this much happiness.*

Then one day Appendai appeared with a small monkey explaining that the mother had died. Penny fed the little thing with an eye dropper, and it clung to her constantly. Blake refused to let her have it in bed with them, so she made a small bed on the floor beside her, waking several times in the night to pat and soothe it. Her sense of apprehension vanished.

"Have to get a second boat boy next season," Blake announced. "I'm having to put in to many hours, but it's a good life, isn't it, sweetie?"

"Oh yes, Blake. It's good, so good. I never want too leave here."

"No reason why you should," he assured her. Then his face clouded. "Guess who's coming in next."

She looked at him questioningly. With a glower, he said, "The Krauts! A whole bunch of damned Krauts. What have I done to have this visited on me? I went through a court martial because of them, you know."

"No, I didn't," she replied, surprised. She crossed to him, and sat with her head on his shoulder. "What happened?"

"It was during the war," he replied, a deep furrow formed between his eyes. "I was commanding a Turkish caique. Actually, it was British, but disguised as a Turkish vessel. We weren't in uniform, and our guns were covered with a large tarp. We were operating in the Peloponnesian Sea in the south of the Greek Islands. The war was nearly over, though we didn't know it then. We sighted a German landing boat late one night. The Krauts were making for one of the islands; a landing party. They had explosives strapped on them, and were wearing camouflage suits. We opened fire and sunk the landing craft. The Krauts were swimming like mad toward shore, and there was no way to pick them off in the water, so I ordered a depth charge dropped. The bodies all drifted to shore where they were discovered by the British' on the island the next day. A doctor examined a few, and said they had been killed by concussion. It was traced back to me, and I was brought to trial."

"Not very sporting, as well as illegal, the Royal Navy contended, to drop a depth charge among ship wrecked men. I contended they were close enough to shore to swim in and start blowing up the island. What saved me actually, was a young radio operator I'd taken on shortly before. He'd been in some minor trouble, and was having difficulties getting on a ship. I agreed to take him on, and had a talk with him. I told him I'd give him another chance if he kept his nose clean. He was properly grateful, and turned in a first rate job for me. At the trial he testified that just before I ordered the depth charge dropped, he thought he had seen a submarine, and had sung out, 'sub on starboard'."

"Actually," Blake grinned, "there hadn't been a submarine in those waters for over two years! All said and done, I got off, but my commanding officer told me my career in the Navy was pretty well ruined, and suggested I not try to stay on after the war. I suppose I should have gone around and picked up those Krauts out of the water, but I couldn't stand the thought of them on my boat."

"So," he added, with disgust, "get ready for the German invasion again, only this time, it's here!"

The Germans arrived, lugging scuba gear and spears by the ton. They brought half a plane load of beer along also, and a case of schnapps.

"Damned cheapies," growled Blake. "They buy the stuff wholesale in Dar, and "ll want us to cool it for them for free. Damned if I will!"

Blake thought of an errand he had to do, and was gone until late in the evening. Penny thought she had never seen a group of men so rude. They took over the barroom, locking arms and singing at the top of their lungs, shattering the exquisite stillness of the night. They yelled at the servants in guttural German, berating them when they failed to understand, and ate like a starving army.

One winked at Penny. "We nearly starved to death during the war, and we've been making up for it ever since."

Penny wondered if he knew how many British nearly starved during that time, also. By the time they retired in the wee hours of the morning, Penny and the boys were exhausted. "They're even louder than the Americans," she thought.

Next morning, Blake, glowering and barely civil, got the boats ready. When they loaded the spear guns on with the scuba equipment, Blake stood his ground.

"One or the other," he said, tight lipped. "You don't shoot fish with scuba equipment on. You wear the tanks, you leave the guns here." He began tossing the guns out of the boat.

The leader of the group ran up. "We have a special permission." He thrust a paper at Blake. "From the Minister of Fisheries."

Blake waved the paper away, not bothering to read it. "Not on my boats," he said, with finality, throwing the last spear gun onto the sand.

The men boarded sullenly, muttering under their breaths. They carried plastic sacks filled with food they had demanded at breakfast after they had eaten to capacity. Having gotten a special deal to forego lunch since they would be diving all day, they had gotten a group reduction from the Major. But the plastic bags were filled with boiled eggs, rolls, butter, and fruit along with bacon and ham. Blake decided there would be no seconds next morning. Let them yell, if they liked.

Penny wondered how long it would be before Blake exploded. She had only to wait until that evening. Blake had returned early, stiff and silent. For the first time, she heard him order a double whisky. The boat with Appendai was long delayed, and Blake made several trips to the beach to check for him. It was dusk before the boat appeared. Appendai, looking worried, had a long conversation with Blake. Penny ran down and asked what had happened.

"That damned Kraut leader!" Blake's face was purple. "The one with the letter. He tried to make Appendai go over some coral where the water was too shallow. Appendai refused, and rightly, too. The bugger grabbed the wheel, and tried to take the boat through the pass out to sea, and hung up the propeller. Appendai had to go over the side to dislodge it. It's all bent up, and they hardly made it back. Wait 'till I get my hands on him!"

Blake went up the embankment in two leaps. The Germans were sitting in the bar, mugs of beer in hand. Blake cocked his head at the tall blond leader.

"This one," he asked Appendai, who nodded.

Blake covered the distance to the man in one stride, and grasping his shirt collar, jerked him out of the chair, and off his feet. With their faces only inches apart, Blake shouted. "Don't you know, you stupid bastard, that when you're in that boat, Appendai is the captain, and his word is law?"

The man sputtered and choked. Blake disgustedly threw him down into his chair, beer mugs flying.

"Look at him," Blake shouted, pulling Appendai next to him. "Take a good look at him, you bloody Kraut. This one African is worth a whole platoon of German soldiers!"

He spun on his heel, and stomped toward the entrance, then turned and glared at the subdued group. "Tomorrow I'm giving Appendai orders that if any of you even touch that wheel, he is to run you through with the fish gaff, and he always does exactly as I say!"

He muttered as he strode angrily to his room. "Wish I could have killed them all off in the war!"

Bob and Ann visited the island often, both before and after the busy seasons. Penny especially enjoyed the times they brought young Adam with them. The two-year-old boy and the monkey, Koko, were inseparable. Penny often stayed at the camp with him while the others went out in the boat. She took him down to the beach after his nap, and played with him in the shallow water. Koko ran up and down the beach, chattering and crying. Much as young Adam loved splashing about, even learning to swim a few strokes, he soon waded ashore and held out his sturdy little arms to the tiny monkey.

One evening after Penny had lovingly tucked Adam into bed, the two couples were sitting in the open air bar before dinner. Blake seemed distracted, not joining in the light conversation. Bob leaned back in his chair and looked quizzically at Blake.

"You're frightfully quiet tonight, old chap. Something on your mind?"

Blake's face broke into a mischievous grin. "I think I've found her."

"Found who?" Bob countered.

"Penny and I went with the Major one evening to see the cock fighting and the following show. You know the one I mean."

Bob nodded. "I took Ann once, and she kept me awake the rest of the night." He winked at his wife and grinned.

"I surely did," Ann laughed. "That was the best lay I've had—before or since!"

Only Blake noticed Penny's face flush before she ducked her head. He looked back at Bob and Ann. "I was telling the Major I thought something of that sort might go here on the island. Nothing fancy, of course. A horse would die of tse-tse fly down here on the coast before we could use him very much, and animals are too much trouble, anyway. They say the little pony, damn near kicks the stall apart on the nights they don't let him at the woman."

"Bob's the same way," Ann giggled. They all laughed.

"Well," continued Blake, "today I found what happens to be the island's one prostitute. As I understand it, she ran away from her husband from one of the northern tribes. She came here with a young buck. He couldn't marry her, different tribe, and all that. So, she's pitched up here, and keeps a hut at the other end of the island. Open to all comers, I judge."

Blake said something over his shoulder in Swahili. A tall lean black woman emerged from around the building. She wore a single length of cotton material wrapped around her, leaving her arms and shoulders bare. She stood with an arrogant expression, her skin so black it looked like polished leather. Her face had been tattooed, leaving welts crossing her cheeks and forehead. Her face was square with unusually thick lips and a flat spread out nose. She showed none of the Arab mixture usually seen in coastal blacks.

"Not much to look at, is she?" Bob commented.

"Who's going to look at her face?" Ann laughed.

Blake spoke a few words in Swahili, and the woman languorously slipped the material from under her armpit, unwound it, and let it fall to the ground. She had small breasts, unlike most African women whose breasts became elongated and flat after their first child. She stood with her legs slightly apart, her pubic hair kinky, and laid flat against her groin like the hair on her closely cropped head. Her chest and stomach were tattooed in spiral designs. She stood staring just above their heads.

"Got three young bucks lined up," Blake said, looking impersonally at the woman. "Think I can come up with some tableaus or the like, if I can control those hot blooded blacks. Fun to try, anyway."

"It doesn't look like she's had children," Ann said. "They get so old and scrawny after a child or two, no matter what age."

"I think you're right," replied Blake. "Probably that's why she ran away from the tribe. You know what happens to barren women."

He turned to explain to Penny. "They're often turned out, especially if the father refuses to return the bride price, with nowhere to go."

Blake spoke again to the woman, and she stooped, picking up the length of cloth and letting it trail behind her, walked off into the shadows.

"The boys will be here after dinner," Blake said. "I'll give them some b'hang to smoke so they'll last longer, then we'll try them out."

Ann was especially animated during dinner. "I'm so glad you're going to have them perform while we're here, Blake. I can hardly wait to see it."

"My God," Bob exclaimed, "That'll all she thinks about, screw, screw, screw. The only time I get any rest at night is when I travel.

"That's all you'd better be getting when you travel," Ann said, sternly. "In case you don't remember, it takes two to screw." They all laughed.

"Hey, that's a song," Ann said, as they filed back into the bar. She sang the words to the tune of, "Tea for Two".

Bob groaned. "Enough, woman, enough. I can see it's going to be a long night."

At an order from Blake, the three men and the woman came into the bar and stood under the shaded light bulb.

"Let's turn off the generator and light the hurricane lamps," Penny said. "I think it will be more interesting."

"All right," Blake chuckled, as he stopped the generator and lighted the lamps. "That's my Puritan wife. Do you know she still comes to bed every night with her undies on under her nightgown?"

"Blake!" Penny exclaimed.

"I can't get Ann to wear even a nightgown," Bob laughed. "Are they ready to start?" he asked, looking at the four blacks standing in a row. The men were grinning, but the woman stood stoically. Blake turned on the tape recorder to a chanting African song.

The woman dropped her dress, tossing it in a corner with the men's shorts and shirts. The men began a slow shuffling dance around the woman, coming closer with each step. One reached out for her, and passed her to the next man as they twirled her between them. The music grew faster, the beat of the drums louder. The men were becoming aroused. One leaped to the table top, and thrusting his pelvis back and forth, reached down to pull the woman up on the table with him.

Ann shouted something in Swahili, and one of the men leaped onto the table while the other placed a high bar stool beside him. He jumped up and mounted the stool, teetering precariously. Their black bodies, wet with sweat, shimmered in the flickering lights. The rhythm grew faster. The men clawed at the woman, muttering under their breath. Her body jerked as they shoved at her.

Suddenly, the stool began to topple, and a moment later they all came tumbling down off the table and rolled on the floor.

The two couples were convulsed with laughter. "Guess that'll have to do for a starter," Blake laughed, wiping his eyes with a napkin. He rose, and handed the Africans some money. They got to their feet, grinning sheepishly, and took the money as they walked out.

"Think you'll have to work on that a bit, Blake," Bob choked through his laughter. "You'll have them falling in the customers' laps."

"Quite," Blake replied. "Maybe I can build a little platform or something, though from what I hear, the guests won't mind one in their laps, as you said. Fellow told me the other day—he lives north of here on the Kenya coast near Malindi—that the Germans are advertising tours labeled, 'Black and White Sex'. Said the Krauts were flocking there, as many women as men, matter of fact."

Blake served brandy all around and settled back in his chair. "He told me one chap had a beach house near the hotel, and every time he walked out of his house he had couples all over the lawn, screwing like hell. He even found one white woman and a big black buck using the hammock on his verandah. He's so disgusted he's got the place up for sale."

"Wouldn't do to have that sort of thing here," he added, glancing at Penny. She looked relieved. "Think it's bad for the morale. You noticed I waited until all the servants had gone home for the night. Heaven knows we have enough trouble with them as it is without giving them ideas like that. Never could touch one, myself."

"I neither," Bob said, "but I've caught Ann looking at one or two sometimes. You know, the ones with a whang half way down to their knees?"

Ann gave him a playful slap. "Not as long as you keep me happy, dear. Now come to bed. You've a busy night ahead of you."

"Here we go again," groaned Bob, "and I came here to get a rest!"

# Chapter 14

Penny and Blake flew into Dar when the fall rains started. They found Major Redwood beside himself. "Damned woman went back to the tribe. Took the boy! Can't find them anywhere. Africans hid her out and won't talk. Threats, money, no good. Said she wants him raised tribal. *My son!*"

He sat crumpled in a chair, his face in his hands. "Never could understand those people." He was almost in tears. "If I ever get my hands on her, I'll kill her!"

"If you send over any more Krauts, I'll do some killing myself," Blake said, darkly.

"Just yesterday," the Major continued, not hearing, "a water buck sprang up out of nowhere onto the runway as I came in to a bush strip for a landing. Had a load of passengers. Ran straight down the runway in front of me. Nearly scraped his horns trying to pull up over him. Close one. Circled that postage stamp strip again, and had committed the plane to a landing, when four impala broke right in front of me. Came down with two impala somersaulting ass over horns on each wing. Tore hell out of the canvas."

"Way back, this nut of a minister went to put out a cigarette. Ash tray missing from the holder, and he proceeded to drop the butt in the opening back of my seat. Told the African next to me to take over the controls. Dived back to get the fire extinguisher."

"Did he know how to fly?" Penny queried.

"Haven't the foggiest. Didn't ask." His wry smile was interrupted by the telephone. He winced. "Blake, answer that. Unless it's an emergency, I'm not here."

Blake listened a few minutes, then held the phone out. "Afraid it's an emergency."

The Major groaned and ran his hand through his wispy hair. Taking the phone in a limp hand, he said, "Three greens aren't on, you say?"

"What's three greens?" Penny asked Blake.

"There are three green lights on the instrument panel that must be on before you can be sure the landing gear is down and the wheels locked into place. If even one isn't lighted, you're taking a chance. It might be a blown fuse or a malfunction in the gear."

The Major's voice grew higher as he talked to the control tower. "Can you see the landing gear? Is it down? Does he have a passenger? Oh, a corpse, is it? Only half the problem if one of the two is already dead." He gave a dry laugh.

Blake broke in. "Ask the pilot if he's got cold feet in his back."

The Major repeated the question over the phone. In a moment he turned. "No. Says the corpse's turned the other way."

Blake explained to Penny that since there were so few mortuaries in Tanzania, that the important dead were often flown into Dar for burial. They piled them in the back seat of the plane, and on the flight in, rigor mortis set in, making the dead man straighten out. When that happened the pilots often complained about cold feet in their backs.

The Major continued talking on the phone. "Tell him to jiggle the knob. Nothing happens, eh?" He paused. "Nothing to do but bring her in."

Minutes passed as they all sat tensely. Finally the Major smiled thinly. "Thanks, friend." he said, as he replaced the receiver. They didn't need to be told the plane had landed safely.

They waited several days for the weather to clear enough to return to the island. Even so, when they landed on the muddy strip the small plane slued badly. On the drive to camp they passed Abhurdamoni's hut. The door to the corrugated tin roofed structure was painted a bright blue. A small thorn fence surrounding the house was held with posts painted the same color of blue. Blake slowed the Jeep, staring, tight-lipped. He glanced at Appendai who was sitting in the back seat. The African lowered his eyes.

When they reached the camp Blake went immediately into the kitchen. The smile on Abhurdamoni's face froze when he looked at Blake.

"Turn your pockets out," commanded Blake.

Abhurdamoni stood, paralyzed.

"Turn them out," Blake's voice was low and menacing.

The African didn't move. Blake reached into Abhurdamoni's dhoti, found a pocket, and flipped it out. A few coins fell to the cement floor. Blake's hand came away with a soiled white handkerchief.

"This is my handkerchief, isn't it?" He shoved the cloth in the African's face, who trembled and nodded.

"And that paint on your house is my boat paint, isn't it?"

The lowered head barely nodded.

Blake brought his hand up sharply across the other's mouth, then across his cheek with the back of his hand. Penny gasped when she saw blood trickle from Abhurdamoni's mouth.

"I never want to see you around here again." Blake shoved the man toward the door so hard he fell to his knees. He half crawled across the floor. With one last backward pleading glance, he got to his feet and ran down the road.

"Oh Blake," Penny protested. "Please give him another chance. He's been so good, and he's so nice. Please?"

"No. Absolutely not. No bloody black's going to steal from me. One of them gets by with it, and there's no end to it. He's never allowed back here, do you understand?"

Blake angrily opened a beer, and sat heavily on a bench. "Part of it's your fault, you know."

Penny started to protest, but Blake cut her short. "I know that as soon as I leave here on the boat, one or the other of them comes up to you saying they're sick, have malaria, or what not, and you let them off and do their work for them. Once you start that, there's no end to it, and you lose their respect as well. I've spoken to you about it several times, but you don't listen." He took a long swallow of beer.

"What will happen to him and his family?" Penny cried. "He hasn't the money to get back to the mainland."

"They'll probably all starve," Blake muttered. "The copra plantation won't hire him after this, and there's no place else he could find work."

He stared hard at Penny. "And I won't have you giving him money or even scraps of left-overs. Do you understand?"

Penny shook her head, her eyes filling with tears. "I'm sorry, Blake. Will you forgive me? I didn't mean to—."

He tossed the empty bottle into the waste basket, and left the bar without looking at her. "Nobody's going to bugger me about," he muttered. "Not even you."

Penny caught the little monkey as he leaped into her arms. She walked down to the water's edge, watching the moon's silver path across the water. Her tears dropped on the clinging monkey. "You love me, don't you, little one?" she wept softly.

Several weeks later Penny saw Abhurdamoni leaning against the door of his hut. His once proud frame was gaunt, his cheeks sunken. Penny turned to Appendai, tears in her eyes.

"Isn't there something we can do for him?" she asked.

He shook his head. "Got T.B. Young son die' last week. No food."

"If I gave you some food would you take it to them?"

Appendai looked frightened, and shook his head violently. "Bwana Captain—." He drew his fingers across his throat.

The busy winter season was drawing to a close. There were few guests. The golden days mellowed with the first rain clouds. Penny felt uneasy with the coming of the rainy season. Ann and Bob were on leave in England, and she knew she would miss them on her trip into Dar. She ran her hands over her flat hard belly. She had lost a good two stone, and was trim as a young girl. She asked Blake to take a stroll with her before dinner, feeling uneasy about the news she had to tell him.

They walked hand in hand along the hard packed white sand.

"Something troubling you, Penny?" Blake asked, stopping to look into her eyes.

"I—I feel I should go back to England—." She hurried on when she saw his expression. "I—I mean—just for a bit. I would like you to go with me, but I guess you can't."

He nodded. They were silent for a while.

"Aren't you happy here, sweetie?" he asked.

"I am! Truly I am. I hate the idea of being away from you, even for a little while. I'll miss you so." She gave him a warm kiss. "It's just that I have to sign the final divorce papers, and I have to do it there. Then there's Alfred. He'll be due his spring holiday soon, and it would be nice to be there then."

He waited, knowing there was more. "I think I should see a doctor. I've missed my period for the third time now, and I'm a bit concerned."

Blake stopped and stared at her. "But Penny, you're much to young to be going through the change of life. You must be pregnant!"

"It might be something else though, Blake. A tumor or something. I've heard of that. But I could be pregnant. What would you think if I were?"

Her eyes searched his face anxiously. "Super! That would be super," he grinned. "I've always regretted not getting to know my first child. I'd love having one about, our child, that is. How do you feel about it?".

"I'd be very happy," she replied, relief flooding her voice. "I've always wanted another baby, but, you know—Hubert."

He nodded.

"Then," she continued, speaking rapidly, "I thought I'd got to old. But, oh, I'd be so happy if I were pregnant!"

That night she took Blake's hand and held it firmly against her abdomen. "Do you feel anything? Lately, I've thought I could feel it moving, but I could be imagining it."

He pressed his hand against her, moving it slightly. "Yes, yes. I think I did feel something. I'm sure I did. Just a slight thump' where I pressed my hand. Let me put my ear there."

He pressed against her. "I'm not sure, really. I guess it's to early to hear a heart beat, but I did feel something."

He kissed her tenderly. "My dear, my love. Just imagine! I simply never thought—. It makes me very happy. I'm proud of you."

"I didn't do it alone," she teased.

Blake made love to her that night at her insistence. He was unusually tender.

A few days before they closed the camp for the season; their only guests were an American couple, parents of a boy twelve and an eight year old girl, Kimberly. Blake took an instant liking to Kim. While Appendai took the parents and the boy fishing and diving, Blake took Kim to the reefs and taught her snorkeling. Penny sometimes went along, marveling at Blake's patience with the little girl. She was a bright child, and learned quickly. In the water her shimmering blond hair spread out like a golden fan. Penny disliked diving when Blake used the spear gun. It frightened her, and she never felt at ease with it about. On market day she stayed at the camp when Blake took Kim out.

With two of the kitchen boys in the Jeep she wound down the road. *What a good father Blake will make. Wouldn't it be great if we have a daughter?*

118

As they passed Abhurdamoni's dilapidated hut they saw a group of people clustered in the yard. Penny stopped the Jeep, got out, and walked over to them. They moved back to reveal a shrouded corpse laying on a crudely lashed stretcher. A small gaunt woman, her face streaked with tears, tore at her clothes. Penny recognized her. It was Abhurdamoni's wife.

"Abhurdamoni dead," one of the cook boys muttered.

Penny moved to put an arm around the woman's shaking shoulders, but the African drew back sharply. Penny quailed at the look of pure hatred the woman threw at her. Penny's eyes dropped, and she fumbled in her purse, withdrawing all the shopping money. She handed the bills to the woman. The African stepped back, and starting with a low hiss that rose to a piecing crescendo, spat in Penny's face.

The bills fell from Penny's hand, and drifted down to the ground. She wiped her face with the back of her hand, trying to push away the spittle and the tears from her cheeks. She turned and ran to the Jeep, letting one of the boys turn it around and head back to camp.

She leaped out of the car even before it stopped, and seeing Blake's boat at anchor, called, "Blake, oh Blake! Abhurdamoni's dead!"

He appeared at the door to their bedroom. Kimberly darted around him, then stopped when she saw Penny.

"Whatever were you doing with Kim in the bedroom?" She asked, forgetting for the moment how much Blake disliked being questioned about his actions.

But he smiled, and said casually, "I took Kim in to look at my cowrie shell collection. You know, the one I keep in the bureau drawer."

"Oh," Penny replied, wondering why she felt vaguely troubled. "Aren't the shells lovely, Kim?" she asked. "There's every kind of cowrie found in Africa in that collection. There's the leopard and—."

She realized Kim wasn't listening. The child kept her eyes down, and avoided looking at Penny, then she ran past her and down the embankment to the water's edge where she sat looking out over the bay.

"What's the matter with Kim?" Penny asked. "She's usually so bubbly and outgoing."

Blake smiled sweetly and gave Penny's shoulders a quick hug. "She's a little tired from so much snorkeling. That's why we came in early today. She's not quite herself."

Penny was reassured for the moment, wondering why she had felt so apprehensive before. "Probably Abhurdamoni's death, and that awful scene back there," she thought, and mentally shrugged.

Two days later they closed the camp and flew to Dar.

"Any trace of your wife?" Blake asked, when they arrived at the Major's house.

"Damn it, no!" he groaned. Penny thought he looked particularly haggard and untidy. "Imagine *my son* living in the filth of a native village! They've probably filed his teeth and tattooed his face by now!"

Blake knew that was an exaggeration since these things were done at puberty rites, but he said nothing.

The Major paced the floor, his face contorted with pain. He gripped the slender glass he was holding until it suddenly shattered, and cut his hand badly. Penny rushed to find a cloth to stanch the blood. She called to the servant to bring water and the first aid kit. She wiped the Major's hand, searching for embedded glass. *I'm glad I wasn't flying with him today.*

As she dressed his hand she thought to herself she had never seen anyone deteriorate so rapidly. His impeccable calm was replaced with nervous jerking, his usually immaculate clothes soiled and rumpled. He had aged considerably in the past months. They spend an uneasy evening, mostly in silence. Penny sat hugging her belly, thinking of the child within her, loving it. She caught Blake's eyes on her, and they smiled fondly at each other across the table.

The following week Penny and Blake returned for the second visit to the Asian doctor's office. She had hoped to find a British doctor, only to discover they had departed, one by one, as the political situation in Tanzania became more unsettled. She had not liked the small nervous Indian whose eyes never quite met hers. At last they were ushered into his office. The doctor fiddled through grimy papers spread out on his desk. Withdrawing one and peering at it nearsightedly, he said in a flat heavy voice, "Yesss, ummm. The result of the rabbit test, Mrs. ummm Blakely."

He produced a pair of horn-rimmed glasses from a heaped up drawer. "Yes," he hissed, again, "you are pregnant."

Penny grasped Blake's hand, her face radiant.

"In about the fourth month, I would say," the doctor continued, laying the paper down. His expression remained grave as he removed his glasses. "I'm afraid I have bad news for you, however." He turned in his chair to gaze through the dust-streaked window.

"The fetus is dead," he said, flatly. "There's no heart beat." Their happy faces faded into disbelief. "There is no doubt about it," he added, hurriedly. "I would recommend—." He stopped to clear his throat and spit into a tin on the floor. "I would recommend we induce an abortion immediately. It's risky. I'd rather have done this a month ago, but it can't be helped. At your age, too—."

Blake rose and leaned over the littered desk. "You must be mistaken, doctor. Just recently, when we were resting, only a few days ago, I felt the baby move. You must be mistaken. Is there another test you could run?"

"No. There's nothing more we can do now. The fetus is dead. There's no doubt about it' I'd suggest we do the abortion here. The sanitary conditions at our hospital are not of the best, and it must be done before the dead fetus poisons your wife, and you lose her, too."

He started across the room. "I'll have the nurse prepare you now, Mrs. Blakely. You should be able to go home this evening. In a week or so you'll be fine. I'll keep tabs on you."

Penny stood up, her face white, her large eyes staring in disbelief. She pushed past the doctor to the door. "Blake," she choked, "Please take me home."

"But Mrs. Blakely—," they heard the doctor sputter as they left the office.

After a silent drive, they walked into the welcome coolness of the Major's house. Penny went into the bedroom, removed her dress, and lay on the cool sheets. Soundlessly, a torrent of tears ran unheeded down her cheeks onto the pillow. Blake came in carrying two cold beers, and offered one to her. She shook her head, not speaking. Blake sat on the edge of the bed and stroked her shoulders.

"Penny, please don't," he said, softly. His fingers wiped at her tears. "I'm sure there's something we can do. Maybe you should fly to Nairobi. They have some good British doctors there, and a modern hospital."

Penny shook her head. "I want to go home—to England—to save my baby."

121

She didn't notice Blake wince. But, sweetie, *this* is your home, with me, here in Africa."

She shook her head, sat up, and leaned back against the pillows. "Oh, Blake, I'm frightened, and I'd be so alone in Nairobi. In Liverpool I have friends and family."

"Sweetie, I know you're upset. So am I, but I have friends in Nairobi. Lots of British women have their families there without any trouble. Have a check-up with a good doctor there. I'm sure this chap here is mistaken. Then when your time comes, you can leave the island, and go there to have the child. You know I'd like to be with you, but I can't. My friends would look after you."

She stared at him in disbelief. "Did you say, 'leave the island'?" Her voice grew shrill. "You can't mean that! Do you really expect me to go back while I'm carrying the child?" Her face was distorted. Blake turned away. "Surely you realize I can't go through a pregnancy there. There's no doctor, not even one like that sorry Asian, and planes can't come in during the rainy season. How can you expect that of me?"

He turned to her, his face a steely mask. "Yes. That's exactly what I *do*_expect of you. That is the home I have made for you, for us. You wanted it as much as I did, remember? You could hardly wait to get back. 'I never, never want to leave,' you said."

"But that was before—," Penny cried. "It isn't as if I were a young woman. I had my last baby over fifteen years ago. Anything could happen—to me—to the child. I can't go back to live on the island."

Her voice had grown hysterical, and she pounded the pillow next to her. Sobs shook her body. Blake sat on the edge of the bed and tried to sooth her, but she jerked away from his touch.

"At least you could move back to Dar and find something to do here," she sobbed brokenly.

"No. Penny," he answered, bitterly. "No I couldn't, or I won't. We're just beginning to make money at the camp. I took it on a percentage, you know, and it's slow building up. I hope someday to buy out the Major's interest."

"There's my three thousand pounds, just sitting in the bank in England," she pleaded. "We could start a little shop or something in Dar. Isn't that what your brother's doing in Liverpool?"

Blake dropped his head in his hands. She hesitated, then rushed on. "I mean, it would only be for a little while. I know you don't like that sort of thing, but I'd be able to hlelp, for a long while, I'm sure. You wouldn't be stuck in the shop all the time and—."

She stopped when she saw the expression on his face as he dropped his hands. "So, you want to make a proper shopkeeper of me, eh? It won't work, Penny. Don't ever mention it again."

"Then you don't really love me, or the child, do you?" Her voice was without hope. "It's just like Abhurdamoni. And he's dead. That's what will happen to me if I stay."

"Penny!" He spoke sharply, and held her arms in a punishing grip. "You're wrong! I love you more than I've loved anyone in my life or ever shall! It's that I'm asking you to share my life, and not to leave me. That's the most I can offer you. I can't change myself for you or anybody, and I don't intend to try. I can't live my life your way. I shouldn't be happy with that, and neither should you, when all's said and done."

"Then I'd like you to check on the planes to London as soon as possible," she said, in a flat voice.

"Very well, if that's what you want." He started toward the door, then turned and crossed over to her, taking her hand. "It would give you a change probably need just now. Get a good check-up and return in a month. I'm sure you'll feel differently when you know things are all right with the baby. We'll get you to Nairobi in plenty of time when you're toward the end of your term."

He left the room, then returned after a time. "All set. They had one seat leaving tomorrow evening. You'll be in London the following day. You shouldn't have any trouble getting on to Liverpool. What about your things on the island?"

"I'll let you know later. Perhaps you could send a few things on. I don't know why I brought all those heavy woolens with me, anyhow. I've no use for them here."

Blake answered a knock on the door to be told by the house boy that a gentleman wished to see the Major, who wasn't home. He closed the bedroom door behind him, and went onto the verandah to find the next door neightbor, a young Italian engineer.

"Sorry, the Major's gone for a few days, Sal." Blake spoke easily in Italian. "He's off running down a lead on a light skinned baby reported off in the bush somewhere. Could I help you?"

123

"Well, I don't know. I—," Sal hesitated. "It's a bit 'dicy' as you British say."

"Like a beer?" Blake asked.

"Yes, gracia."

Blake fetched the two beers, and sat waiting for Sal to continue.

"I'm sending for my family in Rome, and you know how hard it is to get foreign currency out of the country. I've got to get the money to them to clear up some bills and buy passage here. I've been over here nearly a year now, and that's too long to be seperated. Already she's had a child I've not seen yet."

"What can I do to help?" Blake asked.

"I've five hundred pounds here," Sal replied, opening his wallet, and bringing out the pound notes. "I've been buying these on the black market for a long time now. I thought the Major might know someone who could get through customs with this. It can't be declared, you know."

He looked questioningly at Blake.

"Matter of fact," replied Blake, "my wife's taking the eleven-thirty for London tomorrow night. I've a small bag with me, one with a false bottom in it. I think she could manage to do that for you."

"Of course," he added, a smile playing about his lips, "it should be worth something to you for her trouble. It is risky, you know."

"Yes, of course," Sal stammered. "Glad to. What would you suggest?"

"I think a thousand shillings would do it."

"That's more than I would have expected," Sal drew back. "Perhaps I should wait for Major Redwood."

"As you like."

Blake started to leave the room when Sal spoke up. "I've five hundred with me. Would you accept that?" He brought out his wallet and fingered through the bills.

"I'd accept seven-fifty, but no less," Blake responded.

"All right," Sal replied. "But I've not that much with me. Here, take this for now. There's a chap in town can get me the rest, but he's leaving early tomorrow, so I'll go in now and try to catch him."

"Very well," Blake said, as they walked to Sal's car.

"Before I forget it," Sal added, "here's the name and address in Rome. Have your wife deposit it in her bank and send a check on to my wife. Thanks again. I should be back this evening with the rest."

"Right-o. See you later."

He returned to the bedroom. Penny was lying quietly, staring at the ceiling. "Feeling better, sweetie?"

"My dear," Penny's eyes filled with tears. "I do love you so much. This whole thing is tearing me apart. This baby, this wonderful miracle for both of us— something that should bring us even closer than before—is what's tearing us apart." She fought back a sob. "I almost wish—."

Blake touched her lips with his finder. "Don't, sweetie. Everything will be fine. You'll see. We'll be back together soon, and happy again like we were." he kissed her. "Ready for supper?"

"I really couldn't eat right now. Ask to have something cold set on the table. I'll try to take a nap now and eat later if I'm hungry."

He kissed her again, and left the room. Penny closed her eyes and assessed her situation. Always she returned to the same thing. *The child. The child must come first. This small' helpless thing inside me. It must be protected. But I know I can't change Blake. What am I to do?*

Finally she gave up trying to sleep. She showered and slipped on a house coat, a lovely hand woven one in vivid stripes that Blake had given her. She went into the dining room and picked disinterestedly at the cold chicken and fruit. Blake came in from the verandah, and started to say something, when the house boy ran in, speaking rapidly to Blake in Swahili, his eyes bulging, jaw slack.

"Stay here," Blake ordered Penny, and went quickly out the back door.

Penny heard excited voices coming from the road in back of the house, and walked into the kitchen. She peered through the window. There were several men clustered around a small foreign car. She moved out the door and walked to the car. The Africans parted to let her through. The door to the passenger side was open, but all she could see in the dim light was a form sitting there. One of the Africans flicked on a flashlight and shone it full into the car.

Penny looked in to see the blood soaked stump of a neck rising out of a shirt drenched in red. The man's body sat erect, but as she stood there horrified, the body slowly slipped toward the open door. The movement started the blood spurting from the severed neck arteries. The body fell in slow motion onto the sandy soil, and brushed against Penny before it turned the sand dark around the stump of a neck.

She heard Blake's voice, and felt his arms catch her as she slumped down. Blake carried her into the house, and started to lay her on the divan, but she struggled to her feet, and ran to the bathroom and wretched. Blake's voice on the phone calling the police reached her as she returned to the living room and sat, her head reeling, feeling the nausea mounting again. She swallowed repeatedly to keep it down.

He returned and sat beside her, holding her hand. "Penny, I'm sorry you saw that. How do you feel?"

She shook her head, afraid to speak with the vomit tight against her throat.

"You shouldn't have come out. I told you not to."

"Do you know who he—," she stammered.

"The fellow next door, young Sal. Don't know if you've ever met him. We found his head about a meter back, in the road."

"But why—who—?"

"I've seen this before," Blake replied, standing to look out the back door. "The long rains are late coming this year. It's a voodoo thing, white witch doctor stuff to get rain. Usually you see this in the bush, but with all this shifting of tribes the government's doing, a lot of bush natives are coming into Dar to find jobs, and there aren't any. They're starving, and they're desperate. So we're getting an element in Dar we've never had before."

"But, why him?"

"It wasn't 'him', particularly. He was probably the first one who came down the side road after they set up their cordon."

He brought her a drink of water. She gratefully took a sip.

"Better go into the bedroom. The police will be here shortly, and you've blood on your gown." He helped her to her feet.

She avoided looking in the mirror when she reached the bedroom, and quickly shed the gown, stuffing it under the bed.

Blake had followed her. He took out his wallet. "This will take care of your trip. I had a bit of luck today selling some old machinery, and got British pounds for it. This will buy your ticket, and should leave you enough to see you through the month you're in England. I'll probably have to go to the police station to make a report, and I'm not sure when I'll get back."

He handed her the five hundred pounds. "Put what's left after you buy the ticket, in the false bottom of my small case. Don't check it. Carry it with you. Above all, don't declare it."

She looked uncomprehendingly at the money.

Blake continued. "Call my brother when you get to London and have him meet your plane in Liverpool."

A car had driven into the driveway. The police were hammering at the door. Blake held Penny and kissed her, but she didn't respond. He started toward the door, then turned and went into the bathroom. He took out his wallet, and withdrew a slip of paper with a name and address on it. He carefully shredded the paper, dropping the pieces into the toilet bowl, then flushed it. He hurried into the living room.

Long after Penny heard them leave, she lay staring at the dark ceiling. *"It could have been Blake in that car—or even me! Now there's no doubt what I must do."*

# Chapter 15

A week later Penny called Blake at the Major's house. "It's alive, Blake! It's alive!" she shouted into the poor connection.

"Oh, Penny, I'm so glad." He sounded relieved and happy. "How are you?"

"Fine. Just fine. I've had all kinds of tests. The doctor is a bit worried because of my age. He wants to keep a close eye on me, and he thinks I should stay here, dear, until the baby comes. What do you think I should do?"

There was a silence. The line crackled.

"Blake, did you hear me? Are you still there?"

"Yes, Penny. I'm still here." He hesitated. "You must do what you and the doctor think best, I suppose. You know I want you with me—."

"I do so want to be with you, especially these next months, but perhaps I'd better stay, just until the baby comes, and a little while after that."

"Where are you staying, with my mother?"

The phone was silent, ghost voices coming in off the periphery.

He shouted. "I asked where you're staying?"

"Your mother's place is quite crowded you know," Her voice was faint.

"What about my mother's place?" Blake shouted again. "You'll have to talk louder."

"I said it's quite crowded there," Penny's voice was stronger. "She's just the two bedrooms." She hesitated, then continued. "Hubert's been most decent. There's a small side of the house with an outside entrance, and I'm staying there. I'll pay him rent and fix up a small kitchen. After all, it's only for a few months. All right?"

"Very well, Penny, whatever you think best," he replied, dryly.

"Oh, and Blake, I thought it best to leave the divorce as it is. I don't want the child born without a name. It's all right with Hubert. As I said, he's been frightfully decent. Is that all right with you, Blake?"

He was silent so long she thought the connection was broken. She tried again. "Blake, is that all right?"

"I suppose so," she heard him say. A muscle twitched near his eye. "You can wait until after the child comes to sign the final papers. I suppose that's best."

"Thank you, dear," she signed with relief. "I'll write to you every day. Will you write often?"

"Of course. I'll be back on the island soon. I was here to await your call, but I'll call you whenever I come into Dar."

"Oh, please do, dear. I haven't a phone yet. They're frightfully expensive, but I'll have one hooked up right away, and write you the number."

"Let me know when you need money. I want you and the child to have the very best."

"My darling," her voice rose, "I love you so and miss you terribly."

"I miss you too, sweetie. Take care of yourself. Bye-bye."

\*\*\*\*\*\*\*\*\*\*\*\*\*\*\*\*\*\*\*\*\*\*\*\*\*\*\*\*\*\*\*\*\*\*\*

Penny worried about seeing Alfred again. He was in exams when she returned, and anxious as she was to see him, she was glad to be settled and some things worked out before he came home on holiday.

"You're quite grown up!" she exclaimed, when she and Hubert met him at the train station.

Alfred hugged her, nearly lifting her off her feet. "My, you're looking fit," he said, as they walked toward the tube. "It's jolly good to have you home again."

Penny prepared dinner in Hubert's kitchen that evening, and they all ate together. After the meal Hubert found an excuse to return to the shop. *Bless him. He doesn't want to embarrass me while I tell Alfred.*

She sat watching Alfred as he settled back on the divan with his coffee. His voice had deepened and a small nick on his face showed he had started shaving.

"Do you mind if I smoke?" he asked, shaking out a pack of cigarettes.

"May I have one, too?" she asked, her eyes twinkling.

He covered his surprise, offered her the pack, and lighted her cigarette. She went to the side board and poured some coffee. She tried to speak lightly. "I'm afraid your Mother's picked up a lot of bad habits in the past year and a half."

Then her face crumpled and she sobbed. Alfred crossed over to her and guided her to a chair, sitting on the arm. He took her cigarette and placed it in the ash tray. "What's happened, Mum? Has Blake—?"

She interrupted. "No, nothing like that, Alfred, really. I'm—I'm to have a child, Blake's child."

She turned, facing him. "I—we thought it best for me to return here. I'll be thirty-nine when it's born and—."

She stopped, seeing a worried look cross his face. "I'm fine, really I am, healthy as a horse the doctor said. I don't expect any trouble at all."

Alfred looked intently into his mother's face noting her worried look. "How do you feel about it, Mum?"

I'm most awfully pleased, dear, really. I am concerned about how you'll take the news. It's all quite complicated, of course, with things the way they are, but—."

He smiled and squeezed her hand. "If you're happy about it, then so am I. Actually, I've always wanted a brother or even a sister."

They both laughed, relieved, then his face sobered. "What about Father?"

"He's been so good about it, dear, so much better than I deserve. I don't know how I should get through this without him."

She rose, stretching out her hand. "Come, let me show you what we've done." She opened the door to her small apartment.

"Look. It's quite cozy, and I've my own outside entrance. I've a hot plate and a wee sink. Hubert's helped me fix it up. I'll pay him rent, and will help him in the shop as long as I can. He says we're to act as if the baby's his. He's agreed to give the little one his name. Later, when Blake and I are married, Blake can adopt it."

She put her hands on her son's shoulders, realizing she had to reach up to do it. "I suppose I should be most awfully ashamed, but I'm so happy to be having another child, I really can't think of anything else."

She stopped and turned away. "I was truly concerned how all this would affect you, dear," she spoke hesitantly, "to find your mother a shameless hussy."

Alfred stopped her with a hug and a kiss. "You're not even to think that," he smiled fondly at her. "You're the greatest mum ever, and I'll always be proud of you. It can't be easy for you to come back here, the baby and all, and I want you to know I'll stand by you, and look after you as best I can."

Her eyes filled with tears, and she hugged him tight.

"What about Blake, Mum?"

"He's fine," Penny brightened. "He asked me to give you his best, but as you know, he can't leave Tanzania, even if he wanted to. 'Though I don't think he'll ever really want to. He was terribly excited about the baby and dreadfully upset when I couldn't stay, but—," her face clouded, "the island and all—. It's so remote, and dicy getting in and out, especially during the rainy season. Maybe he can find something in Dar later on—." Her voice trailed off.

"You look tired, Mum," Alfred said, rising. "Why don't you turn in? We've lots of time together. I have a long holiday."

She hurried to her feet. "Can't I unpack for you, dear?"

"Oh no," he laughed. "I've done that for myself for a long time now." He stopped, seeing the look of dismay on her face. "I mean—going off to school, and all."

She smiled. "Quite right, dear. I must remember how grown up you are now. I wrote you Blake's mother and brother live here. They're so anxious to meet you."

He turned toward the door before she could see his frown. "Right-o."

He kissed her cheek, and she looked fondly at him as he left the room and closed the door. *What a fine young man he's become. I'm so fortunate.* She sat in the chair, hugging herself and smiling.

The weeks turned into months. Penny wrote ten letters to Blake's one, but his were tender and concerned, planning on her return, telling her the improvements he was making on the fishing camp, and news of the people in Dar. The Major was still looking for his lost son, neglecting himself and his business. The investigation of the murder of the Italian was filed away, unsolved.

Penny spent a few hours each day helping Hubert in the shop, and often had Sunday dinner with Lucy and Fred, Blake's mother and brother. She was fond of them both and they of her. Fred was little like Blake, except in looks, and she discovered there was another brother in Australia, a very successful business man. Though it was never said in so many words, Penny gathered that Blake was considered something of the black sheep of the family. She knew Lucy had written to him, urging him to apply for a U.N. passport and return to England, but that he had replied evasively.

Alfred spent his summer holidays at home, helping his father in the shop. Penny prepared the meals for all of them, and sitting around the table, Alfred could almost imagine they were a family again. He often sat talking to Penny in the evenings after Hubert had gone upstairs. She read parts of Blake's letter to him, glad to have someone to talk to about him. She didn't notice that Alfred seldom commented when she talked about Blake.

She could hardly bear to have Alfred return to school. They had grown so close during the summer. She was quite large now, and seldom left her little apartment except to take her daily walk in the park.

She was having Sunday dinner with Lucy and Fred one still leaf-turning September day, and Fred was talking about their early life on Zanzibar, when Penny broke in with a sharp cry and bent forward. Lucy rushed to her. Penny straightened up, white-faced.

"I think that was a labor pain," she said, smiling faintly.

"We'll get you straight to the hospital," Fred said, reaching for their coats.

Penny stopped long enough to alert the doctor, and to call Hubert, asking him to bring her bag to the hospital. She had a long and difficult delivery, and woke to find Hubert peering at her.

"Blake?" she spoke, her eyes not focusing.

"It's me, dear. Hubert."

"The baby?" she asked.

"A girl," the small slender man replied. "It's a fine healthy little girl."

"Thank you," she murmured, and drifted off to sleep.

The next day they brought the baby to her. Afterwards she sent off a cable to Blake. Three days later he received it, brought by one of the pilots. He read the cable over several times, then crushed it in his hand, and stuffed it in his pocket. His face contorted with pain. "Penny, Penny," he whispered, "Come back soon."

He called as soon as the rains let up enough for him to get a flight out the following week.

"My darling," Penny exclaimed, when the phone woke her late at night. "It's so good to hear your voice! How I wish you were here."

"How are you—and the child?"

"Fine, a bit weak, but fine. Your mother comes over every day and helps out. She's such a dear. I can't think what I should have done without her."

"And the child," interrupted Blake. "How is she?"

"She's beautiful, Blake. She looks exactly like you, the same dark eyes and complexion, only she's prettier than you are, dear," she teased.

"I hope so," he laughed.

"When she squalls, she sounds just like you do when you're mad!" He laughed, sounding pleased. "Blake, I've named her Lucy Anette. I hope you like it. Lucy, after your mother, and Anette from a poem I read once."

"That's a musical name," he said, laughing again. "Are you sure you're feeling all right?"

"I had a rather hard time, and I'm still weak, but the doctor says I'm making good progress. How are you?"

"Things are good here, except I miss you. We had a busy season and I was glad to see the rains come. The Major's having a bad time. He heard the boy's dead, and he's off trying to check it out. He's talking of trying to get out of business in Tanzania, and I may be able to buy him out at the camp. I think we can do it for a lot less if we can pay him off in British pounds there in England. He's thinking of returning to London. I may be sending you some money with friends from time to time to forward to his bank account there. All right?"

She was silent, biting her lip, and blinking back tears.

"Sweetie, are you there?" he asked, anxiously.

"Yes, I'm here, Blake." A sob escaped her. "If you do that, what about me and the child? I can't bring a small baby to that island. That would be impossible. Can't you invest somewhere in Dar, or even in Kenya, where things aren't so difficult? I've been reading so much about the internal troubles in Tanzania—."

"That won't affect us on the island, sweetie, It's a very safe place to raise a child. You come back as soon as possible, and you'll see. Things will be fine. Trust me."

Penny remembered the deadly green mamba that had slithered across the patio one day. Even Appendai had been afraid to get close enough to kill it. She had locked herself in the bedroom until Blake returned and searched it out and shot it to pieces. What if one crawled into Lucy Anette's crib some night! She shuddered.

"Please, Blake. Please try to make some other arrangements. I simply couldn't bring Lucy to a place like that. Please understand."

"Let's wait and talk about it when you're stronger, Penny. I think you'll see it differently later on," Blake said heartily. "Better ring off now. I'll call you when I'm in Dar next, so take good care of yourself and little Lucy. I love you, dear, and I'm most proud of you. Let me know if you need anything."

She replaced the receiver and stood up, bending over Lucy's cradle, tears streaming down her face. *Good-bye, Blake. Good-bye, my love. Oh, please, God. No."*

The months passed. Penny's only joy was her baby. Hubert was enchanted with the child and often stayed with her when Penny had to do errands. On one of Blake's calls he told her the Major was in the hospital in Nairobi, and he expected him to sell out and return to England soon. Again she pleaded with him, to no avail. A letter a month later said he had taken the camp over from the Major, asking her when she was coming. She replied that Lucy was troubled with an allergy and needed to see the doctor each week.

Christmas came and Blake sent a large check for Lucy. Penny opened a special closed account for the child; one that could not be touched for seven years and drew top interest. She told Blake what she had done. He approved.

Alfred was delighted with Lucy when he came home for Christmas. He carried her around so much Penny said she was getting spoiled. Alfred bought the biggest doll he could find for her Christmas present, and wrapped it in yards of paper. He had to open the package for her and they all laughed when he showed it to Lucy. The doll was bigger than she and, at first, it frightened her. A few nights before his return to school, Alfred and Penny were sitting in her apartment. Lucy was sleeping in the small crib next to Penny's bed.

"Mum, I want to talk to you about something."

She poured a brandy for each of them, then seeing his look of surprise, she hurriedly said, "Lucy's stopped nursing, you know. She's on cereal and other things now, and wants more milk than I can give her."

It seemed that Penny downed her brandy quite fast, and she poured another before he was half way through his, but he said nothing.

"She is such a dear. Did you see her laugh when I came in the room the other day?"

Penny nodded. "Yes. Even in so short a time she adores you. Now," she took his hand, "what did you want to talk about?"

"I guess you know at school we're required to go to Chapel every morning?" He looked serious, his hands twisting together. She looked at him inquiringly. "I've always just sat there, usually thinking about something else. I'd never have gone if I hadn't had to."

He stopped, taking a sip of the brandy, then continued. "The first of the year we got a new Chaplain, and, for the first time, I began to listen. It was as if I had never heard it before; the love of Jesus Christ for us—for me! It was the first time I really understood about the Holy Spirit living in a person. It got so I could hardly wait for Chapel. Finally I went in to see the Chaplain, and he talked with me for a long time."

Alfred stood up and took his empty glass to the kitchen. "We're had lots of talks since then, Mum. He's the greatest! I've been reading the Bible and studying every chance I've had. I—we both feel I may have a calling."

He stopped when he saw the surprised look on his mother's face.

"I'm not at all sure yet," he said, as he sat down and put his arms around her shoulders. "It's something one really wants to be sure about, and I've a long way to go yet. But if it should turn out I do have a calling, I'd like to start my pre-seminary studies next fall. It'll take years, but the Chaplain says he's sure I can get a scholarship if I decide to do that. Except," he looked away, "I rather felt I should get a job after this school year, and help out with you and Lucy, if you need me."

"My dear," her eyes were shining, "oh no. We're quite all right. Blake's sent more than enough, and I've savings. You're a dear, but don't give it another thought."

"I shouldn't mind, I shouldn't mind at all. After all, I'm a man now."

"You are a precious man!" She exclaimed, kissing him. "I don't know what I've done to deserve such a son. If you feel the same way next fall, you go right ahead. Surely by then, Blake will have sent for us. I know he'll work out something."

He reached over and patted her hand. "Thanks, Mum."

She brushed his cheek with her lips. "God bless you," she said, shyly.

Soon after Alfred returned to school, the Slades came to England on leave, and Ann came to spend the week-end with Penny, telling her all the news of Blake and Africa. While Penny was tending the baby, Ann opened the refrigerator looking for a snack. The box was filled with baby food and several bottles of gin, nothing more. She noticed Penny had started smoking heavily, and looked sallow and hollow eyed. Later that evening, after Penny had tucked Lucy in, they had several drinks, Penny pouring doubles and chain smoking.

"I hardly had anything to drink while I was carrying Lucy, or while I was nursing her," Penny said, defensively, after Ann had refused the last drink. "But now—I don't know—it helps somehow. Even with Lucy, I get so lonely—."

"Tell me when you're hungry," she added, hastily. "I'll run down to the corner and fetch us some fish and chips. I'm afraid I haven't much in the house."

Ann smiled. "Finish your drink. It's early yet. I've become so accustomed to late African dinners, I find it hard to adjust."

"Do you think," Penny hesitated. "Do you think Blake will ever send for us?" Her eyes, darkly circled, flicked across Ann's face. "Surely he's talked to you about it?"

Ann shifted uncomfortably in her chair. "Of course, dear. Actually, he's talked of little else when we've seen him. But I think he's rather set on staying on the island. He can't seem to understand why you don't come there, 'though I must say I can see your side of it. It's not too pleasant even in Dar these days."

Penny turned her glass nervously between her fingers, then took a long swallow. "Ann, whatever shall I do? I love him so. I wrote him just yesterday that I'd give anything to be able to lay my head on his shoulder. I've sent him ever so many pictures of Lucy and of me, too. I wanted to show him I've kept my figure. See?" She pulled her skirt tight around her. She was still lithe, but her face was strangely bloated and she had an unhealthy color.

"Has he said anything else?"

"He did say," Ann hesitated, "he'd wait two years."

"Two years? And then what?"

"Nothing," Ann replied, seeing tears spring into Penny's eyes. "He said—two years—that's all. He's so proud of Lucy. He carries her picture about with him and shows them to everyone, yours, too. Has he said anything in his letters?"

"His letters are mostly—newsy. *All about what he's doing, and news of our friends.* In almost every one he asks me when we're coming. I don't know how to answer him, so I say nothing."

Penny stood and turned away. "Whatever shall I do? I'm so unhappy."

"If I were you, and planning to stay here, I'd find something to do. I'm sure Blake sends what he can, but it's hard to know how long that will continue."

Penny nodded. "I've thought of that. I've had to dip into my savings several times and it worries me. Blake's mother and brother have offered to help me if I need it, but I haven't asked." She half fell into the chair, sloshing the drink on her dress, unnoticed. "Alfred's so fond of the child. He's terribly sweet with her. Why can't Blake come here so we can be a family?"

"Penny," Ann said, leaning forward, "I think there are reasons Blake would be taking a risk to return here. He's a somewhat checkered past, you know, and he's made some enemies, I'm sure. It's just rumors I've heard, nothing in detail."

"I know, Ann. I know," Penny sighed. "He's not been all he should have, I'm sure. I closed my eyes to it when I was there, but even his brother has hinted at some things."

She went into the kitchen and brought the gin bottle back, setting it on the coffee table. As she poured a drink, she added, "I still love him, no matter what he's done. I think I'll go to my grave loving him."

Ann frowned. "Look here, Penny, you must preserve yourself, both for yours and Lucy's sakes." She picked up the bottle, and screwed the lid on firmly, setting it on the far side of the coffee table.

She turned back to Penny. "Why don't you open a small shop. I noticed the space next to Hubert's shop is vacant. You could open, say, a boutique, and that way, you could keep Lucy with you when you're in the shop. It would give you something to do and give you an income, too."

Penny brightened a bit.

Ann continued, "I could send some lovely African prints that would be a bit different. There isn't a boutique in the neighborhood, is there?"

"No," mused Penny, "not within walking distance, anyway. I don't know much about fashion, but I guess I could learn."

"Great! I think you could bring it off. You get on well with people and you've a good business head. I don't think you ever realized how much you contributed to the fishing camp. A lot of people like you and the way you ran the place."

"Truly," she asked, surprised.

"Oh, yes," Ann smiled. "As a matter of fact, we've been back there only once since you left. It just isn't the same now. We rented a little beach house near Dar where we go for week-ends. It's lovely swimming but there aren't the splendid reefs one finds near the island. It's fine for the children and for us, though."

"Thank you, Ann." Penny yawned. "Excuse me, I must be getting sleepy. You've given me a good idea, though, and I'll look into it first thing Monday. How about some fish and chips?"

"It's settled, Mum," Alfred said excitedly, when he returned home that spring. "I've applied to the pre-seminary and they've accepted me! I'll have a small stipend, and I'm sure to get a part-time job and work holidays, too."

He had lost his boyishness, standing tall and well developed. "How beautiful he'll look in his vestments," she thought.

"Have you talked to your father about it?"

"Yes, just today. He was quite decent about it, though I could tell he'd hoped I would go into business with him. I feel so right about this, Mum, knowing the good Lord will help us all. You'll see."

He turned and looked out the window. "What's the word from Blake?"

Her face clouded. "He's still on the island. I thought maybe he'd settle in Dar, but it hasn't worked out somehow. I can't think of taking little Lucy to live on the island—."

"Of course you can't, Mum. It's a beautiful place, but not right for a small child."

"I was thinking I might start a dress shop in that empty space next to Hubert. I've checked and it's available, and the rent is reasonable. I've been talking to buyers, too, and they've been very helpful. I think I could manage it—just until Blake can work things out," she

138

added, hastily. "I could always get a good price for the stock when I'm ready to sell. It's a good location." She looked questioningly at Alfred.

"That's capital, Mum. I can help get it ready while I'm home, if you like. It would give you something to do, and it would be the kind of place you could have Lucy with you most of the time." He looked fondly at his mother. "It's good to have you in England, but I want you to do whatever will make you happy."

"I'll never really be happy until I'm with Blake again," she said, softly. "Do you understand that, Alfred? I love him so, and Lucy's part of both of us."

"I understand, Mum. I only want you to be happy. Come," he said, pulling her to her feet. "It's a lovely spring day. Let's put Lucy in her carriage and take the air."

They walked through the verdant green park with the yellow daffodils and forsythia blending with the new shades of green. Alfred stopped to buy a few sprigs of greenery for his mother.

"Mum, would you mind—I mean, have you thought about having Lucy baptized?" He hurried on. "I mean, with Easter next Sunday and all, I thought we might slip in. There'll be lots of other babies being baptized then, and—well—I'd feel good about it, and I think you would, too."

"That's a good idea, dear. I'd not like to ask your father to go, but if you'd go with us—?" She paused, then added, pensively, "I always went to church when I was a girl, but after Hubert and I were married, I gradually stopped going. We were married in a church, but Hubert wasn't in the habit of attending regularly. Then, there was the shop and all; animals to be fed and cared for even on Sunday. Maybe I should start back again."

"I think you'd like it, Mum. There's a lot there for you, and for Lucy, too, as she get older."

"I'll be going back to Africa someday, of course," she frowned, then brightened, "but I'm sure there are Anglican churches in Dar. There are quite a few of us Brits there still."

"Capital. We'll take Lucy along tomorrow and buy her the prettiest frock we can find. Then we'll go and talk to the Priest."

A few days later Penny wrote Blake that she had signed a lease on the space and was starting a boutique. He didn't reply. Weeks went by with no word from him. She continued to write each week. The boutique was opened and thriving by summer. Even Hubert found time to help on week-ends. Penny was surprised to find so many women from the church at the opening and they continued to come in and shop. Penny had been taking Lucy to church every Sunday, and when Alfred was home, they all went together. People often stopped to comment on Lucy's looks. Her dark eyes, that had been so brown when she was born, had turned a deep violet, contrasting with her olive skin and ebony hair. She was an usually good baby, but when she got restless, Alfred took her and bounced her on his knee. Lucy would wrap her arms around his neck and quieted down. Alfred came home often enough for Lucy not to forget him between times. It was touching to Penny to see the strong bond growing between the two. She could not help wishing, even so, that it was Blake beside her.

On Lucy's first birthday, Blake called. "I wanted to wish Lucy a happy birthday, and to see how you are getting on."

Penny almost cried with relief. "I'm so glad you called! If it weren't for letters from Ann I'd have thought something terrible had happened to you. I've missed your letters. Just a minute. I'll hold Lucy up to the phone. She's almost walking, Blake. She's so bright."

Penny put the receiver to Lucy's ear. "This is your daddy from Africa," she said. She heard Blake's voice coming over the phone. Lucy laughed.

"Say, 'Daddy'," Penny prompted her.

Finally, Lucy said, "Da Da".

Penny could hear Blake's burst of laughter. She sat with the child on her lap, gripping the phone with white knuckles. "I've been teaching her that for weeks, dear," she said. Then, "Blake, why did you stop writing?"

"Sorry, Penny. I'll do better form now on. I sent a check for Lucy's birthday along with a note, but it may not get there in time. That's why I called."

"Thank you, dear." She hesitated. "The shop started making money from the first month, so we've enough. I'll put the birthday money in the sealed account. You know, I wrote you about it."

"I'm glad to hear things are going well with you, sweetie. I miss you, you know. Buy Lucy a present before you bank the check. There was nothing here I could buy for her."

"Yes, dear, of course. Thank you so much for calling. I miss you terribly."

"Then come to me," he replied, gruffly.

"I can't, Blake! You must know how much I want to, but surely you realize why I can't. Couldn't you possibly come here?"

"That's out of the question. I've explained that. You must come to me," he said, harshly.

"I'm sorry, Blake. I do love you." she waited.

After a moment, Blake said, "Let me tell Lucy good-bye."

She held the phone to the child's ear and heard her say, "Bye bye."

Penny took the phone and said, "Blake?" But the line was dead.

**\*\*\*\*\*\*\*\*\*\*\*\*\*\*\*\*\*\*\*\*\*\*\*\*\*\*\*\*\*\*\*\*\***

Two years passed. Blake would write a spate of letters, then there would be long months of silence. Penny heard rumors that an occasional woman stayed at the camp, but each lingered only a short time.

Hubert and Penny took Lucy to Alfred's ordination. They had presented him with a lovely silver filigreed cross which he wore proudly over his vestments. Alfred had his mother's dark hair and heavy eyebrows, which contrasted startlingly with his creamy complexion and ruddy cheeks and lips. Penny's heart swelled as he entered the sanctuary of the high domed cathedral and knelt with the rest of his class. In one of the most solemn moments, when the priest placed his hands on Alfred's head, Lucy's small voice piped out, "Brother's getting blessed!"

Penny quieted her, but couldn't suppress a smile. "We're all blessed," she whispered.

Hubert sat stiff backed, uncomfortable in his new tight suit. He looked proud but bewildered.

**\*\*\*\*\*\*\*\*\*\*\*\*\*\*\*\*\*\*\*\*\*\*\*\*\*\*\*\*\*\*\*\*\***

Ann visited Penny several times over the years. On her last visit, she said, "Penny, why don't you take Lucy back to Africa just for a visit. Perhaps you and Blake would work out something if you could meet and have a chance to really talk things over."

Penny looked down at her hands. "I don't know why I think this, Ann, but I'm afraid if I did Blake would try to keep her there, run off with her the way the Major's wife did with their son." She gave Ann an anguished look. "I couldn't bear to lose her. You understand, don't you? She's my whole life!"

"Africa's such a strange country," she continued, "more so now, I would imagine, with the drought, and all the political unrest. I haven't any connections there, really, except you and Bob. Blake knows everybody. He could disappear with her and I'd never have a chance of finding them."

Penny paced the floor. "The idea frightened me. I don't know why I think all these things. I just do. Blake can be so——."

"I understand, dear," Ann replied. "Look, if you'd like me to, I'll ask Blake if he could possibly meet you in a neutral country. How about Corfu?"

"Yes." Penny seemed delighted. "I would take Lucy there. I really do want them to know each other. I'm sure if Blake could once see her, he'd——."

"Then I'll speak to him and let you know. I do hope it works out."

"It would be good for me to get away, too." Penny was quite animated. "I've not had a real holiday since Lucy was born. The boutique's done so well I've taken on two clerks, and Hubert would be glad to keep check for me." She hesitated. "Just to see him once more—to feel his arms around me!"

She stopped short and glanced in the mirror. "I hate it that I've got so stout, but it can't be helped now, I suppose."

"Indeed she has aged a great deal," Ann thought. *Her face is puffy and she's taken to wearing muumuus, which don't become her. I suspect she's drinking more heavily than she wants anyone to know. Poor Penny, she deserves better than this.*

"Has Blake changed much?" Penny asked.

"He's grown more cantankerous as the years have passed, especially when the Krauts come," Ann laughed, but with diving so popular these days, he's out on the reefs swimming and spear fishing a lot, so he's kept trim. Even so, he's a bit of a beer belly and a trifle more bald. There's a bit of gray at his temples now, come to think of it."

She gave Penny a hug. "I'll talk to him when we return next month. I know he's lonely, but it would be hard for him to admit it, or to beg. You understand."

Lucy came running in the door from school, stopping short when she saw Ann.

"You remember Mrs. Slade, don't you, dear?"

Lucy made a small curtsy. "You're from Africa where my daddy lives, aren't you?" Her dark eyes danced and long dark braids swung down her back. She had a peculiar way of crooking one side of her mouth when she smiled, as if she smiled more with one side than the other. Ann thought she had never seen so striking a child.

"I've never cut her hair," Penny said, taking the ribbons off and untwisting the braids with her fingers. She took a stiff brush to the thick shining hair, and it fell, glinting with black lights, past her hips.

"What a charming smile, like a pixie," Ann said, after Penny had re-braided Lucy's hair and let her go out for an ice.

"Doesn't she? She usually smiles that way when she's very pleased, or when she's talked me into letting her do something I'd said no to at first."

Blake called a few weeks later. Lucy answered the phone, and after a bit, turned to her mother excitedly. "Mum, Daddy want us to meet him on Corfu. Can we? Please, Mum?"

Penny took the phone, and eagerly agreed with Blake to meet on Corfu the first of the following month. He named a hotel, saying he would make reservations.

They sailed from London on a sunlit late summer day. Ecstatically, Lucy ran from deck to deck. She made friends with many of the adults on board, but seemed to shy away from the children.

"She's spent too much time with grown-ups," Penny thought. *I suppose I must put her in a boarding school soon, but—oh—I hate to part with her, even for those short periods.*

They usually talked as two adults, and Penny, quite truthfully, had explained why Lucy's name was Lambert-Smith instead of Blakely, even though she was actually Blake's daughter. Lucy accepted all this, but also, she heard the pain in her mother's voice when she tried to explain why they couldn't all live together.

Arriving in Corfu, they hurried from the dock and checked into the hotel, asking if Captain Blakely were there yet. No, he was expected any time, they said. She and Lucy had a quiet dinner at the hotel and went to bed early. Next morning she inquired after Blake again. No. Expected. She wrote a short note to be placed in his box.

They went for a walk, soaking in the hot sunshine, enjoying the bright colors and flavor of the island. At noon they returned. The desk clerk shook his head when they appeared.

That afternoon they went for an ocean swim. Penny tried to tell Lucy what the reefs were like off the island in Africa. That night, Lucy could hear her mother's muffled sobs. The next day they explored another part of the town, visiting the bazaars lining the winding narrow streets. Penny tried to be bright and cheerful, but soon fell silent. Lucy patted her mother's hand with womanly concern. "Don't worry, Mum. You still have me."

"You're becoming so grown up. I thank God for you, Lucy Anette," she said, giving the child a hug.

Two days later as Penny was packing to leave, she heard her name called loudly. Running to the door, she found the desk clerk coming down the hall. "Telephone, Madam," he panted. "Long distance from Africa!"

Penny nearly tripped running to the phone at the desk. "Hello, hello! Blake, is that you?"

"No, it's Ann," she heard. The connection was terrible.

"Ann," she asked, "what is it? Where's Blake? He was supposed to meet me here. He's not—is he all right?"

"Yes, he's all right," Ann shouted. "I can barely hear you. That is, he's all right, but he's in jail here in Dar."

"In jail!" shouted Penny. "Whatever for?"

"He tried to leave, to get to Corfu. He really did. But he was picked up at the airport and taken to police headquarters. I've tried for days to call you, but the overseas lines here have been logged for weeks. This was the first time I could get a line through."

"Tell me about Blake," Penny interrupted. "Why was he arrested?"

"Something about the old deportation thing, Penny. They said his papers weren't in order, that some were forged. They wouldn't guarantee he could return if he left. Bob's been trying all week to get him released. There's an American banker coming in next week. He's a foreign advisor to the President. Blake's known him for a long time. We think he may be able to help."

"Thank you, Ann. Thank you for calling. Write to me in Liverpool and let me know what's happening. Lucy and I are leaving here tomorrow. Thanks again, Ann. Give Blake my love."

She dropped the phone. The clerk caught it and returned it to the cradle. "I'm sorry, Madam," he said. Penny nodded through her tears.

Late that night, Penny sat watching Lucy's quiet breathing. She had dimmed the lights, and only a night-light glowed. Pouring the last of the gin from the bottle, she downed it in one swallow, then got up and searched the room for another bottle, knowing there was none. She walked aimlessly about the room, biting her lip, straightening Lucy's dress on the back of a chair. Hesitantly, she went to the door, opened it, and peered out. With one last glance at Lucy, she picked up her purse and let herself quietly out the door.

She stumbled in the hallway and staggered, her shoulder hitting the wall. She leaned against it, then started to return to her room, but changed her mind and continued down the hall. She crossed the lobby and entered a small, dimly lit bar, slipping into a seat in a dark corner. The waiter appeared and she ordered a double gin. She had two and was about to order another when they told her the bar was closing.

She tried to focus her eyes, barely able to make out that there was someone seated at the bar. She rose to leave, stumbled, and half fell against a chair. The man at the bar quickly came to her side and caught her arm, helping her to stand erect. She saw he was black.

"You all right?" he asked, his voice heavily accented. She nodded and he stepped back. She started to sway and he again took her arm.

"I help to room," he stated.

She nodded, and managed a thanks.

"Which room are you?" he asked.

"One twenty three?" she replied' shaking her head. "One thirty two." Her voice was thick.

"Have room key?" he asked, as they crossed the deserted lobby.

She stopped and fumbled in her purse, but failed to find the key. "My room—daughter," she slurred.

"Come my room," the man said. "Rest some. Feel better."

He supported her down the passage way, and holding her with one arm, opened the door and drew her inside. He slipped her dress off and led her to the bed. She sank gratefully onto the pillow and closed her eyes.

"Drink?" she asked, not opening her eyes.

He was removing his trousers. "Not have."

Penny's eyes flew open as she felt his heavy weight on her. His hands fumbled, trying to pull her panties to one side. She stared in horror as she saw his bulging eyes close to hers.

"No, no!" she cried, struggling to move out from under him. He brought his hand over her mouth.

"Like white bitch," he breathed heavily. "You like black man plenty," he stated, pinning her to the bed.

She felt him trying to enter her, gave a hard twist, and freed herself. She jumped from the bed and staggered toward the door. He sprang to his feet, stood in front of the door, grinning maliciously. "You try. You like," he said, moving toward her. He held her face with one hand, put his other arm around her, and kissed her viciously. She managed to turn her head and scream. He jerked away and drew his hand back to hit her. Then, spinning around, he picked up her dress and flung it at her. He crossed to the bed and threw himself on it, staring at her.

She fumbled into the dress and stepped to the door, grabbing her purse from the chair. She turned the knob, shook it, then realized it was locked. With a hard turn she released the lock and got the door open. As she entered the hall, she heard his laugh.

"Not like anyway. Fat drunk bitch."

She hurried to her room. Lucy was sleeping peacefully. Penny turned on the shower and soaped twice, then a third time, running the water hot and cold. She threw her clothes into a pile in the corner and dressed in clean things. Sitting in a chair, shuddering, the tears streaming silently down her face, she was scarcely aware when the first light slid over the window sill.

# Chapter 16

Blake's letters and phone calls were frantic after Penny's return to England.

"I've a house here now," he wrote. "The government's built a hotel near the fishing camp, and they took over the camp from quarters for the staff. You remember the house on the bluff down from the camp that was usually empty? Chap from Nairobi built it and seldom gets there. I'm renting it from him."

"Planes come in every day now and the house is large, three bedrooms and two baths. It's really nice, better than living at the camp, and more privacy. I have two fishing boats and they bring in plenty of money. I supply the hotel with fish and eat my evening meals there. There are always interesting people about, and the British couple who manage it are good people. You would have lots of company. Come and bring Lucy. We can work out her schooling."

Penny replied, "Darling, I do so want to come. I've longed for you so all these years, but, my dearest, when the government took over the camp, couldn't you have moved into Dar? Lucy could have gone to school there, at least for some years, and perhaps I could have opened a little shop. I want to be sure Lucy is provided for, and I need something to do during the day while you're gone. Lucy still has some allergies and needs shots periodically, and—oh—so many reasons!"

"Please, please move into Dar so we can join you. That's all I'll ever ask of you. Do you still love me, even after all these years? I'm not sure you do anymore."

"My dear Penny," he replied. "I'm being neither capricious nor stubborn. There are good reasons for remaining on the island. First off, I'm out of sight here. So many British are being forced out of Tanzania, and by keeping a low profile, I don't attract attention. Also, I like living here and I like my work. I'd rather do this than anything I could do in Africa. It's a good life, and it's a good place to raise our little girl. There are studies we can get by mail to teach her. I can easily provide for Lucy and for you." "Yes, I still love you. If I didn't, I wouldn't ask you both to come. Moreover, the island is a safer place to live than Liverpool, if worse came to worse. Wasn't Liverpool one of the first places they bombed in World War II? Wouldn't it be a primary target in case of an atomic war? They wouldn't waste a bomb on our little island, and we could live in plenty with what we could grow and catch without any outside contact, if we had to."

"After the Corfu experience, I know there is no way I could ever return if I were to leave here, and here is where I want to stay. I think you feel the same way, so what are you waiting for? I long to be with you. You know that. I think we should be raising our daughter together."

"Dearest Blake. A year has passed since that awful experience on Corfu, and I miss you more than ever. I must see you. I can't stand it any longer."

"My shop is doing so well I don't want to interrupt anything at this point, so how would you feel about me coming there for a visit? Perhaps if we could see each other, we could work things out."

"Bob and Ann are here with young Adam and they're returning in two weeks. I could fly back with them and get a lift from Nairobi to their farm. Ann's brother, David, will fly me to the island in their bush plane. I won't plan on this until I hear from you, so if you want me to come, you must let me know right away."

"I love you so. I'm trembling at the thought of seeing you again."

"Dear Penny. Of course I want you to come, you and Lucy. You know that. It would be better if you'd plan to stay. You'll be wasting a lot of money flying here twice, but if that's what you want to do, very well. You will, of course, bring Lucy with you. I've waited quite long enough to see my child. It won't hurt her to miss a bit of school."

\*\*\*\*\*\*\*\*\*\*\*\*\*\*\*\*\*\*\*\*\*\*\*\*\*\*\*\*\*\*\*\*\*\*\*\*

Penny held her breath as the plane circled the runway. It looked just as she remembered it; the flight over the reef spattered ocean, the palms bordering the long narrow island, the landing strip winding out like the tail of a kite.

She had not radioed Blake, but the plane had buzzed the hotel, and David had said they would send a car. Her heart pounded against her ribs as the small plane touched down and turned to taxi back to the airport. As the plane stopped, she saw a small bus drive up and park. She opened the door and climbed out onto the runway. Even with the sea breeze, she was struck by the intense humid heat. She swayed slightly, then started walking toward the low tin roofed building. Her mouth felt dry and her palms clammy.

She saw Blake as he rounded the corner of the building. He was even larger than she remembered. His legs, below the cuffs of his shorts, seemed as big as tree trunks. She started to run toward him and, stumbling, fell against him. He hold her close for a moment, then stepped back, his hands gripping her arms. He looked past her at the plane. David was handing the luggage to an African porter.

"Where's Lucy?" he asked, staring at her with eyes narrowed.

"I didn't bring her, Blake. I'm sorry, but I thought it better not to this time. I hope you're not angry."

Blake's face grew dark. A large vein in his neck bulged and throbbed. His shaking hands bit into her arms, and she shrank back. "He would kill me," she thought, terrified.

"Blake! My arms. You're hurting me!"

He released her abruptly and spun around, heading for the bus. She stood, helpless. David joined her.

"Pretty bad, huh?"

"I'm afraid so. I suppose I shouldn't have come."

"I'm sure he'll get over it. Give him time. I'll be off now, sorry. I've just time to make it back to Arusha before dark. The porter's got your luggage."

"Thank you, David, so much. You're very kind. Thank Ann and Bob for me, too." She kissed him lightly on the cheek.

"Let us know if we can do anything for you, Penny."

She nodded and made her way slowly to the bus. Blake was sitting beside the driver, his face set as marble. The driver opened the rear door for her and she got in, sitting behind Blake.

She leaned over the back of his seat. "Blake, please forgive me. I didn't think you'd be so angry. I only—."

"We'll talk about it at the house," he snapped.

The long ride to the other end of the island was made in silence. The bus turned off onto a narrow road and passed a cluster of huts. A man and a woman stood in a small garden, hoes in hand. They waved at the bus, and Penny and the driver waved back. Blake sat, immobile. The bus pulled up and stopped next to a partially dismantled Jeep.

"Our old car?" Penny asked.

Blake mumbled.

"What did you say?"

"Yes." He stared at her, his eyes hard.

"It doesn't run anymore?"

"No."

"Oh."

The bus door was opened by a tall African. Penny climbed out, hardly seeing the man.

"Welcome, Memsahib."

She saw the outstretched hand, and looked up. "Appendai!," she cried, clasping his hand with both of hers.

Blake muttered in Swahili. Appendai quickly withdrew his hand and started picking up the luggage.

Blake walked to the house, and stood holding the door for her. She walked into a kitchen and through it onto a long verandah with a dining table and chairs at one end, and porch furniture at the other. Appendai started into one of the bedrooms off the verandah, when Blake spoke in Swahili. He turned, and took the bags into another bedroom.

Penny stood looking out at the ocean. It was as beautiful as she remembered it. Blake walked to the front of the verandah where a long line of steps led down to the sandy shore. Resting quietly in the water lay two fishing boats.

"You'll want to get settled," he said, not looking at her. "I have a bit more work to do on the boat before it goes out tomorrow. We'll have dinner at the hotel."

"What lovely boats. Are they yours?"

"I bought one a short time ago. The other belongs to the French Ambassador. I have the use of it in return for keeping it up and storing it."

He descended the steps. Penny watched him wade through the shallow water and climb aboard one of the boats. He bent over the stern tinkering with the motors.

"This is really nice," Penny thought, looking around the house. *It's so much better than that one room at the camp. I wonder if I would dare bring Lucy here? I wonder now why I have resisted so long. We could manage her schooling, really, and I could learn to give the allergy shots when they're needed. Many British wives raise children in more remote places than this, I'm sure. Perhaps Blake is right; perhaps I have been unreasonable."*

Suddenly she felt as if a cold cloud had enveloped her, and she shivered violently. In the back of her mind the word 'yet, yet' played over and over.

Appendai appeared at her side. "Small Memsahib not come?"

"No."

"Pity."

Penny shook her head, looking at the lean African; a bit of gray sprinkling his woolly hair. He pointed toward the bedroom, and Penny walked into the small room with a single bed. Above it, written in colored crayon, were the words, "Welcome Home, Lucy Anette". She pulled the masking tape off the corners of the banner, folded it carefully, and put it on the dresser.

She showered in the tepid water, and taking clean underwear out of her bag, started to put it on, then changed her mind. She opened a dresser drawer, but had put only a few things away when she saw some ladies' underwear tucked away in a corner. She took her things out, laid them on the dresser top, and slipped on a sheer nightgown. She made her face up carefully and brushed her long hair. A strand of white cut a streak from her temple across one side of her head. She had thought it made her look distinguished, but wondered now if she shouldn't have dyed it. She looked at herself in the mirror, trying not to look at her body. It disgusted her. *How could I have let myself get so heavy?*

She lay on her bed, staring at the ceiling. She had not told Lucy she was coming to Africa, expecting to be back before the child's scheduled visit home. Alfred had been hesitant about her coming, relenting when she told him she was not taking Lucy. Hubert was concerned only that she not neglect the shop for too long a period.

*When, O Lord, can I do what makes ME happy? And Blake; he hasn't even kissed me. Oh, what have I done?* Her thoughts raced. *What else could I have done than what I did? Why does one have to pay such a price for happiness? I've known only a few months of perfection out of my whole life!*

She turned restlessly on the bed. *No, that's not completely true. Life with Blake wasn't entirely perfect. There's the long dead*

*Abhurdamoni, and the day that little girl and Blake came out of the bedroom' why has that haunted me all these years? Is this a subconscious reason for not returning to Africa with Lucy? Would I have felt differently if she had been a boy?*

She swung her legs off the edge of the bed and sat up. *After all, what on earth could there have been between Blake and that little girl? Surely I was imagining things. Yet—.*

She heard Blake's step on to the veranda. She listened, tense, hearing the shower in the next room begin to spray, then the bed springs give under Blake's weight. Her body went slack, and she lay heavily back on the pillow. The next half hour seemed an age, her mind bouncing back and forth like a tennis ball between her need for Blake and her fear of confronting him.

*Can I honestly tell him I'll come back and bring the child? Dear God, how can I love a man I don't trust?*

Finally, she rose and walked on bare feet across the veranda and into Blake's bedroom. He lay nude on his side beneath the mosquito netting, his body turned away from her. She listened to the rhythm of his breathing, then lifted the netting, and slid beneath it into the bed. He stirred, and turned on his back, barely opening his eyes. His arm circled her and she laid her head on his shoulder. "My darling, at last!"

She lifted her head and met his lips as he pressed closer to her, shivering as he moved his hands down, pulling her gown down her shoulders and off her feet. He paused a moment, flicking his eyes down her body, and frowned. He lay back against the pillow, his body barely touching hers. She ran her hand down his body, stroking the thick black hair.

"You feel hot," she whispered. "Have you a fever?"

"A touch of malaria, I'm afraid; the price one pays for living in coastal Africa. It will pass in a day or two, but I'm afraid I'll not get an erection until it does. Sorry."

"Darling, I'm the one who's sorry! I shouldn't have awakened you. It was thoughtless of me!"

"No harm. I've slept enough. Let's have a cup of tea. No point' in going to the hotel until after dark. They don't serve dinner before eight, anyway."

He rose and slipped on his shorts. When she had dressed and joined him, he was sitting under a frangipani tree at a table with two chairs. He removed the tea caddy and poured two cups of tea, offering her the coarse sugar and tinned milk. She shook her head, and he helped himself to generous portions. He stared out to sea as he brought the cup to his lips.

"What happened to the Jeep, Blake?"

"I brought it over here when the government took the camp over. I took the motor out and locked it up. No point in handing them everything. One day, when they've forgotten about it, I'll put it back. Really don't need it now, with the hotel transport available."

"I like your boats, Blake. They look faster than the ones you used to have."

"Right. They're the finest fishing boats on the island. I can get to the fishing areas and go farther than the government boats can go. I take a lot of business away from them. That one," he pointed to the larger one, "is a Coronet, the best boat of its kind. You see, it's got a flying deck above the stern. You can spot the big fish from the water there. The other one that belongs to the ambassador I expect to be all mine before too long. He's had a heart attack and doesn't fish anymore."

Penny took a sip of her tea and looked at Blake. "Darling, I—."

"I told you to bring the child!" His voice shook. "Why didn't you?"

"I didn't think it was wise for the moment, Blake. I thought it best for us to talk before I made any decision. I know how disappointed you—."

*"You* didn't think! Before *you* made any decisions!" He jumped up and towered over her. "Tell me why it's to be only *your* decision. She's *my* child too, in case you've forgotten. I said to bring her if you came back here, so why did you come without her?"

"Will you stop shouting at me? I've had quite enough! Lucy would have had a father and you would have had your daughter if you'd tried to come half way! Do you think it's been easy for me? Easy to go back to England and go crawling to Hubert, easy to have to tell Lucy she's illegitimate? Easy to face Alfred? All because you wouldn't leave this damned island, even for a little while!"

"I've explained that," he turned away. "'Though I don't know *why* I needed to explain it. A man's family goes where he is, and that's all there is to it."

He turned back, glaring at her. "Now suppose you go back to England and bring her here. I should think you'd have learned by now I won't be buggered about! I've put up with quite enough of your indecision."

Penny jumped up from her chair and crossed to him. She grabbed his arm, forcing him to look at her. "If you hate me so, how can we possibly have a life together?"

"I don't hate you. I hate the years you've cost all of us, and the unhappiness. I'm willing to do my part if you'll act like a woman instead of a spoiled child!"

"Blake, that's enough! You're the one who's been selfish and self-centered. Oh, you've sent some money, and I've appreciated that, but I've had all the rest of it to do alone simply because you've had your mind set on having everything your own way. You've not considered me—or Lucy."

His face contorted. "Who are you to come here and criticize me? Look at you. Look at how you've let yourself go, then come crawling into bed with me just now. Do you think you can simply pick up where we left off? I suppose I'm expected to act grateful for the chance to make love to you after all these years."

They glared at each other a long moment before they noticed a figure standing on the veranda behind them. They both turned, surprised. A slender, small boned woman stood watching them. She was obviously over forty, but quite obviously, had taken exquisite care of herself. Even before the woman spoke, Penny knew she was an American.

Her flat accented voice was shrill. "I hope you're going to kill him. I'll be glad to help you."

"Jessica," Blake's voice was steel edged, "what in hell are you doing here?"

"'What in hell are you doing here?'", she mimicked. "I'll tell you what in hell I'm doing here. I've come to get my boat, you worthless bastard, and I hope it's the last time I ever lay eyes on you!"

"What are you upset about?" Blake asked, innocently.

"What I'm upset about, you big shit, is getting back from the States two days ago and finding Johnnie and Claude living in a hotel in Dar. They said you'd kicked them out, and wouldn't even let them sail the boat back. What in hell are you doing trying to keep *my* boat?"

"I kicked those two hippie sons of yours out because they were high on b'hang all the time and couldn't get out of bed until noon. Two more worthless sons-of-bitches I've ever seen. As for letting them have the boat, only last week they tried for thirty minutes to get it across the bay with both anchors out. I caught them just before they ruined the motors. If I'd let them start off for Dar in it they'd have sunk her before they ever got there. I wouldn't have cared if they'd drowned themselves, but I didn't want to lose my boat."

"*Your* boat! You thieving bastard. *My* money bought that boat, and you were supposed to teach my sons how to sail it. 'We can double your money in a year', you said. It's been longer than that and I haven't seen a cent of that money yet. I have a boat captain waiting at the hotel and I'm taking that boat with me when I leave, like *now.* The keys, please."

"You're forgetting something, aren't you, Jessica? We had to get the license in my name and my name alone since I'm a citizen and you're not. You signed the boat over to me. Remember?"

"That was only a formality and you know it, you limey son-of-a-bitch! Either give me the keys or I'll go back to Dar and sue you. I'll see you in jail for the rest of your natural born days."

"Sue away." Blake sat down abruptly in the chair and poured a cup of tea.

Jessica walked over and swiped her hand across the table, sending the tea tray crashing to the ground. "Who's the new girl friend? Really, Blake, I thought you could do better than that."

"Jessica," Blake's voice was dangerously soft, "this is Penny."

"The long lost Penny, is it? The one who got knocked up? The one who faints in tents in the bush? Right?" She turned with a derisive laugh toward Penny. "So he can't make love to you. Isn't that what I heard him say when I walked in? Why, he's probably tired, poor dear. He's got women coming in and out of here like it's a turn stile. Some of them are young, dear innocent Penny, some of them *very* young, like children. The only thing he doesn't screw is men and very black women. I will admit he's good in bed, if you don't mind the crowded conditions. Screw, Screw! Oh, I got screwed all right; not always in bed, obviously. He'd better know the *one* thing I'm not going to get screwed on is that boat. You can make book on that!"

She whirled, her high heels digging into the cement as she crossed the veranda.

Penny stared at Blake, her eyes hard. "How could you have talked to that woman about me—about us? And I was about to tell you that I'd—."

Blake strode into his bedroom. He returned in a moment buttoning his shirt, with a jacket over his arm. He passed Penny without a word and went down the stairs two at a time. He waded out to the Coronet and climbed aboard. She heard the motors start and saw the running lights flick on. The boat pulled out into the bay.

She turned toward the bedroom and started to pack.

# Chapter 17

A few weeks after Penny's return from Africa, Alfred knocked at her door late one evening. There was no answer. He hesitated, then turned the knob, and entered. A half empty bottle of gin sat on the coffee table and an overturned glass lay on the stained carpet. Penny lay on the floor, face down. He rushed to her and turned her over. She moaned and said thickly, "Blake?"

"No, it's Alfred. Let's try and get over to the divan. Here, I'll help you."

He got her to her feet. She moved heavily to the divan and slumped down on it. Alfred stood, looking her. "Poor Mum," he said, his eyes filling with tears. "Let me make some coffee."

He patted her arm and stepped into the small kitchen, prepared the coffee pot, and set it on the stove. It perked shortly and he poured a large mug full and brought it back to her.

"Here, drink this," he said, supporting her and holding the mug to her lips.

They were quiet while she sipped the steaming coffee. Settling the empty mug down, he turned to her and brushed the straggling hair back from her face.

"I'm so sorry, Alfred," she said thickly, "to have you come home and find me like this. I thought you were coming tomorrow. I can't think what came over me."

Alfred went to the kitchen and poured another cup of coffee. Handing it to Penny, he said gently, "Drink this. I should have talked to you about this before, but I simply didn't know how."

"I'm all right now," she said, setting the mug down, and starting to rise.

He put his hand on her arm, restraining her. "No. We've got to talk about this now. You've got to stop destroying yourself, for Lucy's sake, if not for your own. You've been drinking more and more, especially since Lucy went to boarding school. You must quit before it gets the better of you. Lucy needs you and I—I need you, too. It kills me to see what you're doing to yourself."

Her eyes filled with tears. "I know, dear, I know. I say every time it won't happen again and then it does. I'm so ashamed."

"My dear, don't say that!" Alfred's voice quavered. "It's living alone like this and not eating properly—."

He carried the mug back to the kitchen. "What happened in Africa, Mum? You wrote that you had gone there—thank God you didn't take Lucy—and that you weren't able to work things out with Blake."

"He was so furious, Alfred, that I had come alone. He had counted on seeing Lucy. I simply wasn't able to talk to him. All he wanted was for me to return and bring Lucy back with me. It was impossible to reason with him. Then there was that dreadful woman saying the most awful things!"

She rose and paced the room nervously. "No, Alfred. It's over. I've held on to a hopeless dream too long. I wonder if the Blake I thought I knew ever existed. I think I made him to be the kind of person I wanted him to be, the kind of person I needed to fill my loneliness, to fulfill me." She slumped onto the divan, her head in her hands. "I know there's your father and I'm grateful to him, but it's rather like living with one's brother, even from the start."

Alfred sat by his mother and put his arm around her shoulders. "You have Lucy and me, dear."

"I know, love, and I'm truly grateful for both of you. Truly I am. It's that it's not the same." She drew back and looked inquiringly at him. "You've not been in love, have you, really in love?"

He shook his head. "No. I couldn't even think about marriage until I was ordained, and for a long time after that. I haven't let myself get involved with girls as yet. I do know, though, what you mean. I look forward to having someone who's truly mine and whom I belong to."

He stood, looking down at his mother, his gentle face grew stern. "When I was a teenager, I thought Blake was the greatest—Africa and all—but, think of it, Mum, everything he's touched has gone sour. Look what he's done to you, and to how many other women, we'll never know. I've come to think he's an evil, evil man!"

Seeing the stricken look on Penny's face, he sat next to her and drew her head onto his shoulder. "Put your faith in Christ, dear. That's the only way out of this I know. Our Lord can heal the hurts, if you allow Him, and make you whole again. I'm afraid of Blake, afraid for you and Lucy. There have been times, seeing you so unhappy, I could have killed him!"

She drew back sharply, but Alfred hurried on. "I've got over hating him. I have to forgive him if I'm to ask forgiveness for my own sins, don't you see? Christ is the answer to everything if only you'll ask his help. Promise you will, won't you?"

She nodded. "Perhaps you're right, Alfred. I've been going to church with Lucy regularly and I've enjoyed the service and the sermons, but I've never really prayed for Christ to take over my life, as you say. Maybe I was afraid it would mean giving up all thoughts of Blake, 'though in my heart, I've known it was over, even before I went back to Africa."

Tears fell down her cheeks and she said, brokenly, "It's that now I've lost all hope and hope was all I had all these years; the hope of loving and being loved."

"I don't know how I can pray when I've done things I know are so wrong. I've committed adultery, borne an illegitimate child. I've wronged your father, and you,—even Lucy. How can I ask God for favors? I can't be truly sorry, for then I'd have to say I was sorry I'd had Lucy, and I can't honestly say that!"

"You don't have to, dear. You see, God can take even evil and make good come of it. You'll see that God loves you even more than you love Lucy and me. He wants only good for you and He'll forgive you so you can come to Him without guilt."

She frowned. "I've always thought of God as the great creator of the universe, and the one who stood in judgment over us."

He smiled, and held her hand. "He is all that, but He's so much more. So many people only see that side of Him. That was why He sent His son to be one of us, to live on the earth, to suffer, and to die—like us. Jesus cared; He showed us He cared. He took all of our sins, our wrong doings, our foolish mistakes, our weaknesses on Himself. When we ask for forgiveness in His name, God sees us as pure and without blemish. He loves us—you—with so great a love we can hardly comprehend it! He doesn't see you as a sinful, wicked woman. He sees you, as I see you, as a beautiful person who's desperately unhappy because you are separated from Him. He hurts with you—for you. He wants to hold you close and comfort you with His Holy Spirit.

"You must read Martin Buber, Mum, to understand the, 'I and Thou', the personal relationship with God, and C. S. Lewis', 'Mere Christianity', and 'The Problem of Pain', along with the Bible, of course. These are men who have found a personal relationship with Jesus, and they can help you to know Him. I've brought some books with me. We'll read them together and discuss them. Each time you read the Bible, you'll find something new, things you'll feel are there just for you. You'll find God isn't some remote force sitting 'way up in heaven putting black marks by your name. He's a good and loving Father who wants you to know him and to have all the riches of the world he so abundantly provided!"

She looked at Alfred and smiled. "After all, I do have you and Lucy. God has blessed me abundantly, hasn't He?"

Alfred laughed and kissed her. "The Lord loves you, dear, and He is grieved to see you so unhappy. Because of His great love for you, He wants to give you all the good things. You have only to let go and let Him fill all the empty places that long so for love, both the giving and the receiving of it. We'll both pray tonight, and every day from now on, all right?"

He started toward to the door, then turned. "I'm to be assigned to a rectory nearer home soon. I'll be able to see all of you more often."

"I'm so glad," she replied. "Thank you, dear. You've given me a lot to think about. Already I feel lighter somehow, as if a great weight had been lifted"

After Alfred left, Penny picked up the glass and returned it to the kitchen, then came back and retrieved the gin bottle. She took it into the kitchen and started to put the cap on, then stopped and stared at it. Slowly she tipped the bottle over the sink, poured out the contents, and dropped the empty bottle in the trash. She went into the bedroom, changed into her night gown, and started to get in bed. She stopped and knelt by the bed, bringing her hands together to her lips.

\*\*\*\*\*\*\*\*\*\*\*\*\*\*\*\*\*\*\*\*\*\*\*\*\*\*\*\*\*\*\*\*\*\*\*\*

Three years passed. Blake did not write, nor did she. The ache to be with him had diminished, 'though there were times, particularly after his yearly birthday call to Lucy, that she longed for the oblivion of the gin bottle. She enlarged her circle of friends, and although she continued to live in her small apartment, she and Hubert went out together, and had people in from time to time. Alfred had continued his studies while serving as rector and would soon become a Priest. She looked forward to their long evenings together when they would discuss the stream of books he gave her to read and when they prayed together.

Lucy was in her third year of boarding school. She loved her swimming lessons. Born with the barrel chest of a champion swimmer, she won most of the inner-school meets she entered. At thirteen, she was long and leggy and wore her braids wrapped around her head, which made her look older.

That spring she returned from school strangely silent. Usually she talked like a magpie, telling Penny everything that had happened to her at school, her crooked smile lighting up her face. This time she sat primly on the divan, sipping tea with a pensive expression, not saying much. Penny came in and sat on the adjacent chair.

"Do you want to tell me about—whatever's troubling you?"

"Yes, Mum, I do, but I don't know where to start."

"As I've always said, 'At the beginning'." She started to laugh, but stopped when she saw the pain on Lucy's face. "What's wrong, dear?"

"Daddy sent me this," Lucy answered, pulling an airline ticket from her jacket pocket.

Penny took it with a trembling hand; it was a round trip ticket to Dar es Salaam.

"Lucy, I don't understand!" She dropped the ticket as if it burned her hand. "Where did he send it?"

"To my school. He's been writing to me at the school for a long time. I didn't tell you because I knew you didn't hear from him very often, and I didn't want you to worry. Most times I don't even answer, but sometimes I do when I've been in a swim meet. He likes to hear about my swimming."

She picked up the ticket and returned it to her pocket. "He wants me to come there and visit him and—I want to go. I promise, Mum," she hurried on when she saw the shocked look on Penny's face, "I promise I'll stay only a little while and come right back. I wouldn't stay even if he tried to get me to. I even told him I wouldn't come unless he sent a round trip ticket."

"Oh, Lucy," Penny turned her face away to hide the tears that sprang to her eyes. "Somehow I feared this day would come, maybe not so soon, and I've dreaded it. You must have been curious about your father all these years. We haven't even a good picture of him, have we?"

She pulled Lucy close and rocked her. "You know how precious you are to me, don't you, dear?"

Lucy nodded and gave her mother a squeeze. "I'm sorry to upset you."

"I didn't mean you to be robbed of a father, dearest," she kissed the top of Lucy's head. "It just turned out that way. No one's fault, I suppose.

"Why wouldn't he ever move to Dar, Mums? We could have all been together then, you said."

"I've never quite understood that either, Lucy dear," she sighed, still holding Lucy in her arms. "There are so many things I've never understood. I've asked myself the same question so many times. He had his reasons but—," she shook her head and smiled. "Whatever happened was worth it. I have you because of it, and that's what really matters."

She went into the kitchen and busied herself with the tea things. "Let's wait and talk to Alfred about this, shall we? He'll be dropping by in the next few days, and after all, you just returned from school, didn't you?"

"All right, Mum," she replied, looking hard at her mother. "It won't make any difference, though. I want to go and I'm not going to change my mind. I'm sorry if it makes you sad, but I have to go. That's all."

Lucy was visiting a friend when Alfred dropped in. He smiled with satisfaction and thanksgiving when he saw his mother. Her eyes were clear and she had lost the bloated look of former years. Her grooming had improved and she looked younger, although she was still overweight.

His smile faded when she turned to look at him. "What's wrong?"

"I need to talk to you." She sat on the divan and patted the cushion beside her. "My, I like it when you wear your clerical collar. You look so distinguished."

He waited for her to continue.

"It's Lucy," she said, hesitantly.

He looked at her in surprise. In spite of being overly stubborn, Lucy had never been a problem. She was a cheerful outgoing girl, doing well at school, and made friends easily.

Penny looked down at her hands. "Evidently she and Blake have been corresponding. I didn't know about it until she returned from school a few days ago. As you know, I don't hear from him anymore."

He nodded and took his mother's hand. "What else?"

"He's sent her a plane ticket to Dar es Salaam, a round trip ticket," she added, seeing how shocked he looked. "I'm afraid to let her go, Alfred. I don't know what to do. Naturally she wants to go. She's understandably curious about her father. I've never said anything to her against him, but she wonders why he never made it possible for us to be together, and I've never been able to come with a really good explanation."

Alfred stood up and walked to the window, frowning. "You're quite right, Mum, about her going. I, too, think she shouldn't go. I'll talk to her."

"I should warn you, dear, she's quite determined. I used to tell her all those stories about Africa when she was young and I thought we'd be going back there. I'm afraid I made it sound all too glamorous."

"I know. I felt the same way about Africa at about her age."

Penny twisted her hands together. "There's no way he could force her, is there? He has been most generous in providing for her. There's enough in her account to pay all the education she'll ever want. Of course, I've added to it from time to time, but most of it is from Blake. She's bright like you, dear. She may even want to go to university."

"I wish you would send it all back to him, Mum. I can take care of Lucy's expenses now, and would be glad to. Your boutique is doing better every year. We could mange."

He sat down and passed his hand the length of his face. "I'm very much against her going there—to him. Let me talk to her. I'm sure I can talk her out of it."

She started to tell him about the young girl, Kimberly, and what that American woman had said about Blake, but she didn't. *How could I even intimate a thing like that about Lucy's father? All there is to it, really, is a vague suspicion and a vengeful woman's hysterics.*

Alfred sat on the steps waiting for Lucy. When she came skipping down the sidewalk, he rose to meet her. As soon as she saw him she broke into a run, her long braids flying. When she reached him he lifted her and swung her around.

"How do you expect to look like my older sister when you let your braids down?" he teased.

"I *am* getting grown up," she laughed. "Look. I'm almost to your shoulder now."

He sobered. "Let's take a walk."

She took his hand and walked sedately beside him. "Mum sent you to talk to me about Africa, hasn't she? I want to go, Alfred, truly I do!"

"I know, dear. You've heard us talk about Africa so much, and Blake—." He looked into her deep violet eyes, seeing the anxiety there. "Naturally you're curious."

He stopped at a park bench and pulled Lucy down beside him. "It's such a long journey for a young girl and—."

She broke in. "Lots of girls at school my age go that far for holidays. One even lives in India and that's a very long way off."

Alfred laughed. "No farther than Africa, Lucy. Seriously, dear, it would be an awful worry to Mum, and to me, too, for you to go. Why don't you wait a few years, until you're older, and I'll take you. Wouldn't you like that? We'll both start saving our money, and—."

Lucy jumped to her feet and faced him. Her eyes blazed. "That's all right for you to say. You see your daddy all the time. But me, in my whole life, I've never seen mine!"

Alfred involuntarily drew back. *How like Blake she looks! That same expression, the narrowing of the eyes, the lips compressed. I've never seen the resemblance so strongly before.*

He motioned for her to rejoin him on the bench, taking her arm, but she jerked away. "Now, when I have the chance, you have to be an old spoil sport and say I mustn't! I think you're horrid!"

She started to cry and he tried to soothe her. "Darling, you can't know how we'd worry about you. It's such a long way—."

She stood over him and glared fiercely. "I'm going to go, Alfred. You and Mum have no right to say I'm not to. He's sent for me, and he's my father, even if he and Mum were never married."

"If you won't let me go," she looked at him from under stern brows, "I'll run away, that's what I'll do. Even if you take my ticket away he'll send another if I ask. I know he will."

She started to cry again and he stood up, put his arm around her, and started walking home. "All right, dear. All right, now. I'll talk to Mum. Don't cry, Lucy, and no more of this talk of running away, understand?"

Lucy sniffed and held out her hand. Alfred put his handkerchief in it. She dabbed her eyes and blew her nose, and handed it back to him, grinning her crooked little grin.

"You're the best brother in the whole, whole world."

\*\*\*\*\*\*\*\*\*\*\*\*\*\*\*\*\*\*\*\*\*\*\*\*\*\*\*\*\*\*\*\*\*\*\*\*

A month later, trying her best to hold back her tears, Penny stood with Lucy and Alfred at the plane gate. "If you need anything, anything at all, darling, get in touch with Ann and Bob Slade. Here's the address and phone number, dear, clipped to your passport. Don't hesitate to call them, they'll be so glad to hear from you. Don't forget to cable when you arrive and—."

"I won't, Mum. You're a dear, and Alfred, too. I'll let you know what plane I'll return on so you can meet me."

"They're calling for you to board now, dear," Alfred said. "God go with you."

Lucy gave her mother a big kiss and a hug, then Alfred. She turned to go but Penny ran toward her and held her in her arms once more. Tears streaked her cheeks. "I love you so much, sweetheart. Take good care of yourself and say hello to your father for me, and to Appendai, and everyone."

Lucy turned at the ramp to wave again, then entered the plane.

"She looks so grown up—and so small," Penny sobbed.

"She'll be all right, Mum. The stewardess promised to look after her, and we got word to Blake in plenty of time to meet her. She's in the Lord's hands. You mustn't worry."

# Chapter 18

The black maned lion was past his prime. The years of drought and the scarcity of game kept him lean and hungry. He and his pride did not migrate, as did most of the Serengetti lions, and as a result, they bore fewer cubs. Each year he found it more difficult to drive off the young lions who challenged his leadership of the pride. Most of the young males were his own progeny whom he had cut off when they became adolescents. Some became loners who tried to gather stray females into their own pride, or take over his. Others went off with their brothers to hunt and live out their bachelor lives together.

One young lion, with his father's thick black mane, stayed on the edge of the pride, the old lion sensing his presence, and attacking him when he came too close. The old lion's ears were tattered beneath tufts of hair. In some places chunks of ear were entirely missing. His body was scarred from the horns of buffalo and the bites of zebra. His right eye blazed out from beneath a long scar left by a giraffe's kick.

He labored to cover the distance between the two prides, then had to fight off the young males he found on his return. He slept most of the day and waited impatiently for the lionesses to make a night's kill. Many times they returned short of breath, their golden sides heaving, with no game. He made the long trek to the second pride in the dark of the early morning, hoping to find a kill there. Since he kept all the females well sired, so far, they had accepted no other male.

# Chapter 19

Lucy's plane had been flying for some hours over Africa. It had touched down in Athens for refueling and a nice couple had invited her to go into the airport with them. She enjoyed hearing the babble of sounds made by a dozen languages and the flash and sweep of national dresses. She felt as if she could sit there for hours watching and listening. Then the plane had taken off, flying over North Africa, the endless sands of the Sahara and the wild and desolate mountains of Ethiopia. Kenya was green with verdant rolling hills, the flat plains interrupted by the snow-covered expanse of Mt. Kilimanjaro. The mountain floated, seemingly unattached above the clouds.

Finally, the announcement came over the loud speakers; Dar es Salaam. With the help of the stewardess, she cleared customs, then hurried through to the main lobby. She could feel her heart pounding in her chest as her eyes searched the crowd.

She felt a hand on her arm and heard a deep voice say, "Lucy Anette?" She jumped and looked up at the huge man smiling down at her behind wire rimmed glasses.

"Are you my Da—?" She knew immediately she needn't have asked. There was no denying the resemblance between them. She felt she would have known him anywhere.

Blake thanked the stewardess profusely, and still holding Lucy's arm, parted the crowd ahead of them with his broad shoulder. He deposited her in the car and asked her to wait there while he collected her luggage.

"Oh, please," Lucy called after him, "send Mum a cable I'm here."

He nodded and walked on to the airport.

Lucy sat in the shimmering heat almost overwhelmed by the sounds and smells of so strange a place. She watched the faces of the Africans coming and going. She loved the white flowing' dhotis some wore and the rich color of the cotton fabrics of others. In spite of the excitement, the heat coupled with the long plane ride, made her drowsy. She was startled when Blake opened the door and slid in behind the wheel. The boot slammed shut, then the back door opened and a tall muscular African climbed in the back.

"This is Appendai, Lucy," Blake said. She turned and put out her hand. Appendai grinned and took her hand in both of his.

"Karibu, Memsahib Lucy."

She liked him instantly, remembering how fondly her mother had spoken of him. "Tell him my mother sends greetings," she said, looking shyly at Blake.

He relayed the message in Swahili, then turned to Lucy. "What a fine looking girl you are! You've no idea how glad I am you came."

He started the car and turned out of the parking lot. "I know you've had a long trip, sweetie, and would probably like a chance to rest up, but—."

"No, really. I feel fine—Daddy?"

Blake's laugh boomed. "By jove, that's jolly good to hear! My, what a beauty you are. How good it is to have you here."

"It's so exciting," Lucy replied, pleased at his reaction. "I never, never thought I'd actually get to Africa—to see you. I'm quite dizzy, really."

Blake laughed. "As I was saying, sweetie, I'm sure it's been a long and tiring trip, but I wanted to take you first off to the island. One of the charter planes is going there to pick up some passengers, so we can ride over. They're waiting for us right now on the tarmac."

He parked the car in the lot of a small hanger and turned to Lucy. "Do you think you can take one more short plane ride? Then we'll be home."

"Yes, Daddy. I feel fine, really I do. You shan't need to worry about me."

"I'll show you more of Tanzania later. All the game, and the people, as well as Dar, but I wanted you to see the island first."

He handed her into the small plane and the props started spinning. "I'm glad," Lucy spoke above the revving motors. "I want to see the island most of all."

Blake pointed out several places of interest along the way. They flew over the curving jutting coast of Tanzania before the plane headed out over the ocean. Appendai sat in the furthermost back seat, his face set in a frozen grin, eyes rolling.

"His first plane ride," Blake laughed. "He came over by dhow. It took some doing to get him to agree to this. He's not sure what to make of it."

They took the waiting Jeep down the length of the island as Blake pointed out places of interest, finally arriving at the house.

"This is your room," he said, "Mine's next door. My pump motor is broken so there's no running water but the boys will bring you what you need."

There was a narrow bed and a dresser, and the boys had added several vases of trailing bougainvillea. "Let me open and close the windows for you. The latch isn't working properly." He laughed. "Things have a way of rusting out this close to the water."

"It's very nice," she hastened to assure him.

"I'll leave you to freshen up, and take a nap if you wish. Come out when you're ready," he said, as Appendai brought in her bags and set them on a low table at the foot of the bed.

"The house boy will unpack for you later." Blake made a quick check of the bathroom. "Don't bother with anything now. By the by," he added, testing the temperature in the water bucket, "how is your mother?"

Lucy's face grew serious. "She's fine, Daddy. She asked that I give you this."

She opened a suitcase and handed Blake a sealed envelope.

"Please take good care of her, Blake. She's all I have—all I have in the whole world. Penny."

He stood holding the note, his face expressionless. Lucy moved to his side and shyly brought her arms up. Blake bent down and she reached up to kiss him. He picked her off the floor and held her close, his face pressed against her neck.

"It mustn't have been easy for her to let you leave."

"It wasn't, Daddy, but when she saw how much I wanted to—."

He kissed her again and set her on her feet. "Take your bath now, Lucy. We've lots of time to talk later."

He took her to dinner at the hotel that night. She had put on her prettiest frock and brushed her hair until it gleamed, letting it fall over her shoulders and tying it back with a white chiffon scarf. She had bought the dress when she was at school with money saved from her allowance. Her mother had never seen it. White, with gold butterflies embroidered on it, it had a gathered neck, and could be pulled down off her shoulders. She pinched her cheeks and bit her lips, peering closely into the mirror in the fading light. Her dark eyes sparkled under heavy bat winded brows. She turned and walked out onto the verandah where Blake waited.

He stood when he saw her, his eyebrows lifted. "How stunning you look!" He embraced and kissed her, and she imagined his lips lingered a moment as she moved closer to him. He stepped back, holding her at arms' length, and looked closely at her, letting his eyes go the length of her body. "You are getting to be a young lady!"

They walked the short distance to the hotel. Blake introduced her to the Hudsons, the middle-aged couple who managed the hotel, then to several Africans who worked in the bar and restaurant. He beamed as he observed the impression she made on everyone. They were invited to have dinner with the Hudsons who joined them on the spacious verandah that stretched across the entire front of the hotel. Blake ordered drinks for them and an orange squash for Lucy.

"All you can get now," he grumbled, "is this Chinese soda. Hope it's not too bad."

Lucy took a sip and smiled. "It's quite good, actually."

"How this country got in a position where all we can get is Chinese exports is beyond me," Blake muttered.

"You know why," Brandt Hudson said. "It's in exchange for that magnificent railroad the Chinese are building for us. Did you hear that after all this, Uganda may decide *not* to ship her copper through Tanzania? How the government's ever going to repay that loan is beyond me. Without the copper, there's not a chance."

"Amin must be crazy," Amilia Hudson shook her head. Turning to Lucy, she explained. "Idi Amin is the president of Uganda, and strange stories have been coming out of there lately. We had a young American engineer here last week. He had been hired' by the Ugandian government to do some electrical work there. Things are so bad, they had to give him an armed escort so he could do his work."

"You know," she turned to Blake, "after Amin got rid of all the Asians, he ordered medals struck to reward the men who did the ax job. He couldn't get them since only the Asians knew how to strike a medal, and they had all been killed or deported!"

Brandt broke in. "This engineer said things are terrible there. Whole villages are lined up and a crudgen given to the second man in line with orders to bash in the head of the man in front of him. He passes it back to the next, who in turn bashes his head in. The whole line goes down this way."

"What happens to the last man?" Lucy asked, shaking her head.

"He's shot," Brandt explained. "Saves bullets that way. The worst thing this chap told us is that when he was riding down the main street of Kampala, there was an army truck in front of his car. There were two soldiers riding on the front bumper, and they were smiling and waving to the people on the sidewalks. As soon as one came close enough, the soldiers took their rifle butts and bashed his head in! He said it was the waving and smiling that got to him."

"They would do that to their own people?" Lucy asked.

"Just what I've tried to tell them here," Blake exploded. "They don't know what oppression is until they find how cruel the African leaders can be to their own people. Amin stays in power through terror, and that's the only way he can hold on to the presidency."

"Surely it won't ever be like that here," Amilia interjected. "There's no comparison between Amin and Nyerere. If any of these African countries has a chance, I think it's Tanzania."

"Let's hope Nyerere can stay alive," Blake frowned. "I heard he keeps a navy gun boat off shore near his house, ready to whisk him away at the first sign of trouble. He did run off, you remember, when the army mutinied. All it took to quell the fuss was two shells from the British!"

They all laughed. "Perhaps you can have a bit of wine with dinner," he suggested to Lucy.

"I'd like that," she smiled.

"What a beauty you have there, Blake," Brandt looked at Lucy. "Your pictures don't do you justice, my dear."

"Thank you, Mr. Hudson," she smiled, one corner of her mouth curving up.

"What an enchanting smile," Amilia observed. "We're so glad you're here. Feel free to come to the hotel any time. You might get lonely when your father goes out on the boat."

"She'll be going with me," Blake countered. "If the clients don't like it, they can go in your government boats. They won't catch as many fish with your boys as they do with me, but that's their hard luck."

"How *do* you do it, Blake?" Brandt asked. "There's hardly a day your boat doesn't bring in more than any of ours. What's your secret?"

"I live right," he answered, winking at Lucy, "and I have a beautiful daughter." She flushed with pleasure as they all laughed.

"Honestly, Lucy, your father's the best fisherman in East Africa. You couldn't sail with a better captain."

"I was hoping you'd teach me, Daddy. I've never been fishing."

"Indeed I shall. We'll start tomorrow in the Coronet."

"What's a Coronet?"

"That was the larger boat with the upper deck. Remember?"

"That beautiful white and blue one?"

Blake nodded. "Right, and beautiful, she is! Did you see the name on her side?"

Lucy shook her head.

"It's the Lucy Anette. I finished repainting her last week, and renamed her."

"He's been working ever so hard on that boat since he heard you were coming, dear," Amilia smiled. "I didn't know you'd changed the name from Jessica, Blake."

"I know it's supposed to be bad luck to change the name of a boat, but what could be bad luck with a name like Lucy?"

"Shall we go in to dinner?" Brandt rose, and started toward the stairs leading down from the verandah.

They crossed the green lawn where a pit fire glowed beneath palms. The sea fell against the sandy shore beyond in slivery moonlit breakers. Servants in white coats manned several long tables spread with large trays of food. Torches lighted the area.

"We have a cook out on Saturday nights," Amilia explained to Lucy. "I think you'll especially like the fish. It's one your father shot last week, a two hundred and forty-eight pound rock cod. We kept it in the freezer until you came. You may not see another that large while you're here."

"Goodness, isn't that a frightfully big fish to shoot, Daddy? However did you manage?"

"It's a record in these waters with a spear gun," he replied. "I must remember to send it to Guinness Book of World Records."

"Would you teach me that, too, Daddy? I'd love to spear a fish. I've seen it done on the telly."

"That I will, sweetie." He moved through the line behind her, heaping his plate high. "I think you'll make a good spear fisherman, but we won't start with one that big right at first, if you don't mind. I would imagine that fellow as well over a hundred years old and you've got to be sure to get dead center of the brain on one that big."

At the end of the long line, they came to an African manning the huge pit. The fish lay on the hot coals, his body slashed with diagonal cuts. Lucy tried to imagine what a fish that size would look like in the water. They returned to the table on the verandah.

"I've never seen a place so beautiful, Daddy, 'though I like the location of your house better," she added. "Thank you for sending for me, even though Mum—."

"Here are the dancers," Blake interrupted.

A group of brightly cotton-robed Africans filed onto the lawn below. They formed a circle, feet shuffling. Three drummers sat nearby. The dancers moved slowly at first, but as the rhythm of the drum grew faster, they twisted and leaped, chanting in tune with a wailing pipe.

Lucy rose and sat on the balcony railing, enthralled.

Later, Blake joined her. "Time to go. That's about all they do, anyway, keep going around in a circle. Wait until I show you the dancing back in the bush. We'll visit some villages where they do ritual dancing—not for the benefit of tourists."

Lucy said her good-nights and thanks to the Hudsons. They were standing next to the assistant manager, an African, whom she had met earlier. She smiled and shook hands with him.

"The young Memsahib is as beautiful as a black maned lion," he said to Blake. "If the Memsahib wishes anything, please to let me know."

"Nothing now," Blake circled Lucy's shoulders, "but thanks."

The Hudsons walked arm in arm toward their apartment.

"What a shame," Brandt said.

"I know," Amilia replied. "She's a lovely girl, and Blake's such a bounder. I only hope she doesn't find it out. She obviously adores him. It's all so new and glamorous to her."

"I hope the child doesn't come down with something. He's living so—dirty, I guess you'd call it. Like letting the pump remain broken, and not having any running water. You know his boys aren't going to haul any more water than necessary up those steep stairs from the well. I was over there the other day to get back some tools he'd borrowed, and the kitchen stank! The floor was dirty and food sitting out with flies about. Imagine having the second boat boy cooking and keeping house for you! I spoke to him about it and he said the' frig was broken. Ugh!"

"What's worse," Amilia said, opening the door to their comfortable apartment, "I think he's just run out of paraffin and hasn't bothered to get more. It's always a shame seeing an Englishman go African, and that's what's happening to him. He was telling me his dog caught a sick rat! Imagine, allowing sick rats about in this country! It's a good way to spread cholera."

"Keep an eye on her, Amilia. You know her mother wrote us when Blake sent for the child. I hadn't the heart to write her what I thought about the girl's coming. It wouldn't have made any difference, probably, and would have worried her, I'm sure. I'll certainly cable her, however, if the child seems unhappy or gets looking unwell."

Blake helped Lucy climb from the shallow water over the side of the boat. Appendai followed with the fishing equipment. The water ran down his blue black skin and stood in droplets on his tight hair. He smiled at Lucy and placed a chair for her to sit on. She watched him as he moved about sorting the gear, remembering something she had read in one of her many books about Africa.

*How perfectly the African is adapted to the land he lives in; his stiff wiry hair protects his scalp from the intense sun and the rain, since it sheds water, his small tight-to-the head ears and his flat nose keep out the dust, his skin doesn't burn or overly react to insect bites and his prominent buttocks stores fat to take him through lean times. Even the yellowish whites of his eyes give him protection from the glare of the fierce African sun. His teeth stay strong and healthy from his simple diet, and most of his illnesses can be cured with native herbs and roots.*

She looked at her own olive skin, so like her father's, yet not so burnt. I *have the feeling I've really come home, that this is where I belong. Even the sea water feels natural.* She brushed the flakes of salt from her slender legs.

Blake had climbed up on the flying deck, and started the motors. He called down to Lucy. "Climb up here. You can see more."

She went up the vertical ladder and sat beside him as he moved over behind the wheel to make room for her. Appendai hauled in the anchors and the boat moved through the placid bay water.

174

"We'll go for fish today. They're getting low at the hotel. Later we'll do some reef diving. We've got to hurry to get through the pass and out of the bay. The tide's going out and it'll not be deep enough for this boat shortly. I wouldn't want to damage a screw."

He shoved the throttles forward and the boat surged powerfully. Lucy leaned back, absorbing the wind and the sun through every pore, watching Blake's face as he sat behind the wheel. *My daddy, Captain Blakely! I've not felt even the least bit strange with him, not, even at first. He's all I ever thought he'd be, strong and kind, and— protective. All those times the girls at school bragged about their fathers, and I had to sit there, and couldn't say anything about mine— except that he lived in Africa.*

*Then they found out I'd never seen him! How hateful they were. I showed them, though. I beat them at everything; in class, too—not just swimming meets._I showed them all right! I wish they could see me right now—and see him. Not one of them has a daddy like mine, not a one!*

"What's that dark place in the water?" she asked, pointing.

"That's a reef," Blake replied, turning the boat slightly to avoid it. "When the tide's out we can stand on it. There's a twelve foot tide here, and the Indian Ocean's more saline than most oceans. The sea life around the reefs are second to none in the world. I'll enjoy showing it to you."

He pointed to a large moving shadow. "That's a shark. You don't see many of those big fellows in here. The entrance is narrow, and they like to be back at sea before the tide's out. Seldom hook one in here."

"What happens if you hook one that big?"

"We could bring him in with no trouble, this size boat, but I won't have a shark on my deck. People who go out for shark are bonkers. There's no sport to it, just a test of strength dragging them in."

She leaned over the side, leaning across Blake, watching the shark's fin cut the water. "Are you scared of sharks?"

"No, not much. If they come too close I bang their noses and they go away."

"I don't think I'd be scared of sharks either, Daddy."

"That's my girl."

Lucy slipped off the knit top, letting the sunbeam down on her bare skin. She was glad she had talked her mother into letting her have a bikini. It was a modest one, but better than the one piece her mother had preferred. She drew her shoulders back, watching the slight swelling under the bikini top. She felt Blake's eyes on her. His arm brushed her breast as he swung the boat toward the narrow passage.

"Take the wheel," he said, as the boat cut into the open sea. "Head her straight out."

He sat with his arm around her, only occasionally placing his hand on hers to correct the direction.

"How wonderful, Daddy. I love it!"

"You're a natural, sweetie. I knew you would be. I'll throttle back a bit and get the lines ready. Keep her going straight. You can check your direction by looking back at the island."

She watched him move across the deck, his knees slightly bent, not faltering even when the boat rolled in a swell. She turned back to find the outline of the island was dimming.

*I hadn't dreamed it would be this wonderful and he treats me like I'm already grown up—not like a child. He's so big and strong and—*. She had heard the word 'virile' but couldn't think of it at the moment. "Sexy", she whispered.

Appendai appeared shortly and motioned for her to join her father on the lower deck as he took over the wheel. Blake had two lines out, the rods seated in sockets off the stern. He was stringing an outrigger to the tall mast rising high and to one side of the boat. "These are for eating fish," he nodded his head at the two rods on the stern. The lines cut the water's surface making washboard ridges on either side.

"These," he added, indicating the heavier rods leading to the tall spars, "are for bill fish. We may raise a sail or a marlin."

"Why is the line held with a clothes pin?"

Blake tossed the bait out, adjusting it so it slapped the surface of the water to the side of the boat's wake. He picked up the other bail, showing it to Lucy. "See? Appendai slit the mullet open and fitted those two hooks inside so just the barbs are showing underneath."

She had to look closely to discover the two metal hooks that protruded from the sewn belly.

"This leader," he held a slender metal wire leading from the mouth of the mullet; is attached to the line, and the line attaches to the outrigger. That's those poles on either side of the boat. He hooked the wire leader to the end of the monofilament. "The mouth is sewn shut so the bait won't bloat up with water. We want the big fish to think it's an injured fish flopping about."

He clipped the line to the clothes pin and raised it with a draw rope, adjusted the bait, and slipped the rod in its holder. "There. Now we can relax."

He opened a gunny sack and drew out a ripe mango. He took his knife and sliced the two sides of the fruit away from the large seed. Cutting criss-cross lines into the meat, he deftly pushed the peeling up, separating the diamonds of fruit. Handing it to Lucy, he prepared the other half. Smiling, they bit into the sweet meat.

"Umm. Delicious!" Lucy devoured the last bite and threw the skin over the side as she had seen Blake do. A large plop and a silver flash sent the hull into the air.

Blake groaned. "We have four perfectly good baits out and that ruddy fish goes for a mango skin." He leaned over the side, pulling and releasing the line, causing the bait to swing up and back. "Here," he shouted, in mock seriousness. "Here's your dinner, fish!"

Lucy laughed as she tried to wipe away the mango juice running off her chin.

"Just a minute." Blake went into the cabin and returned with a damp cloth. He dabbed at Lucy's chin and patted her chin and throat.

"It went farther down," Lucy laughed. The cold cloth felt good against her hot skin. She lowered the straps from her shoulders as he drew the cloth down into the cleft between her small breasts. She watched his brown fingers against her skin. The thick black hair nearly covered the back of his hand. He let his hand rest a moment, then moved it to one side.

"You're getting to be quite a young woman," he smiled, as he bent and kissed her mouth. She started to raise her arms around his neck when they heard one of the lines sing out.

"Strike! Blake cried, as he dropped the cloth and eased a rod out of the socket. "Watch, Lucy."

He brought the tip of the rod back sharply over his shoulder and turned the handle of the reel rapidly. As he pulled the rod up again the fish ran, taking yards of line with it.

"Big one," he grunted, as he fought to hold the rod tip up. "Sit in the chair, Lucy, and I'll let you bring him in. It feels like an intanga. He ran straight out instead of diving like a rock cod would do."

He handed her the rod and placed the end in a sockets attached to the chair. "Hold on tight and keep the tip up. Pull back when he quits running, and reel hard on the way down."

Blake quickly reeled in the other line so the rigs wouldn't get tangled. He shouted to Appendai in Swahili and the boat slowed. Lucy pulled up again and again, reeling fast as she lowered the rod tip. Perspiration broke out on her forehead.

"Keep it up. You're doing fine. Do you want some help?"

"I want to do it myself." Lucy gasped, pulling hard at the rod.

"Easy, sweetie, easy. Let the fish wear himself out. Just keep the line taut."

The reeling in became easier and Lucy relaxed a bit. Blake watched her. Her lips were parted and her eyes shone. He reached over and picked up her long thick braid and laid it on her back, running his fingers over her smooth damp skin. She smiled up at him. The water off the stern roiled as a flash of crimson broke the surface. Lucy gasped.

"Keep the rod tip up. Don't let it go forward," Blake said. "I'll gaff him."

He grasped the handle of the long hook, and catching the leader in his hand, took a swipe at the fish, and flipped it into the boat.

Lucy leaped to her feet. "Oh, he's beautiful, Daddy. He's simply beautiful!"

Blake brought out a short club and slammed the fish hard between the eyes. It gave one last convulsive jerk and lay still. Lucy knelt on one knee.

"Look at him, Daddy. Look at the dark purple spots against the red. Even his eyes are red. He's the most splendid thing I've ever seen."

Blake laughed, enjoying her excitement. "That he is, sweetie. I'm glad your first was an intanga. You'll always remember it, and they are the prettiest fish that hits a bait."

He withdrew the gaff and held the fish firmly as he worked the hook from his mouth. As he put it in the box, Lucy picked up the lure.

"This one's different, Daddy. It isn't at all like the ones you put on the outrigger."

"That one's called a feather jig and the other line like it has a silver spoon. Different lures catch different fish. The reason we used the wired bait is that a bill fish doesn't swim up and hit the bait like the others. He uses his long pointed bill to stun the fish, and as it sinks in the water, he takes it. Wait, you'll see. This is a good time of year for bill fish, and today the ocean's just right."

The line soon sang out again and Lucy landed a dog-faced tuna. Blake let her bring each fish, and boated only one himself when both lines were struck at the same time. The storage box was almost filled.

"Time for lunch, sweetie. We'll leave the outriggers out and pull the other two in. I could stand some rest and I think you could, too."

Lucy smiled gratefully. Her arms ached but she hadn't wanted to mention it. Blake opened two beers. She thought it bitter but the cool taste was good and she sipped it slowly. He brought the lunch basket up on deck and Lucy insisted on serving it. She arranged the food carefully on paper plates and opened a fresh beer for Blake. They ate hungrily. Lucy held her hands over the side of the boat and rinsed them in the sea water. Blake tossed the paper plates over the side and they watched them float for a few seconds and slowly sink.

"Guess we'd better head back," he said, calling up to Appendai. The boat described a half circle and Blake leaned back in his chair.

"The life of a millionaire." he smiled at Lucy.

She leaned back and closed her eyes.

"If you're tired, you can lie down in the cabin."

"No thank you. I like it here in the sun where I can watch the ocean. Besides, something may hit the line and I shouldn't want to miss it."

Blake's laugh boomed. "You *are* my daughter! I feel the same way about it. Let's move back on the deck, though. I don't want you to get burned."

They moved their chairs in the shade under the flying deck. She stared out over the side.

"Look, Daddy. What's that?"

They were passing what looked like a huge dark cloud hovering under the water's surface. "Manta ray," he replied. "They grow big in these waters. I've seen some that were fifty yards across. When you've become an expert diver, we'll take a ride on one. They're harmless for all their size."

Her eyes sparkled. "What fun!" Her face clouded and she turned to Blake. "How could Mum ever have left here?"

"I don't know, Lucy. I did everything I could to get her to come back after you were born but she wanted me to move into Dar. I wouldn't have liked that. Too, I wanted you to grow up on the island and know all this." He waved his hand.

"When I'm old enough, Daddy, I'll come back. You'll wait for me?"

"You know I will," he smiled, running his hand over her hair and giving her braids a playful tug. "Let's not talk about that yet. We've a whole summer ahead of us. You may change your mind about going back to England."

"But Mum—."

Blake leaned over and kissed her. Lucy caught his hand and pressed it against her cheek. "I think you're the most wonderful man in the whole world!"

They trolled for a time before the line snapped out of the clip. Blake stood up and took the rod from the holder. "Bring your chair where you can brace your feet against the stern, and put on that leather harness hanging there. We've got a bill fish on."

She had some trouble fitting into the harness and Blake helped her with one hand. The line was running smoothly off the reel, yards and yards of it. He called up to Appendai and the boat lurched forward. Blake brought the rod tip up sharply, repeating it two more time. The boat slowed.

"Want to be sure the hook's set," he said, as he fitted the rod in the leather sprocket below Lucy's waist. He snapped the harness hooks to eyes on the reel and released the rod to Lucy.

"Brace your feet now. If you think you can't hold him, call out."

The water broke far behind the boat and the great blue and silver fish leaped high out of the water. He shook himself violently, sending sprays of water splashing in the sun's rays. He seemed to be walking on the water with his broad tail, throwing his head from side to side, poised in mid-air.

"It's a sailfish, Lucy. See how big his dorsal fin is. Bring him down now. Give the rod a tug."

"He's so big, Daddy!" Lucy laughed as the big fish splashed down into the water, sending spray on all sides. "I've never seen a fish so big."

"He is that, sweetie. Careful. Don't reel now. He's sounding. Give him line or he'll break it."

He loosened the reel's brake, and the line fed out smoothly. Waiting a moment, he tightened the brake. The sailfish leaped again, but not so high this time.

"He won't shake that hook. Reel in, Lucy, he's swimming this way. Faster."

They watched a moment. The dorsal fin broke water.

"Good. You've got him coming," Blake laughed. "Now pump."

The line cut from side to side, Lucy pumping and reeling furiously.

"Good. Hold him now. Don't let him sound again. He's tiring."

The sail gave one last leap, half out of the water. He was so close Lucy could see his magnificent eye. It was a cold sea blue and as big as that of a horse. He was just off the stern.

"That's it. Don't reel any more. Hold him steady."

Blake slipped on a heavy canvas glove and picked up a flying gaff. He slipped the rope noose over his wrist, leaned over the stern, and caught the wire leader, and threw the gaff hard. The rope lengthened, and the gaff struck the fish, glancing off. It darted away in a twisting dive, tearing the leader from Blake's hand. The line went slack. Lucy started reeling as fast as she could.

"Never mind, sweetie. He's gone. He threw the hook. Let me have it."

He took the rod from Lucy's limp hand and reeled in the lure. The bait hung in shreds and one of the hooks was bent almost straight.

"Damned Chinese stuff!" Blake exploded, as he examined the hook. "Can't buy decent equipment any more."

He glanced at Lucy. Her face was stricken. "Did I do it wrong, Daddy?"

"No, Lucy. You did fine. It wasn't your fault. I probably threw the gaff too soon, wanting to be sure I'd boat him for you. I still think we'd have got him if the hook hadn't straightened out."

She tried not to show her disappointment. "He was something, though, wasn't he, Daddy?"

"Indeed he was. Now suppose you go below and lie down on the bed. It'll take us a couple of hours to get home and you've had enough for one day."

Gratefully, she went below and was asleep minutes later. She was hardly aware of Blake's lying down beside her. Later she only vaguely remembered a dream in which a monstrous blue and silver fish leaped up in front of her, and the feeling of someone gently running his hands over her body.

# Chapter 20

Two evenings later Blake and Lucy were at the hotel for dinner. The Hudsons came onto the verandah, bringing with them a tall distinguished looking African. Blake rose to greet them, extending his hand.

"Hello, there. It's been a long time! It's jolly good to see you again."

"Good to see you, Blake. I was aware you had settled here. You are well?"

"Very well, especially since my daughter is here with me. Lucy, this is Maasseemma. He's a genuine Masai. I'll introduce you to more of his people later on."

"Mr. Maasseemma," Lucy beamed. "How do you do? I've read about your people. It's super to meet you."

He bowed and took her extended hand. "It's a pleasure. I did not realize your father could produce so lovely a young lady, but the resemblance convinces me it is so."

"Come, Maasseemma," laughed Amilia, "she's only thirteen. You'll turn her head."

"I was thinking of my son, Katenga, who is in the U.S. attending Stanford. She would most likely turn *his* head all the way around!"

Blake laughed, pleased. "Sit down, all of you. We've time for a drink before we go into dinner. Let me order for you."

"What brings you here, Maasseemma?" he asked, as they sat around the table.

"My last vacation," he replied, his face serious. "I return to my tribe in a few days."

"I didn't realize that, Maasseemma," Amilia said. "Just for a visit, surely? Not—."

"No. Forever." He stared into his drink, his long slender fingers pressed against the glass. "My people need me. I am returning to be a Masai, at long last."

"But, why? You've risen high in the government and surely you can do more for your people here than if you join them permanently."

He straightened in his chair and looked pensively across the expanse of lawn toward the sea. "I have decided. Our president speaks of all Africans being brothers, that we must be concerned with the peoples of the whole continent, but my people do not want to live in the twentieth century—and they must—if they are to survive. The old way of living like nomad cattle herders is becoming impossible. We must stay in one place and farm the land. It is our only hope of survival. My people will not listen to me unless I again become one of them. That is what I must do."

He glanced at the others at the table only briefly as he spoke. Blake thought, for the hundredth time, that this was what confused most white men about the African. It wasn't that he wouldn't, look at you, it was that he looked at you when you didn't expect him to. He lived with a different rhythm.

"Can you discard western life so easily?" Brandt asked. "Can you really go back to a mud hut and to rubbing yourself with animal fat?"

"My people are always surprised when I return to the tribe. I spend a good part of each year with them and take my family, so that my son will know his roots. They are always surprised that I remember so much. But I lived with them until I was twelve, until my father took us to Zanzibar, to work on the clove plantation." He smiled at Blake, who nodded. "Any tribal boy of twelve knows all there is to know of tribal life. He knows everything by that age. Oh, there may be a few of the elders' secrets kept from him, but that is all. I returned in time to undergo the warrior's ritual and slay the lion."

Lucy's eyes widened. "You have killed a lion? How?"

He made a fierce face and drew his hand back over his shoulder. "With my spear, as all good Masai do, my dear. My son must do this also, regardless of how much western knowledge is in his head."

Blake leaned forward, his eyes narrow. "And your wife?"

"One of the things that decided me," Maasseemma grew serious, "was when I finally persuaded my mother to visit us in Dar es Salaam. She had never been there or seen our home. She insisted, though, on taking the bus and I met her at the bus station. She held on to her dignity, but I could tell she was frightened. She was my father's favorite wife, and after his death, hers was a very respected voice in the tribe. My people listened to her words. Still, she was frightened to go there."

A look of anguish crossed his face and he turned his head. "When we drove to the front of my house and I stopped the car, I saw my wife and our servants standing by the front gate. I thought, 'Isn't that a good thing! They are there to welcome her.' Then I realized my wife was there with a change of clothes for my mother—and a can of insect spray! She was going to de-bug my mother before she could enter my house! My mother would have been terribly insulted. I could not permit that. Later my wife and I quarreled about this. Although she has never been out of Tanzania, my wife has grown to far from our people. She must return to being a tribal wife."

No one spoke until Amilia suggested they go in to dinner. After they ordered, Brandt spoke, as he served the others large chunks of fruit from an adjacent tray, "You say you are going to teach your people to farm. Surely you must know how the Ujamaa Village experiment is breaking down. How can the government think of shifting three million people, almost the entire population of Tanzania, onto cooperative farms? They've had to leave their ancestors' spirits behind, their medical herbs, their cultural roots, and when they get to the land assigned to them, there's often no housing, no water, no promised plows. That's why so many are filtering into Dar. There they find no work and turn to robbery and to prostitution. Let's admit it. The African is not like the Chinese you chaps seem to admire so much. The Ujamaa Village plan isn't working."

Maasseemma laid his fork down and folded his hands above his plate. "How can a government anticipate a five year drought? We have a good chance yet, if the rains return. We have much to learn from the east. If just two million people in Tanzania could jump from the hoe to the oxen plow, it would be a revolution. It would double our living standard, triple our product! That is the kind of thing China is doing, an ancient culture dealing with the difficulties of feeding seven million people."

"But what about the Arusha Declaration?" Blake interrupted, his fork clattering on the empty plate. "You're nationalizing the banks, the mills, the sisal estates, and redirecting the school system to train students who will return to the land, to community farming. All this is breaking down, too, isn't it? There aren't enough lorries left running nowadays to distribute the produce if you could come up with it." He laughed derisively. "Are you sure that railroad with twenty thousand Chinese laborers isn't a Trojan horse?"

"Much of what you say is true, Blake." Maasseemma walked over to the tray and helped himself to more of the fruit. "I think sometimes our own ministers are sabotaging the program because

Nyerere has asked them to sacrifice also, and to go out into the villages and get their hands dirty. Yes, we have problems. But we must work, work, work!"

He stood at the table, plate in hand, staring earnestly in the distance. 'Freedom and work', we declared at the time of Uhuru. We must no longer say that. We must say, 'Freedom is work!'"

At Amilia's suggestion, they returned to the verandah. Brandt returned to the subject. "But Africans don't like to work, Maasseemma. They never have."

"It isn't that we're lazy," he replied. "Most of us don't get enough protein; milk, eggs, meat."

Blake laughed. "But if you give the African chickens, he asks only, 'Where can I sell them?'"

The Masai smiled and shook his head dolefully. 'I know. Africa is in a mess. There is a devil somewhere in Africa. I am a good superstitious African and I believe in devils. I think we will have to decide whether we will give priority to Africa or to our association with foreign rulers. Our only choice is, again, to be dependent on foreigners. We must not let this happen. The Chinese will leave when the railroad is completed. We believe that. For the rest, we must work through our problems in our own way."

"If only the European," he continued, in a low passionate voice, "would be willing to come here and *assist*. If only he could work *with* us. But no, he must be in charge and run everything, or he won't come."

"Thousands of people will starve this year if the long rains fail again," Blake said grimly. "And you'll find there won't be a white face among the dead."

There was silence at the table; each one looked down, staring into space.

"That is all the more reason," Maasseemma said, softly, "why I must return to my people—to starve with them, if necessary."

He glanced at Lucy. Her eyes were wet with tears. "There! Enough!" he cried. "You must help me celebrate my last holiday. May I be your host for coffee and brandy? For you, young lady, might I suggest a bottle of our best Chinese Great Wall Orange Squash?"

After breakfast next morning, Blake brought an arm load of diving equipment onto the verandah. "How would you like to learn to scuba dive today, Lucy?"

"Really? Indeed I would. It looked such fun on the telly. I can hardly wait."

"It is fun, but it's also very dangerous. I want you to learn all the safety rules first. They can save your life. You must do exactly as I say. Will you remember that?"

"I shall. I'll be most careful, I promise."

"All right. First, let's fit this harness on you, after you get your bathing costume on."

In her excitement she neglected closing the door to her bedroom. Blake, busy with the scuba equipment, glanced into the room, watching her strip out of her clothes. She was slim and lithe, but he saw soft curves were forming. A narrow stripe across her breasts and buttocks were noticeably lighter than her otherwise tanned skin. He watched as she caught a glimpse of herself in the mirror. Pulling on the bottom of her bikini she paused, and cupped her small breasts, forcing the nipples outward with her fingers. He heard her sigh as she studied her profile in the glass, then, she quickly put on the top and snapped it at her back. He was testing the regulators when she returned to the verandah.

"Appendai has the bottles on the beach. We'll go down there."

He fitted the harness on her, adjusting the webbing over her shoulders, and tightened the buckle around her waist.

She followed him down the steps. "I'm so excited, Daddy."

"You're a good swimmer and that's a big part of it. Remember to move slowly and keep me in sight. Don't ever go deeper than I go. I'll keep track of our down time and our depth. Your job is to keep track of me."

On the beach he showed her how to fit the bottle into the harness holder and how to attach the hose with the regulator on it.

"The regulator has a valve on it that permits you to breath the bottled air when you inhale, and send the air out into the water when you exhale. Breath naturally; slow and steady. Don't gulp, and above all, don't panic. If you get in a tight situation, stop and think. There's always a way out if you stay calm and don't start flailing about. You've practiced enough in the pool at your school with the mask and snorkel to know how to clear your mask under water, and to breath

187

through a mouthpiece. This is much like that except you don't have to worry about keeping the top of the snorkel above water when you want air. You can go and sit on the bottom and be one with the fishes!"

Lucy placed the regulator in her mouth and took a breath, hearing the valve click into place when she exhaled. After a few breaths, she removed the mouthpiece. Blake reached over and turned the air off at the top of the tank.

"Good. Now get your flippers on and we'll strap you into the harness. I want you to learn to put on your equipment by yourself. Sit down and slip the straps over your shoulders, then buckle the waist straps."

She snapped the last buckle and tried to rise, but the weight of the tank was to much for her.

Blake laughed. "Hold on a moment, I'll help you."

He swung his harness on and reached down to help her up. "Reach in the back and turn the air on. The emergency valve for when you run out of air is next to it. Don't get them mixed up. Test the regulator again before we go into the water."

He buckled a weighted belt around her middle, then placed a belt solid with weights around himself. He showed her how to release the belt. "If you need to come up quickly, take off the belt and hold it in one hand. Remember, never hold your breath. Keep inhaling and exhaling steadily, and never shoot to the surface. You can get an embolism that way. Do everything slow and easy."

Lucy nodded, and copying Blake, put the regulator in her mouth, and followed him into the water. They swam for a good part of the morning, Blake teaching her how to ditch her equipment and to dive down and put it back on under water. She saw a few stray fish and retrieved some cowrie shells. She loved swimming just above the bottom, arms at her sides, flippers barely moving as she felt at one with the sea and all things that lived there. Blake motioned with his thumb. They broke surface and removed the regulators, treading water.

"You did fine, Lucy, but I think we've had enough for one day. Tomorrow we'll dive the reefs."

"I love this, Daddy. I could stay in the water forever!"

The next morning Blake steered the small boat out toward the reefs. Appendai had taken the Coronet out for two days with sport fishermen. Lucy had waited impatiently while the big boat had been readied, afraid Blake would change his mind and go with Appendai.

Finally, they put all the diving equipment on board and she asked permission to sit on the bow of the boat. She gazed down into the clear water as they pulled away from the island. It was like looking through a pane of glass far down to the waving sea grass separated by stretches of serrated sand. A large green sea turtle broke the surface ahead of the boat. Blake cut the motors.

"Slip these on, Lucy," he said, as he handed her her mask and snorkel. "Hold on to the sides of his shell. A bit of pressure will turn him. Go ahead. It's fun."

Lucy slipped over the side with Blake just behind her. He outdistanced her getting to the diving turtle, grasped the shell, and steered the animal back toward her. He placed her hands under his and gave the shell a sharp push upward. The turtle's head came out of the water, followed by Lucy and Blake.

"You've got him now," Blake laughed. "Go ahead."

Lucy tipped the shell downward, keeping the turtle just below the surface. She turned him right and left as he paddled furiously, trying to escape her. Finally, he made a determined dive downward and Lucy was unable to tilt him up. She held on as long as she could, then with her lungs hurting for air, let go, and came gasping to the surface. Blake caught her in his arms and help her as she choked and coughed before getting her wind.

"That was great," she laughed, hugging Blake and kissing him. Blake's lips parted and she felt the tip of his tongue on her mouth. She parted her lips and felt his tongue touch hers. His arm tightened around her and she pressed her body close to him. Blake broke away, pointing to the drifting boat, and swam toward it.

"I'll race you," Lucy cried.

He had barely touched the boat's stern when Lucy caught him. He circled her waist with his arm. His other hand came up and rested over the small protuberance beneath her bikini top. He looked down at his hand on her.

"Does that feel good, Lucy?" he asked, watching her face.

"Yes. I like it. It makes me feel warm all over."

*That feels so good when he does it. It's different from touching myself. I could stay here forever, in this warm water, with his hand moving over me. It's like a warm soft dream, and I want to melt into him—to be part of him.*

She pressed against him.

"The boat's getting away again," he laughed, and swam over to catch it. "Come on. I'll give you a boost over."

"Let the ladder down," he called, after she had climbed aboard and soon they were on their way through the clear water toward the reef. She stood beside him, with his arm around her waist and her head against his chest. He kissed her once more and she responded eagerly.

Shortly he stopped the motors and dropped anchor. As he helped her on with her tank, he said. "There are two things you want to watch out for. The lion fish and the stone fish. The lion fish is easy to see as long as you don't put your hand into a crevice without looking first. It's got long wavy fins that are brown and gold, and each one has a poison sack that'll hurt, and make you pretty sick. The stone fish is harder to see. He lies motionless on the coral and is like a chameleon; he can be red with purple spots, or orange with black spots, or whatever. If any part of you touches him you won't live thirty minutes, and you'll be screaming in pain all that time. It's best not to put your hands on the coral at all and don't stand on it either. Did I frighten you?"

"A bit. I'll be careful."

"Good. Sit on the edge of the boat and fall backwards. Wait in the water until I join you."

She went over with a splash and sank down. The tank and the weighted belt weren't heavy or cumbersome in the salt water. She stopped a few feet above the bottom, only a short distance from the reef and she stared in wonder at the waving fan coral above the giant brain coral. The colors were brilliant.

Water washed against her as Blake fell past her. He started swimming, bubbles driving upward from his hose. She realized how much the water magnified an object. Blake looked a fourth again bigger than he really was. She watched him as he turned and beckoned to her. Her eyes widened as she stared at him. Except for his harness and the knife around his calf, he was naked. Her eyes riveted to his genitals. She had never seen a man nude before.

He beckoned again and she swam to him, taking his hand. They circled the long reef. The myriad of colors and exotic fish made her head reel, feeling unable to take it all in. Each portion of the reef was different, different in form as well as color. Blake swam down, stopping just above a green and yellow coral that lay flat on the ocean floor. He put one hand out to stop Lucy's descent, and with the other, drew a finger across his throat. She stared, but could see nothing, although she knew the sign meant danger. She held herself motionless while Blake pulled his knife from the sheaf strapped to his calf. He swam with the knife down to the coral, and thrust quickly into it. The top of the coral convulsed and a gaping hideous mouth came open. The sides of the stone fish heaved, it's flat top pinned to the coral by the knife's point. Its face contorted, long tendrils hung from it. Slowly the color of the fish faded as its jerks diminished. Finally it lay inert, its body a lifeless beige color. Blake lifted the knife and shook the fish off the point. He looked at Lucy. She nodded and drew her forefinger across her throat. Blake replaced the knife and swam ahead.

They entered the wide mouth of a cave. A large shape moved on the far side. He motioned for her to approach cautiously. She inched forward, barely moving her flippers. As she drew closer, she saw the shapes of three large fish sitting motionless on tucked under tails. Their open mouths were as large as their bodies. They looked so huge to her, even larger than Blake. Several brightly colored fish dated in and out of their moving gills. One of the giant fish turned his head so that his eye looked directly at Lucy. She held her breath. The fish pushed its body up with its tail, turned, and swam toward her. She whirled and beat her flippers and arms as fast as she could, and was at the cave's entrance when Blake caught her. He held her fast until she stopped struggling.

When she was quiet he took her hand and they swam back to the anchor chain. She climbed the chain until her head broke water. A moment later Blake appeared. They removed their mouth pieces and shoved their masks above their foreheads.

"Are you all right, Lucy?"

She was trembling and breathing hard. "Yes, but I was so scared! Were those big fish sharks?"

"No," Blake smiled. "They were big rock cod. They're harmless. That's a cleaning station and they often go there. Didn't you see the clown fish cleaning their gills?"

"Oh dear, I panicked, didn't I? They looked big enough to swallow me! I'm sorry."

"That's all right. I'm glad I caught you. If you had come to the surface as fast as you were going, you could have hurt yourself badly. Now, take it easy and follow me. I saw some big lobsters up near the ceiling of the cave and I want to get a couple for dinner."

"Are we going back into the cave then?" she frowned.

"Yes. You must. If you stopped now you might never be able to bring yourself to go into a cave again. It's like falling off a horse; you must climb back on."

She tried to still her shaking. Blake climbed the ladder and reappeared in a moment with the spear gun. She watched him as he descended, his genitals swaying as he stepped down each rung. She had her regulator and mask in place when he joined her at the anchor chain.

"Remember to stay absolutely still if you feel scared. Even if it had been a shark, that's the best thing to do. If you start flailing about he will think you're a wounded fish and that will trigger him. You must steel yourself. Ready?"

He pulled himself down the anchor rope and swam toward the cave's entrance and she followed. Once again in the cave she hung motionless as she watched Blake float upward. The cocked spear pointed toward the ceiling and the point flew from the gun. A large lobster struggled on the point of the spear. Blake grasped the shaft and forced the spear head into the sand on the floor of the cave. He took his knife and drove it just below the lobster's head. It lay still. Lucy moved aside as the three large fish filed past her and out the mouth of the cave.

Blake pulled the lobster off the spear point and handed it to her. She took it gingerly, the spiny points sharp against her hand. He shot twice more, missing once, and bringing down another lobster with the second shot. Lucy swam to the top of the cave where the water stopped a few inches from the coral ceiling. She saw a half dozen lobsters clinging to it. Blake motioned that it was time for them to leave and she turned and swam to the cave's entrance.

She stopped suddenly. Her last intake of air had produced nothing. She adjusted the mouth piece and inhaled again. Nothing. Her eyes felt as if they were bulging from their sockets. Blake swam to her and took his regulator out of his mouth. In the same gesture he tore Lucy's regulator from her mouth and placed his own between her lips. She inhaled deeply. He reached over and turned a knob on her tank, then replaced his regulator with hers. She blew hard to clear it of water, then inhaled, nodding as bubbles floated up from the hose. Blake replaced his mouth piece and they swam slowly to the boat.

Blake removed his tank at the foot of the ladder and handed it to her. He climbed into the boat and reached down for the tanks, hauling them over the side. By the time Lucy had climbed the ladder, Blake had his shorts on.

He pushed aside a few wet strands of hair from her forehead. "I think we both need a beer."

"I'd enjoy that," she replied, flopping into the deck chair.

He returned with two beers and sat next to her. "You did well there. You didn't panic."

"What happened? I breathed but there wasn't any air."

"You had used up a lot when we were in the cave the first time. You breathe harder when you're scared. I turned on your emergency valve and gave you enough air to get back to the boat. You did just the right thing. You didn't panic and you stayed still. I'm proud of you. I know a lot of grown-ups who couldn't have done that."

She smiled with pleasure. "Thank you." Then she added, mischievously, "Do you think I'm grown up enough to swim like you did?"

He looked puzzled.

"I mean—starkers?"

He laughed. "Any time. I prefer to swim that way when I can. I enjoy it more."

"I've always wanted to, but I'd never the chance." She was laughing with him, looking sideways at him through long lashes.

"You have now. You see that little outcropping of coral there?" He pointed to rocks jutting up near the leeward side of the boat. "On the other side is a small stretch of sand. We'll have lunch there. Rest a bit while I get the things out of the ice box. I'll swim our lunch over and meet you."

She watched him move about the boat, stopping occasionally to rub his hands over his hairy chest and shoulders. He seemed to be caressing himself.

*How good I feel with him. It's as if there's only the two of us in the whole world. And he loves me more than anything. I know he does.*

"All right," Blake grinned. "Off with your costume and over the side." He began to unbutton his shorts.

She slipped out of her bikini and stood on the gunwale. Glancing back, she saw him standing, naked, holding the cooler. His eyes were on her slender body as she dove cleanly into the clear water and swam with long easy strokes toward the coral island. She waded onto the strip of sand as Blake rounded the island, swimming on his back, one hand holding the ice chest balanced on his stomach. She helped him carry it to a sheltered spot under a coral ledge where they ate.

When they finished they walked to the water's edge and rinsed their hands. Lucy squatted by the clear shallow water watching a cloud of small iridescent fish weaving in and out of the submerged coral. Suddenly Blake's hand scooped a shower of water on her. She gasped, then laughingly splashed him with one hand, trying to hold his hand with her other one. They grappled in the shallow water, then stumbled back together, falling on the sand, their arms about each other.

She brought her arms up around his neck and turned her face to his. He leaned down and kissed her, gently at first, then with passion as he felt her tongue searching for his. His hand came up, rubbing back and forth across her chest, coming to rest on her breast.

"The boys will be after you one of these days, sweetie, or have they already?"

"There's a boy down the street," she said, shyly, holding very still. She liked the feel of his hand on her, the gentle massaging. "He's always teasing me and wanting to see my 'chicken': says he'll show me his 'rooster'. But I wouldn't."

"Did you want to?"

"I was sort of curious but I didn't like him very much."

Blake turned away and pulled himself into a sitting position. He caught her wrists and pulled her up beside him.

"Do you ever play with your own 'chicken'?" he asked, smiling at her.

"Sometimes, but Mum said I mustn't. She said it wasn't good for me."

"All little girls do. Doesn't she know that?"

Lucy shook her head.

Blake stood and pulled her to her feet. "I think it's time you knew a few things, but not from some shirt-tailed boy down the street.

"Come," he added. "Let's take a swim."

They sailed back to the island in the late afternoon. They climbed, laughing, hand in hand up the steep steps. A figure rose to meet them on the verandah.

"Mimi," Blake cried, dropping Lucy's hand and bounding up the remaining stairs. He wrapped his arms around the small woman, lifting her off her feet, and swung her around. Lucy stood on the edge of the verandah, watching with narrowed eyes.

"Who is this lovely child?" the woman asked, speaking with a thick German accent. She casually circled Blake's waist with a possessive arm.

"This is my daughter, Lucy Anette. You know, I've written to you about her. Lucy, this is an old friend of mine from Munich, Countess Mimi von Frome."

Lucy extended a limp hand and withdrew it quickly.

"Sit down," Blake said. "Let me offer you a drink."

Lucy watched the woman. Tiny, wearing an exquisitely tailored dress and very high heels, her reddish blond hair was perfectly in place. A gold bracelet set with diamonds circled one wrist and a large star ruby surrounded with emeralds flashed in the late afternoon sun.

"She's ancient," Lucy thought, noticing the fine lines around the woman's eyes and the deep parenthesis at the corners of her mouth. "Her teeth are all crooked and stick out, too."

Mimi accepted the drink with a tiny, almost childlike hand. Lucy noted that the flesh was flabby around her upper arms.

"What would you like, Lucy?" Blake asked.

"I think I'll bathe and rest a bit," she replied, moving toward the bedroom. She stopped at the door and turned around. "Mayn't we eat here tonight, Daddy.? I don't feel like going to the hotel."

"Would you join us for dinner here, Mimi?" Blake asked.

"Sorry. I'm here for only one night with my sister. We fly to Arusha late tomorrow to go on safari. I just wanted to pop over and surprise you—for old time's sake— Couldn't you and the child join us at the hotel?"

Blake looked questioningly at Lucy. "I'd really rather have something here, Daddy."

195

"Very well. I'll have the boy prepare a fish curry for you. I'll go on over to the hotel, but I'll be back later on. You'll be all right, won't you?"

"I suppose so," she replied, walking into her bedroom. She closed the door with more force than was necessary. As she sponged off, wishing there was some way to take a long hot shower, she heard Mimi's high excited voice interspersed with Blake's low rumbling tones.

"How long has it been, Blake? I was trying to think just yesterday."

"Ten years, anyway," he replied. "I remember you were the first woman I'd had since my wife went back to England."

"I remember. You said you'd waited over two years for her and the two years were up, and more. We had a lovely week, didn't we, Liebling?"

"Indeed. I've thought of it often. And now you're here, but you've brought your sister. I hope you've separate rooms."

"I asked for two rooms, but they were so crowded at the hotel, we are sharing one. I'd hoped—."

"We'll work out something—for old time's sake," Blake laughed. "What's happened to that wealthy husband of yours?"

"Ah, Kourt. He's doddering, my pet. He's senile half the time and thinks I'm his first wife. Not that' *that* means anything. He's not capable—. But then, he's so very rich!" Mimi giggled.

"So you take lovers?"

"What else can one do? Even so, it is very difficult. I must always travel with a relative. Usually it is one of his family, but this time I pleaded for my sister. I'm meeting Jock on safari. My sister is broadminded, thank goodness."

The bracelet jangled as she lifted the glass to her lips. "Jock is not so good in the bed as you, my pet, but he is—how do you say—more available. He's young and quite innocent, really. I'm glad he's not to meet that beautiful daughter of yours. I think I should lose him."

"She's just thirteen and not ripe yet," Blake laughed. "Still, I'm glad, too, she's not to meet Jock. Maybe, I'll teaching her a few things myself first."

"You are a dirty old man," Mimi laughed. "But you are right. I had an uncle who taught me. I've never regretted it."

196

Lucy lay on the bed, the sheet cool against her bare body. She heard Blake in the next room, water splashing as he changed for dinner. She heard his and Mimi's fragmented conversation as they talked through his open door.

"You could come here and scrub my back like you used to," he teased.

Lucy heard the stiletto heels cross the verandah. There were sounds of muted laughter. "You still rise to my touch, don't you, love?"

"Hey, I said my back! You're on the other side."

"There's nothing so interesting there. I like the front better."

"You'd better stop that," he laughed. "I'll be going to dinner with my shorts tented!"

"Let us dine quickly and hurry into the bed," Mimi called from the verandah.

"Right-o," Lucy heard him say. "In a moment."

He opened Lucy's door softly. She closed her eyes and lay rigid.

"She's sleeping," she heard Blake say, as the door went shut. "We can come back here after dinner. She sleeps soundly. We won't disturb her. I'll tell the boy to leave her dinner on the stove. She may wake and eat later."

Lucy lay, listening to the kitchen sounds, then heard a soft, "Memsahib?" at the bedroom door. She didn't answer. The boy left and she heard the back door close. She twisted and turned on the bed. The sheets were wrinkled and damp with sweat.

*What does he want with that wrinkled old bag?*

She jumped from the bed and walked into the kitchen. She lifted the lid from the pan on the stove. Taking a long spoon, she took several bites of the fish curry, then wrinkled her nose, and clapped the lid back on. She walked out onto the verandah, then ran down the steep steps to the water's edge. Standing still for a moment, she looked down at her naked body.

*Why would he want her when he could have me? Oh, why am I his daughter? Why couldn't I have been his wife? I'd have made him a better wife than my mother did! They couldn't have drug me away from here with wild horses. I'd have stayed and even had my baby on this island, if I'd had to.*

197

She plunged into the tepid water, swimming with long hard strokes. *I hate her, hate her! 'Countess', is it? I could kill her! I hate her. I hate—him!*

She swam harder, trying to escape the revulsion of her own thoughts. She rubbed her hands on her body, forcing the salt into her pores. *I feel dirty, so dirty!*

She turned on her back and floated, watching the last rays of the sun bobble across the still water. She felt a sudden pain in her abdomen and turned over quickly, jack knifing in the water. She turned on her back again and felt hot tears sliding down her cheeks. The pain hit again.

*I could die out here and he wouldn't even know until it was too late. He probably wouldn't care! I wish I had never come here.*

She swam slowly toward shore, stopping now and then when the pain hit. She made shore and walked hesitantly up the steps. Once, she stopped and gagged, wanting to vomit. She went into Blake's bedroom and sat on the edge of the bed. "Mrs. Hudson," she thought.

She slipped into a dress and thongs and left the house, walking toward the hotel. She stopped once and gagged, leaning against a palm tree to steady herself. Walking around in back of the hotel, she stopped at the door of the Hudson's apartment, and knocked softly. Amilia opened the door.

"Lucy, child! You're white as a sheet! Come in, dear. What's wrong?"

Lucy stumbled past her. "Bathroom," she gasped.

Amilia put her arms around Lucy's shoulders and led the faltering girl through the bedroom. She held onto her while Lucy vomited again and again. She gave her a glass of water, telling her to rinse her mouth, then led her to the bed, and eased her onto it.

"You're hair's all wet, child. We'd better dry it. You'll get chilled." She went into the next room and called Brandt on the phone, asking him to come to the apartment, then returned to Lucy and rubbed her head with a large towel.

"Slip out of that dress, dear, and put on one of my nightgowns."

She helped the girl into the gown and covered her with a light blanket. Lucy lay back and closed her eyes. "Thank you, Mrs. Hudson. I feel so much better now."

"You'll stay the night, dear. Call me if you need me. I'll be in the next room."

Brandt came in as Amilia closed the bedroom door. "Lucy's in there," she said, answering Brandt's questioning look. "She has a badly upset stomach, but she doesn't seem to be running a temperature. Something's terribly wrong; it's as if she's in a daze. I wonder where Blake is?"

"I just came through the dining room and saw him with the Countess and her sister at dinner. I wondered why Lucy wasn't with them, but I hadn't a chance to stop and ask. The Countess is an old girl friend of Blake's, isn't she?"

"Every woman Blake's ever met is an 'old girl friend'," Amilia said, disgustedly. "I wonder if that's what wrong with the child? She's become so enamored of him."

"Surely you're not suggesting—?" Brandt looked startled.

"I'm not sure *what* I'm suggesting. I only know I was afraid something like this would happen. What should we do? I've told her to stay the night here."

"I think we should cable the mother. I don't like the way things are going. Did I tell you one of our boys said there was a chicken head, nailed to the tree in front of Blake's house this morning? It would be like Blake not to have paid any attention to it.

"A chicken head!" Amilia shuddered. "I wonder who wants to put a curse on him? It could be one of Abhurdamoni's family; the sons are old enough for that now. They've always known Blake was responsible for their father's death."

"Yes, it could be. I've seen stronger men than Blake sicken and die with this sort of thing. You remember our cook in Mombasa? He was healthy one week and dead the next, and it works with white men, too."

"I know. I was thinking of that British judge. He finally had to leave and go to Dar, didn't he? Every time he returned to Mombasa, he fell ill. He ended up leaving Africa altogether, didn't he?"

"As I remember, yes. It's a strange business, that."

"You know," Amilia lowered her voice, "Blake's too stubborn to leave this island, much less stay away for good. I know we can't explain it, but we've both seen it happen too often not to believe it. They either get sick or have a fatal accident."

"And it always starts with a chicken head, at least, in east Africa."

They sat silent for a moment, then Amilia spoke. "I think you're right. We should cable Penny."

Brandt started to leave.

"Wait. You know the Slades are friends of hers. Why don't you get them on the short wave. I'm sure they're at the farm. Tell them what's happened and ask them to call Penny. Perhaps they could meet her plane and fly her on over here. Tell them Blake knows nothing of this, but we think it best. I understand the Slades were planning on coming on over in a few days, in any case, to see Lucy."

"That's a good idea," Brandt replied. "I'll get in touch with them right away. Then I'll tell Blake Lucy's not feeling well and is here for the night."

"Good. With luck, Penny should be here by the day after tomorrow. I'll keep an eye on Lucy until then—as best I can. Tell Blake he can look in on her tomorrow."

"That's fine, dear." Brandt gave her a brief kiss. "I'll have your dinner sent in. Watch her for any fever. The way that man's living it wouldn't surprise me if she's seriously ill."

Amilia turned back toward the bedroom. She opened the door and walked to the bed. Lucy turned in her sleep, pulling the cover off. Amilia spread it back on, tucking it in. She felt Lucy's forehead. It was cool.

"Mum," Lucy murmured, and twisted fitfully on the bed.

Blake stopped at the apartment the next morning. Lucy was sitting up in bed, picking at a breakfast tray. He bent to kiss her, but she turned her cheek to him.

"How's my girl?"

"My tummy hurts," she replied, not looking at him.

"She slept well," Amilia said. "Some time in bed and a bland diet should put her right as rain. But look at her poor skin; it's parched. Really, Blake, you—."

"Sun's good for her," Blake laughed, and patted Lucy's head. "You'll be fine by tomorrow. Take it easy today, sweetie. I promised Mimi some fishing before she leaves this afternoon, so I'll be off shortly. You get some rest. We'll go out with the spear gun tomorrow. You'd like that?"

He turned to Amilia. "Thank you for taking care of her. We should bring back enough fish today to stock your larder. I'll look in when we return."

He came back late that afternoon. Lucy was sitting in the living room in her robe. "Mrs. Hudson went to the house and brought some of my things down. She wants me to stay here one more night."

Blake nodded. "That's fine. Do you think you'll be fit to go out on the boat tomorrow?"

She hesitated a moment, then smiled with her mouth tilted upward at one corner. "I'm sure I shall. I'll be at the house shortly after breakfast,—Daddy."

"I'll be going to the plane to see Mimi off, so I'll see you in the morning." He started to kiss her, but she bent her head over the magazine in her lap.

The next morning she was up and dressed when the Hudsons came out of their room.

"You look rested, dear," Amilia said, "but are you sure you want to go out in the boat today? Perhaps tomorrow—."

"I'm fine, Mrs. Hudson. Truly I am. I'm sorry to have been such a bother. But I especially want to go today. Blake—Daddy's going to teach me to spear fish. It's important that I go."

"You're no bother, child. Don't hesitate to come any time and especially if you're not feeling well. Wouldn't you like some breakfast?"

Lucy shook her head. They walked to the hotel lobby and Lucy waved as she started back to the house.

"Message, Bwana," the clerk called from behind the desk.

Brandt hurried to the short wave set and placed the ear phones on his head. Shortly he joined Amilia, who was sitting in the dining room.

"That was Bob Slade," he said. "Penny will arrive in Dar at noon today. Her son's coming with her."

"I'm glad to hear that. He's a priest in the Anglican church, isn't he?"

"Yes. Fine young man, I've heard. Bob and Ann will meet the plane. David will fly them all over here after that. I wish we could have kept Lucy another day."

"I tried, dear, but she wanted to go, and I couldn't think of a good reason for her not to—"

She nibbled a piece of toast. "I wish I could shake this awful sense of apprehension. Something about Blake and the girl keeps nagging at me. I can't place my finger on it."

201

He looked at her worried face, and smiled faintly, patting her hand. "One more day won't hurt, and then things will get sorted out, I'm sure. You're not to worry."

# Chapter 21

Years and the prolonged drought had made their mark on the black maned lion. He returned to the first pride one day with only the flesh of a flamingo in his belly. It was not his favorite food and he had left part of the carcass to the vultures and the Maribou storks. His stomach rumbled. He lay close to a young female who had borne four cubs a scant three months before. Only one remained alive. It nuzzled the old lion's stomach, mewing with hunger, but the male batted it to one side with a hard swipe. The cub yelped in pain and surprise, a red streak forming on its side. The lion rose and walked over to the cub, scenting the blood. The lioness moved quickly between the two. She sensed the old lion was hungry enough to devour the cub, a thing not unknown in times of famine. Two of the other lionesses joined her and the three drove the old lion off. He paused once, looking back, but the females charged again, and he trotted off toward the high country.

When he reached the second pride he found a young golden lion standing in front of the lionesses, his head raised high above his shoulders, his tufted tail erect, and twitching dangerously. The old lion roared, the sound carrying a mile or more. He circled the intruder, trying to reach the lionesses, but the young lion charged, leaving a deep gash on his flank. He ran a few paces and stopped, hesitant. The young male roared, the sound climbing higher and higher until it split the ears.

The group of Masai warriors camped nearby grew silent. They had covered themselves with ashes, making geometric designs with red ochre that leaped out of the gray-white ashes. Eerie light fled up and down their wild faces. A last gourd passed from hand to hand. In his turn each warrior bent his head over the gourd filled with warm cattle blood and laced with milk and urine.

Their thick hair was elaborately braided, stiff with ochre and animal fat. They glanced at one another as the reverberating lions' roar died away. With few words they grasped their spears and fitted their arms into shield straps. Each had one leg wrapped around the upright spear shaft as they stood, stork legged, in a tight circle around the dying camp fire. The moon was full, making the low hills a contrast of deep shadows and bright surfaces. They had to travel now to find the lion.

This last secret rite was the climax of seven years of becoming warriors. During all these years the young men had lived apart from the village. Their hair had grown long and was braided in intricate styles, pulled low over their foreheads with a beaded knot lying between their eyes. During this last rite each initiate would undergo his duel with the lion. If he survived he would enter the final ceremony. His head would be shaved, care taken to preserve each strand lest it fall into the hands of an enemy and used by a witch doctor to cast evil upon him. With his head clean shaven he would be an 'old man' and an elder of the tribe.

One young warrior stood even taller than the others. He was naked except for the beaded bracelets that indented his biceps. His nostrils flared as he caught the pungent scent of lion. Before they had left the village to search out the lions, one of the young girls had brushed against him. His loins had grown hot. He, like his father, has been to the States to school. He wondered if he could ever again take a woman in primitive sensual pleasure. The exotic discoveries of western indulgences were still with him. Remembering the pink and white California girls and how they had coveted his lean muscled burnt sienna body, he shook himself and turned his face toward the hills where the lion roared.

The old lion turned and slowly made his way toward the south. At dawn he came upon a herd of wildebeest. They were migrating in a long galloping line as far as the eye could see. He was not swift enough any more to hunt by chasing the prey, so he crept as close to the moving line as possible, and settled himself upwind, hidden behind a low bush. He lowered his head and only the tip of his tail moved across the ground to betray his presence. For almost an hour he waited before a yearling broke from the long line and veered toward him. He waited, trembling. The calf leaped to clear a bush.

With a roar that stopped the wildebeest in mid-air he sprang and covered the few yards to the terrified animal. The animal whirled, but before he could touch the ground, the lion leaped on his haunches. His claws too sharp to hold, they cut deep ribbons across the sloping back, ripping the muscles. The wildebeest, eyes rolling, faltered. His hind legs sagged. The lion leaped across his back and bit deep into his neck, severing the spinal cord. The twitching animal lay still, mouth open, eyes glazed. The last of the single file of wildebeest thundered by, hardly glancing at their dead brother. They knew they were safe from the lion now. He circled the kill and tore into the soft underbelly.

The Masai followed the lion spoor in the soft morning light. Here and there drops of blood clung to the tips of the tall grass. Maasseemma glanced at his son. Their eyes met. The lion's spoor was large. The animal would weigh close to five hundred pounds. Maasseemma could not help but wish it were not so big a lion. That meant he would be old and experienced. He looked away lest the young man sense his apprehension.

An elephant, his tusks held high and trunk extended, crossed in front of them. They drew back until he had passed, then fanned out to pick up the lion spoor again.

"I can still track, anyway," he thought. "I wonder how it will be when we meet the lion?"

They heard the old lion feeding in the tall grass. He was intent on the kill, filling his empty belly, unaware of impending danger. Silent, crouching down, the Masai formed a large circle. They paused while the circle was completed, then crouched down. There was no sound except the faint rustling of the yellow grass as they closed the circle. The lion's head rose above the kill. His nose wrinkled and he sniffed the air. He came cautiously to his feet, raised his head, and looked around. An ash white body moved a few yards away, catching his eye. He crouched low, paws gathered under him, body tense.

The warriors leaped upright. Yelling in high-pitched screams they danced the circle closer. The lion rose and roared, showing his long yellow incisors. He turned away from the advancing line of leaping warriors only to find the circle closing in around him. He twisted back and ran for an opening between two of the advancing men. A spear whistled through the air and pierced the ground at his feet, the quivering shaft upright. He bit the spear, broke it, and spat it out. He circled, pivoting on his back paws, ripping the grass from the earth.

The circle was tight now. There was no space between the screaming men. The initiate stepped forward, standing very close to the lion. He forced the shaft of the spear into the ground, standing it directly in front of him, the steel point above his head. He raised the shield to eye level. Trembling, but unflinching, he screamed at the lion, taunting him. The lion roared and sprang upon the unmoving

205

warrior. The point of the spear entered his broad chest, just missing his heart. The weight of the lion bore the man backwards. The thick cowhide held against the lion's ripping fore claws, but his hind claws found their mark and dug deeply into the exposed thighs of the man.

Maasseemma leaped forward, spear raised, and drove it deep behind the shoulder of the lion. The animal stiffened, and with one last powerful rake of his claws, fell heavily on the prostrate man. A half dozen warriors drove their spears into the black and golden coat. They pulled the limp animal from the form beneath and helped the warrior to his feet. Blood streamed from his thighs as he swayed between his companions. Maasseemma reached down and pulled the spear imbedded in the lion's heart. He pressed the flat sides of the point against his son's cheeks, leaving blood marks on either side. He untied a small bag from around his neck and shook some herbs from the pouch. Bending down, he took a handful of earth which he mixed with the herbs and saliva making a paste. He knelt and plastered the paste on the deep wounds of his son's legs. The young man was limp with relief as the pain subsided.

Two of the warriors skinned the animal out with flensing knives. They placed the hide over the shoulders of the victor. Maasseemma led the jubilant leaping dance around the fallen lion and the warrior.

# Chapter 22

Lucy stood on the verandah watching Blake as he worked on the small boat below. He looked up and saw her. She waved.

"We'll be ready shortly," he called.

She went into the bedroom to change clothes. Appendai was pulling the Coronet out to sail to the hotel where the guests waited.

"Pick up the gun there," Blake called to Lucy as she came down the steps. She picked up the lethal weapon and stood looking at it closely. Blake started the motor and waved for her to join him. She waded out to the boat and handed the gun over the side, then hoisted herself over.

"Had breakfast?" he asked.

She shook her head.

"Go below. There's some tea and fruit there. We're going to some new reefs today, some you haven't seen yet. We'll spear fish there.

He spun the wheel and headed south. Lucy stood looking at him for a moment. She hadn't been in that direction before. They passed a dhow in full sail.

They're coming to the island for water," Blake said. He waved, but there was no answering wave from the sail boat. "There's no water on that island where they live."

She looked at the small island as they passed it, watching the children with their nets hauling in a few tiny fish.

"I used to let them take water from my well, but it's too low now with the drought. Don't know where they're going to find any. They may try to sail upriver to fresh water. They're hippos there. Did I tell you? They must have come across to the south end of the island years ago when there was a barely submerged strip of sand between us and the mainland."

He looked and realized Lucy had gone below. She came up on deck after a while and sat under the awning. Blake glanced back at her occasionally, but each time, she looked away.

"Feeling all right, sweetie?" he asked.

"I'm fine. I just want to stay out of the sun for a while. How far are we going?"

"We'll cross the reef barrier down here a way, then head for a big ocean reef. I think you'll like it. The fish are bigger there."

He idled the motors outside a long stretch of breakers. White foam broke over the wave tops and lapped at a near-by coral pinnacles, sending spray up the straight sides in cascades. A mixture of fish eagles and cross-billed storks perched atop the coral. One of the eagles threw his head back and screamed like a gull. He rose, wings spread, and swooped down onto a cloud of fry.

"Anchovies," Blake pointed. "We should be seeing porpoises on the other side of the barrier. Anchovies are a delicacy to them."

He revved the motors and pushed the gear forward. "Here we go!"

The boat surged forward and rode high over the reef on the crest of a wave. It fell into a trough with a thud, the motors shuddering, then straightened out, and rolled smoothly across the open sea. Lucy joined him at the wheel, her eyes sparkling.

"We made it!"

"Yes. That's always a close one, but going this way saves a long trip around the end of the island. Look, there are the porpoises."

She leaned over the side of the boat. Great fins arched above the surface in undulating rhythm. She counted seven of them racing beside the boat. Suddenly, one leaped across the bow, it's gray and silver body sending rainbow spray across the deck.

"How graceful he is," she cried.

"They're really animals, not fish, you know. They breathe air through blow holes on top of their head, like whales."

He throttled the motors down and peered into the water. "They bear their young live, tail first, so they won't drown before the mother nudges them up to the surface to breathe. They're quite intelligent, and best of all, they keep sharks away."

"There's the reef," he pointed a short distance off the starboard. "See? It's a quarter mile long and the water's not too deep. The tide's just right. There won't be any current."

He threw out the anchor. "Let me show you the spear gun." He picked it up and loaded it with a steel pointed arrow. "See, you pull back here. Try it."

She pulled as hard as she could, but couldn't cock it.

"I'll have to do that for you, I guess." He took the gun from her. "I'll cock it when it's time. All you'll have to do is pull the trigger.

208

Be sure to lead the fish a bit. An arrow travels more slowly through water than through air. Gauging distance is dicey under water, remember. Things look much closer and bigger than they really are. Don't try to tie into anything too big. You need a brain shot for the big ones and you'll want some experience first."

"Can this spear kill anything really big, like that rock cod you shot?"

"This is the same gun I used on that one. It has plenty of power."

"Someday I'll shoot one that big, but I'll start with the small ones, like you said."

"Good girl. Now' into the scuba gear. Want to slip off your bathing costume?"

"I'd rather not this time. Maybe later," she said, as she put on her flippers and fastened her tank harness.

"Over you go," he said, as he helped her onto the edge of the boat. She pressed her mask against her face with one hand and fell backward with a splash. The reef was to her left and she swam toward it. It was thick with fish. They swam unconcernedly past, darting in and out of the reef's cervices. Blake caught up with the spear gun cocked and ready. He passed it to her as she swam along the reef. A parrot fish swam at an angle coming towards her. She looked at Blake and he nodded. She held the gun and hung motionless in the water as the brilliant fish swam closer. As it began to turn, she aimed the spear and pulled the trigger. It missed by a foot, falling behind and well below the target.

Blake swam over, retrieved the arrow, and reloaded the gun. He gestured for her to point the gun well ahead of the fish. She nodded and continued swimming along the reef. A large damsel fish, a velvety pink-orange, swam past. Lucy aimed quickly and pulled the trigger, but the fish turned as the point glanced off its side. Blake retrieved the arrow and gestured for them to go up. At the surface they took their mouth pieces out and pushed their masks up.

"It's harder than I thought," she said.

"Yes, it is. But you nearly got the last one. You're learning. Let me take one. You need to stay quite still until the fish comes close. Take your time aiming. Follow me, I'll show you."

They adjusted their masks and jack-knifed down again. Lucy swam behind Blake and stopped as he halted near the reef. A school of tuna swam toward them, swerving as they met Blake. He turned slightly, aimed the gun, and shot. The point impaled the silver and yellow fish. It thrashed and fought against the shaft, slowly sinking in the water, blood drifting from its side.

Lucy sensed something behind her and turned. A long nosed, grinning mouthed shark was coming toward them. It swam in Blake's direction, nosing down. Blake turned, holding the speared fish, and saw the shark. He grabbed Lucy's hand, and hugging the reef, they inched their way up. Two more sharks joined the first. They were all over ten feet in length, and to Lucy, looked like leviathans.

Blake stopped half way to the surface. He pushed Lucy back against the reef, and taking the spear impaled fish, thrust it as far from him as he could. The lead shark dived down and caught the fish in his slit mouth, chewing on the head, and thrashing wildly, tossing bits of fish in all directions. The spear drifted downward while the remaining two sharks knifed through the water like torpedoes. One pulled the remaining body of the tuna from the mouth of the first shark. The third darted in and out, snapping at the small floating bits of flesh.

Blake pressed Lucy against the reef, protecting her body with his. The sharks continued their frenzied turning and snapping. One bit at the spear, nearly severing the metal shaft. The water churned from their circling bursts of speed. The tide drifted the remaining pieces of fish nearer the reef. The tail of one of the sharks glanced off Blake's chest. Lucy pointed, her eyes wide, as she saw blood seeping through the scrapes. Blake looked down, then made the gesture for up. Holding her wrist tightly, he slowly treaded upward. They got to the top of the reef. The tide was going out and a few pinnacles of coral were exposed. Blake stood on top of one of them and pulled Lucy up beside him.

"Whew! That was close! Are you all right, Lucy?"

"I'm all right, but I was scared down there. Does your chest hurt?"

"No. Just a scrape. A shark's skin is like sandpaper. But I thought we'd better leave when we did, although it's usually better to stay still when sharks are feeding. But' with the blood—. They can smell blood a mile away."

He rubbed his chest, wiping off the last of the blood. "We'll stay here for a while. They've nearly finished the tuna and they'll leave shortly. Sorry about the scare."

After a while he replaced his mask and slid into the water. He returned shortly. "They're gone. We can go back to the boat now. Don't kick a lot going back. Put your mask on and keep a sharp eye out. If you see them, stay still until they swim off. When they're feeding, they'll snap at anything."

Cautiously they covered the distance to the boat, kicking only occasionally. Once aboard, Lucy sank in a chair. Blake opened two cans of beer and they sat, drinking silently.

"We'll have lunch and then pull the boat closer to that island over there. There's another reef over there and we'll be well away from the sharks. The water is shallower, too. Are you game to go down again?"

"I'm game. I'd really like to shoot a fish this time."

They sailed for over an hour, the small island slowly looming larger. The tide was well out now and the tops of the reefs lay exposed in the afternoon sun.

"We can snorkel here," Blake said, as he shut off the motors and threw out the anchor. "We can see all we want without having to go deep. It's a good place to get your fish."

Lucy picked up her flippers, then paused. "Daddy—."

"Yes?" He stopped and looked at her.

"Daddy, I—." She looked away for a moment, then back at Blake. The words came tumbling out. "Why did you want to spend the night with that woman—that Countess? How *could* you."

Blake laid down his mask and snorkel and moved by Lucy, an amused smile on his face. "Oh, so you heard. You weren't so sound asleep after all. Do I hear a note of jealously in your voice?"

He started to put his arm around her, but she jerked away angrily. "Maybe I am jealous. I don't know. But, do you do that sort of thing all the time? When I think of my mother—all those years—so unhappy because of you and all the time you were having women, not even caring about her—or about me!"

She saw his eyes narrow as he took a step toward her, but the words kept pouring out. "And I thought you were so great! So super! Why, you're nothing but a—a—."

Blake's hand hit sharply on her cheek. "That'll be enough, young lady! What I do is my own business. Your mother never learned that, but you'd better."

Lucy cringed. The red marks of his fingers on her cheek spread as her eyes filled with tears. Blake's voice shook. "Don't start telling me what to do or sitting in judgment on my actions. I won't take that from anybody, not even you!"

Lucy stared at him, her eyes filled with hate. "Nobody's ever slapped me before in my whole life, and you'd better never do it again!" She lunged at him, beating her fists against his chest. He caught her wrists and held her struggling body away from him. Suddenly he broke into laughter.

"All right, all right. You're my daughter for sure! Now, calm down. I'm sorry I hit you; lost my temper for a moment. I'd forgotten you're a mere child and there are things you don't understand."

He released her and turned away. She stood, glaring at his back, rubbing her chaffed arms where he had held her.

He turned back to her. "Come now, sweetie, let's forget this happened. When you're older you'll understand about these things. For now let's get going while the tide's out. We're missing the best time for our dive."

He picked up the gun and dove off the side, bobbed up in a moment, and began fitting his mask. He held it away from his face and called, "Come on, Lucy, or I shall go without you."

She watched his broad back jut above the surface as he swam away. *How horrid he looks with all that ugly black hair all over him—like an animal. How could I ever have thought he was so great? He's awful, absolutely awful.* "I hate you!" she screamed at the submerged form.

Her eyes narrowed, her lips compressed to a thin line. *So I'm just a child, am I? I shouldn't question anything you do, is that it? Well, I'll show you!*

She jerked on her flippers and splashed over into the water, mask and snorkel in hand. She adjusted them quickly and swam in the direction Blake had gone.

She caught up with him near the reef wall. He cocked the gun, loading a new arrow, and handed it to her. She swam slowly, peering ahead. A Moorish Idle, long fin trailing in the water, swam toward the reef from the open water. Lucy held still, pointing the gun at the moving fish. It swam slowly toward them. She turned her body so the spear point held the fish in its sights as it swam toward Blake. She moved the spear a few inches to the left and pressed the trigger.

The point of the arrow plunged into Blake's chest. His hands came up and gripped the shaft, trying to twist it out. The snorkel fell from his mouth and his bulging eyes stared at Lucy. Slowly, his hands dropped away, dangling in the water. Blood spurted from around the shaft and hung in crimson cords in the water. His body went limp, and in slow motion, turned and floated to the surface, face down. Lucy dropped the gun and kicked to the surface, gulping air.

# Chapter 23

They found her at dusk, sitting in the boat. Blake's huge body floated nearby. Shark fins cut the surface in circles around it. The body jerked as the sharks' teeth tore into the flesh, scattering chunks that floated to the top of the water. Appendai brought the Coronet along side and the Slades held it fast to the smaller boat. Penny was the first one in the boat with Lucy.

"Mum", she cried, holding her mother tightly. She sobbed as if she would never stop. Alfred crossed into the small boat and Lucy turned to him pressing against his chest.

Bob Slade spoke to Appendai in Swahili. They each took a grappling hook and fished Blake's body into the Coronet. The diving mask had been dislodged. His face was hardly recognizable. Large chunks had been torn from his stomach and legs, but in his chest, still protruding, was the spear shaft, the point imbedded in the ribs. David reached down, twisted the spear out and tossed it, spinning, into the water. It sank slowly.

Brandt turned to Appendai. "Take the other boat and go back to the hotel. Tell Amilia to have their rooms got ready. They'll all be staying there tonight. Tell her to have six boys take lots of wood over to Blake's house."

Bob and David looked at him questioningly. "I think we should cremate him tonight, don't you? We shouldn't send the body, with that spear hole in it, back on the plane to Dar. There'd be too many questions asked."

Bob nodded in agreement. "It would be tomorrow before we could fly anyway. It's too late tonight. And you know bodies don't keep well in this climate. I think cremating him would sound very logical. There shouldn't be too many questions asked."

He turned to Appendai. "He drowned. Do you understand?"

Appendai nodded. Tears stood in his eyes. He went below to the cabin and returned with a blanket and some rope, handing them to Bob.

"Asanti," Bob said, and clapped his hand on Appendai's shoulder. "Now go over to the other boat."

He turned to Ann. "I think you should go with Lucy and the others. Talk to Lucy as soon as you have the chance. Make sure she doesn't mention the spear accident to anyone, even her mother and brother. Tell her we think it better to say he drowned. Make her understand why; police investigation—that sort of thing."

"Blake should never have expected a child Lucy's age to handle a spear gun," Ann replied. "Shall I mention the cremation to Lucy?"

"No. I think that would be too much after what she's been through today. Give her one of my sleeping pills and make sure she's asleep before you come back to the house. We'll wait for you and the others."

After Ann had boarded the small boat, Appendai started the motor and guided the boat toward the end of the island, going back by the long route.

It was midnight. Penny and Alfred stood with the Slades and the Hudsons by the bier. Blake's blanket wrapped body lay on a low wooden platform at the water's edge under bright moonlight. David lighted a paraffin torch. It's flare caught the grim faces surrounding the bier. He held the torch out to Penny, but she shrank back.

*Dear Lord, how can I set fire to his body? He is—was the only man I've ever loved.*

Appendai stepped from the shadows and held out his hand. David handed him the torch. He held it high above the bier and began chanting in a mournful minor key. The other Africans joined in. He thrust the torch into the wood beneath the body and it ignited and blazed. The blanket burned off quickly, and Blake's mangled body was brightly lit before the flames hid it from view. The pungent smell of burning flesh was blown back by the freshening sea breeze.

They heard a muffled cry and turned. Lucy stood in the shadows, her white nightgown catching the fire light. Penny rushed to her and held her in her arms.

"We thought you were asleep, dear. Come away."

"No. I want to see him for the last time." She moved away from her mother, closer to the bier. The fire reflected in her dark eyes. *It's gone, all gone, and I don't feel anything. My dreams of my father— and Africa—gone. All I feel is empty.*

They stood in silence as the Africans continued their wailing chant.

Alfred moved close to Lucy, putting a protective arm around her shoulders. *I'd planned to read from the Book of Common Prayer, but somehow this seems more fitting. May God forgive me; I cannot mourn his passing. I can but commend him to God's infinite mercy.*

The fire blazed and snapped. They stood, as if hypnotized, seeing visions in the flames. Ann slipped her arm around Bob.

*If I hadn't been so happily married all these years, I'd have enjoyed a roll in the hay with that man! What awful thoughts to have at this moment. Although Blake wouldn't have minded, I'm sure, were he to know.*

Penny stared at the flames, then looked at Lucy. *How could he have drowned? He was such a strong swimmer. I wonder if I shall ever be able to talk to Lucy about it?* She studied her daughter's face. It was set as marble. She could detect no emotion. The expression in Lucy's eyes seemed as old as time. *She's in a state of shock.* She brought her hand over her mouth, stifling a cry. *That's the way Blake looked when I pleaded with him for Abhurdamoni. Just like Blake!*

Alfred caught the look on Penny's face. He caught Lucy up in his arms. "We'll go now. Ah, dear Lucy!"

"Yes," Brandt said, as they all turned back toward the hotel. "Appendai will see that the fire keeps burning long enough—."

After breakfast the next morning Brandt asked everyone to come to the Hudson's apartment. They were all seated, having a second cup of coffee, when Brandt came in with a sealed envelope. "Only a short time ago," he began, "Blake asked me to keep this for him. I've no idea what's in it, but I think we should open it now, if you're all agreed."

There was no objection, so Brandt opened the envelope. He examined the papers for a moment. "Here are the two boat titles, made out to Lucy Anette. He picked up a flimsy sheet of paper and unfolded it. Everyone in the room recognized Blake's squiggly handwriting between large margins.

Brandt started reading. "'On my death, I wish everything I own to go to my daughter, Lucy Anette, and ask that Bob Slade be my executor. I ask that Appendai be provided for, as well as any of his minor children should he die before they reach age fourteen.'"

"That's all there is." Brandt handed the paper to Alfred, who glanced at it, and passed it to his mother. Penny shook her head.

Lucy reached for the paper and read it carefully, then handed it to Bob.

"I'll have this probated right away," Bob said. "Although it's not witnessed, I don't think there'll be any trouble. Blake has no family in Africa and I doubt his mother or brothers would contest it."

He glanced at Penny and Alfred. "I doubt they would," Alfred replied, "but we'll talk with them about it when we return to Liverpool."

Bob continued. "You realize, Lucy, that none of the money can be taken out of Tanzania. It will be kept here for you until you are of age. Blake probably has some money in a checking account and they're the two boats in your name. Those, and the fishing and diving equipment, the hotel might buy, if you want to sell."

He looked at Brandt, who nodded. "We'll give you a fair price."

Bob turned to Alfred. "Is that agreeable? He's no property I know of. The house and land belong to the government and there's not much in the way of furniture. We'll pack his personal belongings and hold them for further instructions."

"That's agreeable to me," Alfred replied, "though what Lucy can ever do with the estate, I don't know."

"I do," Lucy stood up. They all turned to her. The dark circles under her deep violet eyes made them look even larger. She looked years older than when she had arrived a short time ago. "I intend to come back to Africa as soon as I'm old enough, and I intend to stay here forever."

"Oh Lucy, no!" Penny interjected. "You mustn't—."

"I'm sorry, Mother, but that's what I want to do. After all, I'm Blake's daughter, too. I'm part of him, too. I never want to live anywhere else and I know I won't change my mind."

Penny brought a handkerchief to her eyes and turned away.

Lucy looked at Bob. "Could you please not sell the Coronet? And' not all the fishing and diving equipment? Could you rent that much to Mr. Hudson instead of selling it, and pay Appendai to work? In five years I'll be back and then I could manage everything. I'd be ever so grateful."

"I suppose we could," Bob hesitated, "if that's agreeable with you, Brandt, and you?" He looked at Penny and Alfred.

Penny sat shaking her head, but Alfred, looking from his mother to his sister, said, "We'll agree to that for the present. Lucy may well change her mind before she's of age, but for now——."

Lucy whirled on him. "I won't! I won't change my mind!" Her eyes blazed. "Ever!"

"We'll leave it that way, then," Bob concluded. "I imagine you'll want to pack now since you feel you must leave today, 'though you're welcome to stay."

He looked around. No one spoke. "We had Lucy's things brought over this morning." He looked at Penny. "Is there anything of Blake's you want to take with you?" She shook her head.

Lucy slipped out of the room and skirted the hotel. Penny saw her go and followed a way behind. Lucy walked quickly across the lawn and took the familiar path to the house. She went into Blake's bedroom and opened a dresser drawer, removing a box containing the cowrie shell collection. Returning to the verandah, she found her mother standing there.

"I'm sorry, dear," she said, as she slipped an arm around Lucy.

The girl stood watching the two boats bobbing on the water below. Appendai appeared on the deck of the Coronet and Lucy waved to him. He stood, a forlorn figure, and brought his hand up in a salute. The spot where Blake has been cremated was covered by high tide. Bits of charred wood floated along the shore.

"Let's go," Penny murmured.

"What you don't know, Mum——, what you don't know——." She turned away abruptly and walked across the verandah toward the hotel. She stopped before stepping onto the path and looked back at the ocean.

"I'll be back," she said. "You just wait. I'll be back!"

Penny followed on the path behind her. She couldn't see Lucy's face as it broke into a wide crooked grin, but she heard the sound of a harsh dry laugh, and she shivered.

Printed in the United States
1422300001B/403-405

9 781403 328939